Contents

adjective

Having all the required or desirable elements, qualities, or characteristics; as good as it is possible to be.

The tight feeling in my throat had developed into an actual lump and no amount of forced coughing would clear it. I twisted the cap back on the bottle of water I'd been guzzling in an attempt to dislodge it.

It was hot and sticky and the early signs of cramp had set in. I had considered stretching my legs with a trip to the loo, but had been warned about the facilities on trains and let's face it, I just wasn't in the mood to be faced with anything grotty.

The motion of the carriage as it rattled along the rails was anything *but* calming and the man in the seat opposite kept staring at me with a strange expression. Like he was contemplating something. It made me feel like I had something on my face. Exhaling, I silently willed him to go back to his half-completed crossword. He also had a remnant of something at the corner of his mouth, possibly a bit of sandwich that had sat there for at least the past hour.

My insides twisted and I scowled, turning away to look out at the passing countryside, forcing my mind elsewhere.

I felt exhausted; my last few weeks of exams having zoomed by and I couldn't shake that feeling of anxiety. Those nervous knots about the thought of seeing my father were tightening in my stomach again. We hadn't spoken over the last few months, hence the probable reason for said lump.

Being train bound and on my way to spend the summer with dad was creating all sorts of crazy inside me. After my parents separated a couple of years ago, pops had moved to Yorkshire, to the arse end of nowhere.

He now still lived in the arse end of nowhere, but with his new wife, Rachel. Brutal right?

It was hard to swallow, during my earlier childhood, my family had seemed perfect to me.

My dad was my hero, he'd check for monsters under my bed, clean me up when I got cuts and scrapes and be there when I had fall outs with my friends. He was my rock; the one I went to if I needed something fixing.

When he left, I'd been lost, like a huge void had appeared in my life and I had nothing but school work to fill it with.

I'd adjusted, eventually. I'd had to for the sake of my GCSEs at the time.

Of course, people break up, 'I do' is not necessarily forever. But it still stings, especially as the child on the outside looking in. It takes time to get your head around something like that—and then there's the added complications.

Breakups were never plain sailing, dad now lived on a *farm* of all places, with cows and shit. He came from a family of Northern landowners and after things had broken down with my mother, had decided to return to his roots.

Over a thousand acres of rustic farmland. I didn't even own a pair of wellies; I would be so out of my comfort zone. Country life just wasn't me. The house I shared with mum in London was in the thick of everything; school, friends, family, shops. It was handy and I *liked* handy.

When dad left, things became even more complicated, especially after he re-married; the new Mrs having baggage of her own you see. Baggage that was boy shaped and unfortunately rather nice to look at.

I had met them both once and I'm not going to lie, they were *not* people I had warmed to. *Especially* the boy. I still didn't understand how someone so physically gifted could be such a sarcastic, condescending dickhead.

Huffing bitterly, my belly flip-flopped at the thought of my stepbrother, Connor. I knew I should just bat the image away, push it far from my mind to stop it fuelling my angst. But it was impossible. Every time I closed my eyes, his face was in there, contaminating my emotions. It made me want to bleach my brain.

To my misfortune, he ticked every physical man preference box I never knew I had.

Gritting my teeth, I hated that rotating thought that he'd also be there all summer. He'd try and come between me and my dad, I just knew it. My father had said in one of his emails that Connor had started working at the farm early last year. The jealousy I'd experienced after digesting *that* news had almost pushed me towards a full-on tantrum. Something I hadn't experienced since my earlier teens. But I suppose jealousy does that to a person.

Shoving the bottle of Evian on the table in front of me, I regretted my decision to ride backwards as the train raced through a tunnel, bouncing shadows around the carriage.

To distract myself, I pulled out my iPhone and scanned through my messages, rolling my eyes at yet *another* message from my mother.

Everything OK sweetie?

I sent her a thumbs up and a kiss. Mum was a worrier who would call my phone on a loop if she didn't receive a reply within a nanosecond.

She started to type again, responding with a winking face, a fist bump and a duck for some weird reason. Mum really hadn't grasped the concept of emojis just yet.

Poor mum. She still wasn't over my father's 'betrayal' as she had labelled it. She didn't say it out loud but it oozed from her.

Mum doesn't know the meaning of poker face and is an open book. That's right, Eleanor Williams has two main loves in life. Eating lunch with her friends and a bottle of Vodka. The rest she just makes up as she goes along.

I do love her though. She does *try* to be a good mum, in her own way.

The carriage shook again as the train left the tunnel and my stress levels jumped up a notch. What I wouldn't give for a quick squirt of Rescue Remedy or some sweets: a sugar coma would be a great distraction.

Thinking back to the last time I saw dad at his anniversary party, I shoved my head back against the seat and rested my eyes.

Dad and Rachel had hired out a function room last year in a local pub. It had been a quiet, low-key event and nothing like the other parties I had been to. I'd arrived overdressed and had immediately felt out of place. Strappy dress and heels all the way for me. I'd been stared at and not in a good way.

My being there had also felt a little on the odd side, considering the occasion was to celebrate my dad being with someone *other* than my mother. He'd been so pleased though. He'd literally beamed at me during the entire event. Smiling was not something I had seen him do when he was with my mother. The change was uplifting and it had been a relief to learn that I wasn't being replaced by a new family; one I certainly hadn't signed up for.

The 'party' if you could call it that was pretty basic, which of course it should have been, it wasn't like one year together was a milestone or anything. Just an excuse for a 'do' was my thinking and what did one wear to a 'do', a party dress! Or so I had thought, I still felt annoyed by getting that one wrong.

Rachel had seemed nice enough. She was taller than me which wasn't difficult considering my five-foot two height and she had mousey hair and clear blue eyes. She was younger than my mum and I was relieved to see that she possessed her own boobs, standard skin tone and normal lips. The way my mum had spoken about her had conjured up the caked-in-it clichéd Wag. Dad was in no way a footballer, but he was well off and wealth encouraged the wrong type of woman.

Rachel had been sweet and kind and had paid attention to me and not in a fake active-listening type of way. She was encouraging about my aspirations and asked me questions. I hadn't felt like I'd had much of a voice over the last few years, especially through the tougher times during my parents' breakup but *she* had listened, like *really* listened. The night after the party, I had decided that her presence in my dad's life should be seen as a positive thing.

For both my father and I. Her son however, conjured up an entirely different response.

Connor Barratt was the main reason I'd had second thoughts about spending the summer with dad. *He* was my go-to thought when I was feeling shitty about the whole idea. The concept of spending my entire summer with someone so obnoxious had forced me to unpack and repack my case several times over the last week. The fact that I also found him so physically attractive, only added to my torment. And I had *never* chased a boy, ever! Why would I? I usually had to bat them off.

I half-heartedly scanned a text from my friend Lisa as I recalled how awkward I'd felt in his company. He'd been totally indifferent and I just wasn't used to that kind of response from members of the opposite sex. Bizarre doesn't even come close.

I also hadn't actually realised who he was at first and so had been totally unprepared. Yes, dad had told me that Rachel had a son, but his use of the word 'child' had conjured up something entirely different in my head.

'Child' is a word that in *no way* should *ever* be used to describe someone like him.

As we'd sat down to dinner, he was seated at the opposite end of the long table and sure, I'd noticed him as a fitty but I'd assumed that one of the annoying kids sat closer to Rachel would have been hers. Not the guy placed so far away. It was only after we spoke that I realised that the seating plan was probably done on purpose. He definitely had social issues and rarely spoke during dinner. He had watched me with a brooding expression and never returned any of my smiles, his face a hateful mask of relaxed indifference.

After the main meal had finished, I'd found him leaning against the bar like he was posing for a photo shoot, a bottle of beer in his hand. I remember approaching him fairly confidently until that punch of heat had hit me in the stomach, like an actual fist. Or at least how I imagined that would feel. It knocked me out of my comfort zone.

As I had walked closer to him and was given more detail, I admitted that he was certainly one of the hottest guys I had ever seen. Clichéd I know, but frustratingly true nonetheless.

Connor Barratt oozed confidence, his expression switching in and out of a, bored 'anywhere but here' look.

Tall and broad shouldered with black hair sticking out in all the right directions, he was major league hot.

His deep, dark eyes were set in a strong, masculine face that was flawlessly crafted. It was an almost beautiful face yet it boasted a strong nose and high haughty cheekbones. The guy was borderline pretty. Not that I would *ever* have said that to his face. He was also well muscled and I imaged there'd be impressive abs beneath the T shirt he had been wearing.

Connor had towered above me, over six feet tall and was a definite gym goer. His skin was also naturally tanned which must have been inherited from his dad's side, either that or he spent most of his days outside. His mum was whiter than Lisa and he certainly wasn't the sunbed type like my friend Niall. Niall didn't go anywhere without a quick thirty-minute top-up and was constantly golden.

The guy was seriously hot, and let's be honest, I'd seen attractive guys before but he made even the most macho, sporty guys at school look like first years.

Once dad spotted me lingering by the bar, he'd briefly introduced us before dashing off to help Rachel with her mother.

I'd stood before him, the silence circling us like a shark's fin, you could almost taste the brooding intensity that surrounded him.

The pull I'd felt was strong yet he was *nothing* like the usual type of guy I was attracted to. My ex-boyfriend Andrew had been tall and beanpole-like, with hair and skin whiter than my own. This guy was the polar opposite of that.

When I look back, rude doesn't even begin to describe it. I can honestly say I was floored, having warded off attention from the majority of teenage guys since I'd first developed boobs at thirteen. And please believe me when I say I don't consider myself overly vain but I do tick some boxes. I'm petite in stature with natural wavy white blonde hair, pale blue eyes and an above average complexion. I'm also kind, considerate, funny and nice. What's *not* to like?

Shaking off the indulgent thought, I pursed my lips, feeling annoyed how I appeared to be overthinking the subject. At the end of the day, Connor had blatantly decided that he had a problem with me *before* we'd even met, and in my opinion, there is *nothing* worse than judgy people.

He had been so sarcastic, making me feel like a stupid little girl attempting to speak to her first crush. He'd compared me to a doll, muttering something about Barbie. How do you recover from something like that? No amount of flirting would work. I'd probably just end up embarrassing myself further.

When I'd told my friends, Lisa had thought it hilarious that there was at last one boy out there around my age, that *didn't* fancy me.

'Harlow's looks are already fading', she'd put on our WhatsApp group, next to a pic of me where I *certainly* did not look my best. One of those unfiltered shots taken when you aren't ready. Not that I needed filters of course.

I blinked my way back to the present and the carriage jostled, knocking my water over. I shot out a hand to catch it a little too late as I felt the splash of dampness on my jeans. Shit.

The woman next to me tutted and I murmured an apology whilst frantically dabbing the table with a spare napkin.

After soaking up the carnage, I settled back into my seat whilst properly securing the cap back on the bottle, ensuring no further mishaps. I'd already soured my relationship with the woman in aisle seat 13B after flicking a piece of ham from my sandwich at her only minutes after boarding. She had now thankfully gone back to reading her boring looking novel. The cover looked like it was one of those books people read to battle insomnia. Mrs Lang spoke about them in English Literature all the time.

My phone pinged, yet another text from Lisa banging on about our school nemesis, Samantha and how she'd thrown up in Matthew Mason's lap at last night's party.

I rolled my eyes. I was so done with high school. I just wished I didn't have another year of A-Levels to get through.

Samantha Jones was Primrose High's very own Regina George and had made my last few months pretty shitty. Her boyfriend's wandering eye had been the catalyst to that drama.

I shuffled back into my seat, staring again at my partially distorted reflection through the window of the train.

Some people seem to view me as some type of genetic lottery winner but on the inside, I'm just the same as any other high school girl; confused, flailing and terrified about what to do with the rest of their life.

'Just because you're beautiful, don't think it will do you any favours in this world," my mother had once lectured, her own world being somewhere at the bottom of the vodka bottle she'd thrashed around to embellish her point. 'It's more likely to cause you problems.' Mum hadn't matured well with age and the drinking had only added to her insecurities.

I now realise that she was right and that her words were not just the rantings of a women whose husband left her for a younger model. Being what society deems 'beautiful' doesn't give you an easy ride. *Nothing* does, life is hard no matter what. There is no perfect.

The carriage swayed again and I tried to recover from that seasick feeling. The woman next to me would probably go ballistic if I added the contents of my stomach to the stain I'd caused on her white leggings. I blamed her choice of outfit, who wears white leggings these days? Everyone *knows* white clothing encourages stains.

Pulling my gaze away from the window, I thumbed my reply to Lisa's text about Samantha. I didn't really give a shit to be honest. I'd left all that nonsense behind me now, but my friends still stalked the popular girls on Facebook and they enjoyed feeding me the titbits.

Nope, this was a fresh adventure for me, I was moving on to pastures new having no idea what summer on a farm would feel like. Yes, I knew I'd have *some* challenges to deal with; one boy shaped and annoyingly good looking for starters. But I'd manage, I was a fairly adaptable girl. As long as didn't have to deal with much dirt or spiders. I was terrified of spiders and would never understand why they existed.

The speaker bled into the carriage and a muffled voice announced Pickering as the next station. I gathered up my rubbish and stuffed it into my rucksack. I was beyond grateful to be leaving my seat.

13B placed her book on the table and grunted before standing to allow me to pass. I thanked her, apologising again for the sandwich fail and she shot me one of those forced smiles.

As I approached the luggage rack, struggling to remove my case, a tall, balding man helped me and I thanked him, savouring the gentleman-like behaviour.

After a minute or so, the train slowed and the station platform appeared. Dormant butterflies started fluttering in my stomach. I was now really looking forward to seeing my father and decided that I would embrace the time.

My visit would also provide me with the opportunity of travelling to Scarborough for a day to check out their Uni campus. They had a teaching course that I was interested in learning more about. Future plans and all that.

I stepped cautiously over the gap, noting that my painted toes were verging on talons and wondering fleeting if I'd packed a nail file.

As I struggled across the platform towards the exit, I scanned for my father, but he was nowhere to be seen. I exhaled sharply, disappointment thrumming in me as I shuffled further down another corridor towards the main exit.

It was a bright afternoon and my eyes had to adjust after the darkness of the carriage. A fresh breeze blew against my face but it was tinged with the faint smell of diesel fumes which wafted across from the platforms.

As I moved forward, dragging my case, there was a drop off point with a line of taxis and clusters of people who were hugging.

I blew out a breath. Bully for them. My spirits dipped further. Had I been forgotten about?

I tutted. I hadn't exactly expected a huge welcome banner and balloons but being on time would have been nice. I had purposefully texted dad my ETA earlier that morning. I felt disappointment chew into me as I searched for my iPhone which I then dropped. It clattered against the pavement and I bent swiftly to check for possible damage. My new phone was my life.

As I straightened, it was then that I saw him.

I cursed under my breath, my body stiffening, the dreaded realisation that dad had sent *him* to pick me up was like taking a bullet.

Why on *earth* would dad send *him*, I'd rather *walk*. My father knew how I felt about this particular person after the party.

I frantically searched the conscious part of my brain for any *other* reason he was there. Of course, he *could* have been there to meet someone else, but I seriously doubted it. Did the guy even *have* any friends?

Connor was leaning against a battered black Ford Ranger; I recognised the model as Lisa's now ex-boyfriend drove one and holy shit, he was still gorgeous. Couldn't he have put on weight or shaved his head into one of those styles which guys thought looked good but totally didn't? I straightened to my feet, holding my phone protectively to my chest whilst eyeing him warily. I had probably gone pale with the shock.

He pushed lazily off the truck and strode towards me with a dark expression; like he'd been kept waiting; impatience radiating from him. He had that aura of control and held himself like he was so used to calling the shots. I still hated him on sight. At least my head did, my body was another story.

My mouth opened and closed in a fish type motion and I attempted to shoo my tongue out from its hiding place.

He looked uber-league fit in scuffed work jeans and boots and a checked shirt with the sleeves rolled back, revealing tanned muscular forearms. I noted he had a sleeve of tattoos on his right arm and a further jet of excitement fizzed in me. I had to get a grip before I melted in a full-on swoon.

What the actual hell? I didn't even *like* tats! The hot wave rushed from my belly to my chest. The top he'd worn to my dad's do had been long sleeved and so I hadn't noticed them the first time I saw him.

Connor held the stance of a confident guy who was so sure of himself and his body screamed 'bring it on'. He had a definite Cowper 'monarch of all I survey' air.

As I continued with my summations, I realised how very different we were, he was a pillar of strength; graphite to my porcelain and I was reminded about the rules of 'setting one's sights too high'. Wait! Where did *that* come from? As if I'd want a relationship with someone who was so severely socially impaired.

I swallowed back the reoccurring lump in my throat.

His eyes narrowed as he spoke. There wasn't even the *hint* of polite on his insanely, perfectly sculptured face. He hadn't shaved either, rough stubble covered his jaw, which made the guy even sexier.

"About fucking time. I've stuff to do that doesn't include babysitting you all day."

Heat stung my cheeks as the words rolled across my bones. His voice was a low, rich, rumble. I remember the sound, its timbre, the depth, that pitch. He didn't have a defining accent, which only made him more mysterious. Goosebumps broke out on my skin and I went all hot and cold at the same time.

He seemed taller, broader than the first time I saw him.

Connor's gaze skated over me, rudely looking me up and down. Of course, guys did that all the time, but their expressions usually beamed appreciation not distaste. It made me feel conscious of my free from make-up face.

"I thought dad was coming to meet me?" My voice was much breathier than intended. Connor's eyes were glued to my lips as he came closer, in touching distance and he looked pointedly at me. Like he was humouring a small child or something. "Well?" I prompted.

"Mike's a busy man. He can't afford to drop everything just because you decide to visit at last." His tone was icy.

I grimaced at his harshness, hating the fact that I found him so attractive. Why on earth didn't I see him for the pig he was?

His jaw was strong and at that point thrust out at a challenging angle. He was obviously pissed off, but I saw a tell-tale sign that he wasn't as immune to me as he would have liked. It should have given me more confidence. It didn't.

13

I buried the observation and decided against rising to the bait. He was just one of those guys who got off on confrontation. I'd witnessed it first hand at the party.

"And you were nice enough to come in his place. Well, thank you Connor; you really shouldn't have," I said sweetly.

He snorted. It wasn't a pleasant sound.

"You're right about that. I shouldn't have and I didn't offer either." Pig, pig pig!

He just stared down at me with a mean scowl, making no move to take my stuff. The fact that he wasn't a gentleman did not surprise me at all. I shifted my feet under his scrutiny.

"Well, you're here now and so thank you," I repeated, attempting to be the bigger person. Something I rarely did. I too could be stubborn.

His eyes glittered as he leaned his head towards me; his expression now a mixture of annoyance and amusement. I didn't like either.

"You can drop the fluttery eyelash crap. It won't work on me," he bit back, his mouth pulling into a tight line.

I felt that bubble of unvented frustration burst. He was actually *impossible* to be nice to and I experienced an impulsive desire to kick him; a reaction which was alien to me. I reminded myself I was the nice girl. I didn't do angst or temper. The guy obviously rubbed me up the wrong way and I had to get a grip if I was going to be staying in the same house as him. I so hoped our rooms weren't close. If I was lucky, maybe he slept in a barn or something.

I shook off the thought. Damn it, why did he have to be so fit? Why couldn't he have been fat and sweaty or skinny with spot encrusted skin?

His next words momentarily fazed me. "Had a little accident?" he questioned with a cocky smirk.

My brows knitted as I tried to grasp his meaning. "Sorry?" I said through tight lips. I was frowning so hard my forehead hurt.

The smirk doubled in strength and he glanced downwards, motioning toward my crotch with a flick of his hand. I swallowed, my eyes dropping.

I think I died a bit inside as I realised that he was referring to the damp patch from the water spillage which was still evident on my jeans.

I attempted to laugh it off, but it came out like a pig snort, the voice that followed paper thin. "Very witty. I get what you're insinuating and no I didn't pee myself," I replied, shooting him my best shit eating smile.

My neck also ached from trying to retain eye contact. He was so tall; the top of my head barely reached his shoulder.

He rasped a hand across the light stubble on his jaw. That too was sexy.

"Insinuating? Such a big word for such a little girl," he sneered with a lopsided smile.

I chewed my lip, feeling totally out of my element. He was such a nasty shit. I didn't cope well with conflict at the best of times, let alone with someone I appeared to be so uncontrollably attracted to. God only knew why of course. It appeared my mind and my body were stood in two totally different picket lines.

I paused, mentally coaching myself through my next words. "Not really *that* little. I'm seventeen a few weeks." The severely pathetic comeback left my mouth before I could swallow it.

Even to my own ears my words sounded ridiculous. Next to his mature masculinity, I felt every bit like the school girl I was and he wasn't even *that* much older than me. What was he... twenty, twenty-one? I should have remained mute in the presence of such male sophistication.

I cleared my throat as he took a small step forward, his body looming and yet I didn't step back; I was rooted to the spot. My reaction to him should have been applauded. Lisa would be well impressed. I usually never let anyone stand so close to me. I silently saluted my backbone.

His eyebrows were raised and his face held a, 'that's the best you can come up with' expression. "I stand corrected Little Miss Mature, now hurry the fuck up and let's go. I've got to get back." The 'tone' was back. I wanted to punch him in his rock-hard stomach, even though it would probably shatter every bone in my hand.

I glanced around again in the hope that my dad would suddenly materialise and save me from being in this impossible boy's company, but of course he didn't.

I continued to worry my lip. Now I had to sit in a car in a small space with all this moodiness? Maybe I could just ignore him, feign interest in the passing countryside or something?

"Grab your shit and follow me."

He turned away and I was toying with the idea of telling him where to go but thought better of it.

"You're friendly," I mouthed at his back, grabbing my stuff. My sarcasm couldn't be any thicker if I had tried. He stopped suddenly, twisting back towards me. I almost plastered myself against his chest.

"What did you say?" he snapped, angling his head down at me.

"You deaf?" I blasted hotly.

He blinked as if momentarily shocked, but he must have heard me. My words had the originally desired affect and then some. He shot me a look of pure venom, which forced me to back up another step.

"What did you say?" he demanded again, now extremely angry. I must admit it, I regretted my bitchiness.

"I said 'you're friendly', I was being sarcastic," I informed him as cool as I could muster, my voice wavering slightly.

Some of the tension left his body as he studied my face. "I can assure you I'm not —friendly that is," he drawled out slowly, a twist to his lips. No shit Sherlock.

I wafted a hunk of hair off my cheek and my eyes darted to his as I awarded him with a 'you don't say' type of look. "As I said, I was being *sarcastic*," I muttered again, locking my eyes to his.

His smile didn't sit well with his sour expression.

Showing me his back again, he swivelled on his heel and walked towards the car, leaving me to clamber along after him, juggling all my shit. Thank God there were wheels on my suitcase. It suddenly felt like my joints were held together by bits of elastic. He must have seen I was struggling and yet he still didn't offer to help me. He really was a first-class prick.

I felt frustrated as it was a whole new experience for me, guys usually bent over backwards to please me. There was no doubt about it, the boy was hard work, *impossible* even. It was like plaiting fog.

As we got to the car, he opened the boot and rolled his eyes before snatching my case and lifting it into the vehicle like it weighed nothing, the muscles in his arms bulging.

I still thanked him of course. I was determined not to allow his lack of manners to stamp out my own.

After closing the boot of the car, he stalked off towards the driver's door and I swiftly moved to the passenger side and opened the back, not relishing the idea of riding shotgun. I threw my rucksack onto the seat which was cluttered with assorted tools.

"In the front, I'm not a fucking taxi!" Connor bit over his shoulder as he negotiated his large frame into his seat. He almost had to fold his body in half to fit behind the wheel.

His use of language made me curl my fingers into fists, pushing my manicure sharply into my palms. I hated the F word and rarely used it.

Obeying his barked instructions, I slammed the door and moved to the front.

I felt a twinge of moisture develop in the corner of my eye before reluctantly climbing up into his stupidly big car.

At this rate, the chances of us getting along was up there with winning the lottery.

I took a deep breath and told myself not to cry.

Two

We sat in silence as Connor started the engine and I felt very aware of his strong thighs so close to my own. He was gripping the steering wheel so tightly his gnarled knuckles were white.

My jaw ached from how tightly my teeth were clenched.

"So where is dad? Is he OK?" I asked eventually, wanting to ease some of the tension.

He flicked a lazy glance at me.

"Why the sudden concern?" he returned dryly.

I clipped my seat belt on as we pulled out into traffic, baffled by his response. It was a simple question after all. "I'm sorry?"

He shot me a sideways glance before refocusing on the road. "You should be. You haven't given a shit for the last year."

My jaw dropped at his rudeness. My God he was spoiling for a fight. They guy totally did get off on confrontation.

Fury jetted into my system, to the point where it was almost painful; he had crossed the line and I wanted to scream at him.

"I don't think my relationship with my dad has anything to do with you," I bit out, my voice wobbling slightly. He must have heard the tremor as he shifted awkwardly in his seat and jammed the vehicle into a higher gear.

"If you say so," he put in dryly, suddenly passive aggressive. The guy's changeable behaviour was giving me whiplash.

A cocktail of emotions swirled inside me and I glanced out of the window at the passing countryside, weighing up the decision on whether to challenge him or not. I decided to bite the bullet. It was now or never. I wasn't sure of the adult way of going about it, but the air definitely needed clearing. We were destined to have it out, whatever 'it' was of course.

"Have I done something to offend you?"

His response was fast. "Nope."

"Then why are you being so mean to me? I don't get it?" I could almost feel the groves my frown was making on my face.

18

His dark eyes glanced towards me fleetingly. "I'm not being mean to you; this is me. It's just how I am—with people of a certain type that is."

He then actually smiled. Not the type that could go onto a dental commercial or anything, more of a slight twitch of his mouth, but it was there.

My eyebrows shot sky high and I shot him a withering look. "You've met me like—once and you think you know my type?" I snorted in disbelief. It wasn't a ladylike sound but I was past caring.

His face continued to wear the weird smile. "I 'like' saw you coming sweetheart. And don't take that as a compliment."

My eyes flickered with annoyance as he mimicked my 'like' but I ignored it. "Oh, I wouldn't dream of taking anything *you* said as a compliment and what the hell does that mean? You're going have to help me out here because I'd don't think we speak the same language. You've totally lost me."

He hadn't of course. Connor Barratt had obviously made up his mind about me and whatever label he'd decided on, it wasn't nice. No doubt it was something to do with the radio silence between my dad and I over the last few months, but it takes two people to communicate and my father hadn't exactly been that forthcoming either.

There was a beat of silence and I pulled out my iPhone as a distraction.

"I wasn't speaking in fucking riddles. My point was that it's amazing how quick the tide turns when you want something."

At first, I hadn't a clue what he was referring to but then thought about the iPhone 14 in my hand. Dad did order it and send it by special delivery when I dropped my old one down the toilet. A twinge of guilt seeped into my conscience.

I quickly re-pocketed the offending item with shaky hands.

Connor continued his line of attack.

"And if you think you're just going to sit on your arse all day with everyone else running around after you, you can think again. There are no free rides in farming. It's not a place for useless people."

His comment needled me. He spoke to me as if I was some type of fat lazy lump.

I exhaled sharply. "How can you say that? You don't even know me," I pointed out tightly.

He pursed his lips and relaxed his death grip on the steering wheel. The sight of those long fingers caused my tummy to do that flip-flop thing again. I noticed his knuckles appeared to be scarred.

"I know a lot more than you think." he assured me confidentially. He was such a smug bastard.

He was so arrogant and I longed to wipe the smug smile off his face. Why the hell was I attracted to him when he was being such a dick? I twisted my fingers together in my lap to stop myself strangling him. I shouldn't give two shits really but my mouth just kept on moving.

"Don't you think you're being a tad judgemental? You should shine the light in your own corner when you're talking about free rides. Isn't it my father's money that bought the farm *and* the house you and your mother are living in?" I bated nastily and instantly regretted it. Dad had told me how Rachel had been forced to leave her husband with nothing.

He didn't like that at all and his reply cut into me. With a roll of his eyes, he muttered a curse before blasting.

"You're such a child. I work twelve to fourteen-hour days. I pay my way, always have done. We weren't all born into the perfect privileged life and anyway, that's a completely different fucking conversation."

Boy he liked the word fuck.

I clamped my lips together before I gave in to the instinct to push him further. I appeared to have opened up a wound. A thick tense silence sat between us and I bit my lip, warding off the 'you started it' comment that was dying to push itself out there.

I concentrated on my phone again, I needed to do something with my hands.

Connor continued to stare forward, watching the road before saying, "Nice phone. Latest model?"

He really was a sod; the guy missed nothing. *Yes*, it was the latest model *and* the most expensive, but I needed one that was the most reliable. That is what I had told myself at the time anyway. Plus, it was me, all my friends *expected* me to have the best of everything.

I decided to ignore him, he had obviously pigeonholed me as a spoiled bitch which was so far from the truth it was unreal. I had a monthly allowance from my father and I usually budgeted really well. And again yes, dad sent me gifts from time to time, but he was my *father*. That's what they do! Connor of course wouldn't understand due to his own father being totally fricking AWOL. Dad said they *never* saw him and that he wasn't allowed near the family anyway.

Ignoring him, I checked for messages. I had several more texts from Lisa and one from dad which I must have missed earlier, apologising and explaining that he would have to send Connor to get me. I felt a twinge of annoyance that I'd missed that particular message as I could have at least prepared myself for seeing the moody git again, even if only slightly. I also had a text from my sort of ex Andrew, but I thumbed delete without reading it. I couldn't be dealing with any more shit than what was right in front of me or I'd explode. One thing at a time.

"So where is Rachel?" I questioned, lowering my phone.

Connor shot me a sideways glance. "My mother's in Edinburgh with my Gran for the week."

"OK."

There was a moment's pause before he spoke again.

"*She* should have been the one here to get you. But instead, I'm left with the shit jobs," he announced with an exasperated sigh.

I ignored him and turned to look out of the window, hating the fact that picking me up was deemed to be one of the 'shit' jobs. FFS!

The engine of the car growled into the cab of the Ranger.

"So how was your journey? First class by any chance?" Connor suddenly asked, cutting back into my thoughts. His attempt at small talk almost knocked me off my guard.

"No, I travelled with the other peasants," I began sarcastically, "and you *actually* care enough to ask me?" I put in, feeling out of my element. I wasn't usually so quick to temper.

"Nope, just making conversation," he returned in a bored tone which made me want to thump him.

Instead, I released a puff of air, feeling thoroughly exasperated. I hadn't expected us to get along, step-siblings sired by the 'other woman' rarely did (so I imagined), but I had literally *just* arrived and here we were at daggers drawn. It was going to be a bloody long summer.

"Well, it could use some work," I muttered, not really bothered how he took that.

He exhaled sharply, his nostrils flaring as he aggressively overtook the car in front of us. "What the actual fuck? Stop mumbling, if you have something to say, bloody well say it," he snapped back.

I lurched in my seat and flicked a wayward strand of hair behind my ear, a rush of adrenalin egging me on. "I said your ability to converse could use some work. As quite frankly—you suck at it," I delivered tartly. I was starting to get annoyed at having to repeat myself. He had obviously decided to pick and choose what he heard, a typical boy thing.

He cleared his throat noisily and roughly changed gear, the car revving with an insistent snarl, reflecting the mood in the vehicle.

"Do you even have a license?" I stated under my breath, checking the speedo, noting he was pushing sixty when we were only on a narrow, single track country lane. My fingers were now clawing the seat for stability.

He ignored me and I stared moodily at his profile, wondering whether to repeat the question but knew that he'd probably just speed up or wobble the steering wheel like a proper dick. At least he kept his eyes on the bloody road.

There was another moments silence before he answered. "My ability to converse is fine," he drawled defending himself against my earlier jibe, shooting me a quick glance. He suddenly sounded wounded which was odd. Had I successfully landed a blow? I sure hoped so but doubted it. He was like a rock.

I cocked an eyebrow. "Really? Well, where I come from it's usual to say hello and greet new members of the family in a *friendly* way. Not be a complete obnoxious twat to them," I sniped briskly, amazed at my own daring, I rarely used mean language, but the guy brought out the nasty in me.

His lip curled but resentment radiated from him in waves and he shook his head.

"I must say after everything I've heard about you, Mike left out the part about you being a bitch." His insult still didn't melt the hormones ranging in my gut. Surely the nastier he was to me, the more I could fight the attraction?

My palms prickled like I'd grabbed a nettle and I moodily shoved my phone back into my pocket.

How dare he call me a bitch when he was being such a mean bastard! Steam must surely be coming out of my ears by now.

I opened my mouth to give him hell, but failed miserably.

"I'm not a bitch at all. I am merely reacting to your boorish behaviour." I replied in my best haughty voice.

He sniggered at that one and shot me a knowing smile. "Boorish? Where are we, the 50s?" His eyes sparkled. I appeared to be amusing him now. I felt dizzy, the guy was certifiably schizo.

Connor pulled over at a passing point to allow a car through which *amazed* me. His recent behaviour having not suggested he'd be a courteous driver.

"You just don't like the fact that I'm not floored by that perfect face of yours. I imagine you have all the boys behaving like complete dicks over you."

I felt semi-elated at the backhanded compliment and reigned in my response, as he was right. I'd *never* been treated like this by a boy, it was unique and not in a good way. I cursed the fact that I'd dressed down in a pink tee and skinny jeans and of course the no make-up face. I felt like a soldier without his armour.

I turned away to stare out of the window again. He'd hit the nail on the head and it niggled, oh how it niggled! He was the devil but a clever one at that.

My eye started to do its twitchy thing, a tic my GP had related to stress.

I blew out my reply on an exhale. "It's not my fault that all guys act like sex mad maniacs around me." I was past caring how conceited I sounded.

Connor didn't reply at first, he was too busy concentrating on passing a row of parked cars as we drove through a Beatrix Potter type village.

"High school boy's maybe. Don't tar us all with the same brush. Now who's being judgemental, *Harlow*?" He quirked a brow; dammit, even his eyebrows were sexy.

My stomach muscles bunched as he said my name for what must have been the first time.

I inhaled again, giving myself a moment to recover before I replied. This had to be the most fired up situation I had even been in. Goosebumps prickled my skin.

He beat me to a response, stating. "Bet you enjoy it too, lording your virginity over the male of the species, like an expert tease." His teeth flashed in a gleam of white. Thoroughly pleased with his own judgement. His words were like poisoned darts and I decided against challenging him, knowing that whatever come-back I went with he would top it.

We drove in silence with the radio on low in the background and I wondered what he'd do if I turned the volume up, to drowned out the nothingness.

We sat there in the semi quiet through most of an Ed Sheeran song and I wondered how long to veto conversation until it started to get to me. As a Foo Fighters tracked started up, I was riddled with the urge to speak. I *hated* uncomfortable silences.

"How far is the farm?" I questioned, truly believing that he couldn't throw *that* comment back in my face.

I was wrong. "Not far. You won't have to suffer my *obnoxious* presence for much longer," he jeered, repeating my barb from earlier. So, I *had* hit a nerve, one point to me!

It appeared the guy could twist anything.

I ignored his tone. "So, you work on the farm?" It was more of a rhetorical question as I already knew the answer.

"I do." He deadpanned.

I moodily folded my arms across my chest to stop myself from jabbing him on the leg. It was a solid, mouth-watering leg. I couldn't imagine I'd do much damage to it any way, my fist would probably ricochet off and I'd hit myself.

"You know you could meet me half way instead of the one-word answers," I puffed, feeling thoroughly fatigued, the journey having started to take its toll. I felt a trickle of sweat run down my back and I cracked the window open.

"What do you want to know?" he replied, his voice dripping with feigned innocence. I played it safe, not wanting to be lured into a false sense of security.

"What type of work do you do there?" I questioned, keeping my tone even. I didn't want to appear too interested.

As usual he shot me down and gave me a bland look before steering the car in through a pair of tired looking gates.

"It's a farm, what do you think I do? I work —hard. Not that you'd know what *that* looks like."

I smirked. Me, Harlow Williams *actually* smirked. So that's how it felt, part of me wanted to check the mirror to see how my faced looked. I *never* smirked.

"You're a farmer, so what. The work can't be that hard, it's not like you're saving lives or anything." I knew what I was saying was a pile of bollocks, the words even felt wrong in my mouth, but I couldn't help myself.

He suddenly looked even larger in his seat.

"Spoken like a true ignorant city girl that has no idea about the importance of agriculture."

His city girl comment made me want to yank a clump of his hair in frustration.

"You know, you're actually becoming quite predictable now. It's boring. You don't like me. I get it and that's fine," I stated. "I suggest we keep out of each other's way while I'm here. OK?"

His next words were totally unwelcomed for two reasons. One, him being part of the deal and two, being expected to work on what was actually my holiday.

"Not OK, since we'll probably be working together. As I said, you don't get to sit on your arse all summer. That's not how it works in farming sweetheart."

I gritted my teeth and did not say another word.

I *hated* the way he said 'sweetheart' like I was anything but and I *despised* the way my body responded to his gruff voice.

My legs felt weak, I was so glad I was sitting.

My eyes searched beyond the glass of the window as realisation hit me like a sledgehammer.

I was here all summer with my dad, the woman who stole him from my mum and a guy I fancied, who *hated* my guts.

Great. It was going to be a blast.

Three

The farm was *nothing* like I expected and I closed the window as the stench of dung abused my nostrils.

Connor had pulled the car up in front of a large stone-built house and I unclipped my seatbelt and clambered out of the door.

A cluster of cows mooed, the sound penetrating the calmness and the horrendous farm odour intensified. It was so strong you could almost taste it.

"You'll get used to it." Connor assured me with a half-smile as he strode around the back of the vehicle with an animal-like grace. I shot him one of my best unimpressed looks.

I retrieved my rucksack from the backseat and turned to fully take in my surroundings. There were two large barns, both appearing to be damaged; part of the roof was missing off one and the other had scaffolding erected around a worn breeze blocked section. I could see the hairy bodies of cows that were housed there; aka the probable source of the smell. The other barn was full of haphazardly stacked hale bales that screamed 'health and safety breach'.

Various items of machinery cluttered the pebbled yard, all of which had seen better days and there were a couple of old cars which were rusted through.

I narrowed my eyes against the sun and attempted to shield my gaze with the palm of my hand.

Connor rustled around in the boot of the car. The only vehicle which looked like it had any life left in it, was a bright green tractor. It had one of those spikey attachments on the back that they use to churn up fields. I hadn't a clue what it was called. The huge tyres were daunting; I could so imagine Connor at the wheel—shirtless and sweaty—what the heck? I swallowed. Where did *that* come from?

As my stepbrother started to drag my case from the car, fear of the unknown beat within me like a drum. I looked around again for signs of human life. There was no one, just us, the cows and I could see sheep in one of the distant fields, their coats like cotton wool stuck against a green background. The place was seriously run down. Had dad lost all his money or something? The farm was a proper shit hole.

Connor slammed the boot and started towards the house, this time carrying my case. He had probably forgotten that it was mine. I quietly fell in behind him, shooting invisible daggers into his broad back.

Although old and a bit worn looking, as I got closer; I accepted that the house was fairly pretty. In a rustic kind of way. It had ivy taking up most of the crumbly stonework and looked to be around two storeys tall with four large Georgian type windows on the front. The place had obviously been extended at some point as two newer sections sat on the side like spider's legs. I shuddered as I thought about how many actual spiders lived in it.

It was light-years away from the large family home I now shared with mum, but it was OK, and I embraced the twinge I felt at the prospect of exploration.

Connor pushed through the large wooden front door and I shuffled into the building behind him. A sweet smell of baking hit me and mixed in with the foulness of the outside air. It was a strange combination.

"Anna!" Connor bellowed across the hallway as he dropped my case at the bottom of some stairs. He didn't even turn to check I was with him; he just stalked over towards a mahogany side table and started leafing through some letters with a sour expression. It was like I wasn't even there.

My grip tightened on my rucksack, and I fleetingly wondered who Anna was; his girlfriend, perhaps? I felt a spike of something indescribable at the thought. Surely not jealousy?

There wasn't much light in the hallway and it felt cold which was strange considering it was the beginning of July. The floor was made of stone but was partially covered by a deep red patterned rug and the stairs leading up were part carpeted. You could see the polished wood peeking out at the sides. The walls were also panelled with wood. It looked a bit like the Head's office at school and it wasn't the tidiest of areas; there were walking shoes and wellies strewn around the floor. There was also an abundance of coats hung messily on the wall near the front door.

Two other doors sat on either side of me which were open, possibly living rooms?

I was just about to ask Connor about my room when a flustered woman appeared in the open doorway down the corridor to the front of us.

"Fantastic! You're here," the lady I assumed to be Anna shrieked, whilst bustling purposefully towards me. She was a large woman with a strong Yorkshire accent, dressed in shabby jeans and a flour dusted sweater. I noted her bare feet and that her hair was falling from what you could only call a chaotic bun. She looked *exactly* like you'd imagine a woman who lived on a farm to look.

Connor grunted a reply and started opening one of the letters. I ignored him and stepped forward, only to be pulled into a bear of a hug. Her hair smelled of cooking oil.

"I imagine you're Anna?" My statement was muffled against her neck as she squeezed my tired body and I felt her nod before she set me back with hands on my shoulders, her face assessing.

I put her around the sixties mark as she nodded. "Stunning child, absolutely beautiful," she said with saucer wide eyes.

Her gaze roamed over me from head to toe. "You look *exactly* like your pictures honey, such a pretty little thing. Isn't she Connor?"

My eyes darted to Connor to find him watching us, his gaze hooded, giving nothing away, the letter in his hand suddenly forgotten. Our stares met and tangled.

His lips twisted. "If you say so."

His reply was bland which was typical and his face was now as unreadable as a book with the pages glued together. He was such a sod. My inner tantrum stomped her feet.

Anna's eyes narrowed into slits which added a few more lines to her crow's feet and her grin became much meatier. "Ignore him sunshine, almost twenty-two and he's already like a grumpy old man is Connor," she began before she suggested. "Why don't you take her case up to her room Con and I'll give her the tour. Oh, and you need to call Andy about the new creep feeders you ordered."

She bellowed this over her shoulder, my God the woman was loud. I pulled my eyes away, breaking the connection. Connor grumbled something under his breath as he threw the letter back on the table. I watched him from the corner of my eye as he prowled towards me, his stance screaming irritation. Did the guy *ever* smile? At least he appeared to be doing as he was told for a change. I fleetingly wondered about his relationship with my dad. Was he a prick to my father too? I didn't take too kindly to that thought and so I dashed it away. As far as I knew, they were on good terms and worked well together.

I side-stepped to allow him to grab my case and murmured a quick thank you as and he set off up the stairs, taking them two at a time, the muscles in his shoulders flexing with the weight of my stuff.

"So, you two had a fall out again?" Anna put in gently, releasing me and turning to eye his retreating form; her 'thoroughly in need of a pluck' eyebrows sky high.

I nodded, "You could say that," I replied whimsically.

She pursed her lips. "You'll get used to him. He acts as hard as nails, but he has a softer side once you get to know him."

I almost choked at that one but managed to recover myself. The thought of my stepbrother possessing anything soft was surely a joke. A warmth pooled between my legs and I allowed my mind to wander no further.

Anna wiped her hands down her jeans before saying, "You forget about Connor for now and let's get you settled. Would you like a shower before your dad gets in?" The woman offered. I almost jumped up and down and clapped my hands with glee.

"Yes please, that would be great."

I re-hooked my rucksack over my shoulder as Anna gave me a brief tour of the layout downstairs. The kitchen was based at the back of the house and was rather messy from baking. The two rooms on either side turned out to be a florally decorated living room and the other was my father's study. I breathed in the scent; you could definitely identify an essence of dad. It was decorated with oak wood flooring and mahogany panelling on the walls. There was an array of masculine looking furniture with leather bound books which were shelved floor to ceiling. I spied dad's traditional work desk with the green leather surface sat against the far wall and his worn Chesterfield. The room was large and full of natural light and for some reason I preferred it to the softer more feminine room which surprised me. I was usually all for the girlie stuff. The patio doors also gave you a peek into the back garden where there was a variety of shrubs and flowers; a possible place for sunbathing, I mentally filed away.

Anna chatted about life on the farm and how she had been the live-in cook for the last two years since my father bought the place and got it back on its feet. Really?

This was back on its feet. I would have hated to have visited when it was off its feet.

At least I'd been reassured that the place was at a 'work in progress' phase and dad wasn't broke, thank God. The timeline Rachel gave me was interesting as it confirmed that dad must have bought the farm before he and my mother officially split up. This in turn, was proof that he *had* been seeing Rachel for longer than we thought. When mum had eventually found out about the 'other woman', he'd said it had only been for a matter of weeks. At least that is what I thought I'd heard during one of their rows.

I decided to push the thought from my mind, water under the bridge and all that.

Anna was still chelping on. She was a lovely woman, very warm and welcoming and I started to relax again; the lump in my throat officially gone.

As we climbed the stairs, my eyes were drawn to the various paintings which lined the walls. They were mostly of landscapes, possibly places in Yorkshire and quite old fashioned but they suited the house.

I followed Anna down the long landing and she pointed out my dad and Rachel's room and also where she slept. We took a few corners along the way which highlighted just how big the house actually was. I could hear the low beat of music coming from one of the other corridors and it instantly pricked up my ears. I sure hoped mine and Connor's rooms were a respectable distance apart. Yes, he was attractive but I didn't want him too in my face. We were also classed as family now and I needed to keep reminding myself of that fact. I wasn't here to win over a boy, I wanted to build on my relationship with my father and I was certain Connor would mess with that if he could.

In spite of the weird crush that I appeared to be experiencing, I needed to keep Connor Barratt at arms-length, for my own sanity if nothing else.

"Well, here we go. I hope it's OK for you. I washed and pressed the bedding myself." Anna beamed, stopping outside what would be my bedroom for the next few months.

"Thanks Anna. I'm sure it's lovely," I replied, following her gesture for me to go ahead. I starting to drag my suitcase inside. Connor had left it by the door which was a relief; the thought of him in my room infecting it with all that testosterone did funny things to my insides.

It was smaller than my bedroom at home, but it was perfect. Decorated mainly in white and pastel colours and the bed was a double which was an added plus. My bed back home was only a single.

There was a white wooden dressing table with a large mirror and a tall wardrobe, not that I'd brought that much with me, anything for an excuse for some online shopping.

I scooted around with my eyes wide; the carpet was thick and luxurious under my sandaled feet and I smiled my approval at Anna before trotting over to peek out of the window. The view overlooked the main yard where I'd come in. Not a garden view, but still not bad. You could still see rolling hills in the distance. We really *were* in the middle of nowhere.

Anna still lingered in the doorway, beaming at me. Blatantly happy I was pleased. To be honest, I wouldn't have had it any other way. The place could have been a dungeon and I'd have made sure I appeared grateful. My manners were always impeccable. Well, with normal people anyway. I decided to file my unusually rude behaviour with Connor in the 'extraneous circumstances' section of my conscience.

"Well, I'll leave you to shower and then see you downstairs later. I'm sure Mike will knock on when he's back. We had a bit of an emergency in field four—oh and Rachel's isn't back until next Thursday—her mum's been poorly."

I nodded my understanding and thanked her again and she left, taking the smell of cooking with her.

I clicked the door firmly closed and turned my back against it, the wood was hard against my sticky back. A cocktail of emotion still bubbled within me. I was here at last and was determined to make the summer work. Any grudge bearing for dad leaving my mum was over. There was no point dredging up the past. I now had the opportunity to make up for not having been in touch during my exams, and to be honest, I didn't really feel that guilty, dad could have made the effort too.

I pushed the thought out of my mind and hefted my case onto the bed to unpack. As I placed a handful of toiletries on the dressing table, I realised that I hadn't been told where the bathroom was. I rescanned the room, noticing a door at the opposite side of the bed and slowly moved to open it. It was a bathroom. The fact that it was en-suite kicked my excitement up a notch, as the thought of sharing with a smelly boy was not something I would have welcomed. Even one I would jump at the chance to see naked in the shower it appeared. I rolled my eyes at my automatic sex starved thoughts.

The bathroom was cute and small with a white toilet, a sink and a shower but it was perfect and immaculately clean.

As I started to peel the clothes from my body, I had a promising feeling that I was going to like it here. Well, most of it, if only I could arrange a truce with my tetchy stepbrother. There was no *real* reason for us to dislike each other after all. Maybe I was partly to blame? I canned my moment of self-reflection and padded barefoot to the shower. I would need to play it by ear.

As I stepped under the spray, I made the decision that I'd attempt to clean the slate and get on Connor's good side. He had to have a good side after all. Didn't everyone?

I sat at the dressing table, finishing off blow drying my hair whilst a million thoughts swam around my head. I felt thoroughly refreshed after showering and had put on clean underwear and a pale blue sundress with spaghetti straps. It was A-Line and fell below my knees. It was also slightly creased from being stuffed in my case but if my dad, Anna and Connor were the only ones around, I'd still be more pristine than them.

I wanted to look extra nice for my father and so applied a minimal amount of make-up and a squirt of perfume. After struggling with a couple of different styles, I left my long hair loose and it fell past my shoulders in soft, shiny waves.

Eyeing my appearance in the mirror I smiled. Yes, my looks had caused me problems in the past, but would I really have it any other way? Those that were not so lucky had their own problems. Teenagers were cruel and would find fault no matter what. It is probably human nature to think that beauty and perfection is everything?

My mind rolled back to Connor's comments about boys behaving like dicks around me. A picture of Samantha Jones's spiteful face passed fleetingly through my thoughts. I retrieved my phone and re-read a couple more texts about last night's party.

I was so glad I hadn't gone down the serious boyfriend's path yet. Getting the right grades for Uni had been my focus during my first year of A-Levels. Sure, there had been a brief thing with Andrew and I'd kissed a couple of other guys, but that was it. That other thing could wait. High school boys were really immature anyway.

I fluffed my hair and applied lipstick, almost smudging it as I heard a bang on the door.

"Come in."

The door swung wide and dad rattled into the room like a tornado. I set the lipstick on the dressing table and shot to my feet to greet him, a smile lighting my face. He was so pleased to see me; I was instantly alive with happiness. He met me half way and swung me into his arms. It felt amazing; he smelled of hard work and cut grass and was dressed in dusty work overalls.

"I'm so sorry I wasn't there to collect you sweetie. Everything OK? How'd you like your room? Did Connor get you on time?"

I laughed, "How many questions was that? Slow down."

He set me back on my feet and peered down at me through his mop of sandy hair. His face was full of affection and it tugged at my heart strings. I felt wanted.

"All is good and yes Connor was there on time and I *love* the farm and my room too, it's very me." My response was babbled, but there was so much I wanted to say.

He shot me a smile before strolling over to the chair of the dressing table, spinning it around and sitting on it backwards.

We chatted as I sat on the bed and it didn't feel uncomfortable at all, even when he asked how mum was doing. It felt natural. As if we had never been apart.

Dad explained why he had invested in the farm and that he had also purchased other bits of land in Yorkshire as a new business venture. Dad had been born on a farm and my Grandad had been a wealthy business owner. He had obviously decided to follow in his dad's footsteps as I'd thought. Dad used to own property down south too but sold it to raise the capital for all the farming stuff he needed to replace here.

We must have sat there, catching up for around half an hour before he checked his watch and explained that he needed a shower before dinner. He spoke about Rachel's disappointment that she couldn't be here for when I arrived and I listened and offered my sympathies that her mother was unwell again.

33

Dad stood and dusted off the chair, giving my arm a squeeze. "So, I'll see you at dinner kido. Anna serves it at seven sharp and it's just us tonight. She needs to pop to the village."

"No Connor?" I asked, unable to stop myself.

"No, he goes to the pub on Thursdays."

I felt a strange mix of disappointment and relief that Connor wouldn't be there, but at least it would give me more uninterrupted quality time with my father.

"See you in a bit," Dad smiled and turned to leave.

"Yes—oh and dad," I began. He peered back at me from the doorway. "I'm so glad I'm here. It's going to be a great summer."

His face lit up again at my blatant 'olive branch' attempt.

"It will be. You never know, maybe you'll want to stay longer, you know you're always welcome." He paused, his eyes searching my face. "Anyway, see you at dinner, I want to hear all about your exams."

I nodded, not even slightly worried. I was confident I had done fairly well, considering the shit I'd had to deal with at the time. "Cool. I'll fill you in later."

As dad closed the door gently behind him, I checked the time on my phone and saw that I had an hour before dinner. This was the perfect amount of time for a walk in what was left of the sunshine.

I sent my mum a text to say I'd arrived and wondered if I'd receive a response. She usually started drinking around supper time. I glanced out of the window to double check the weather and decided against adding a cardigan to my outfit, I didn't want more creases. After briefly rechecking my appearance in the floor length mirror, I left my bedroom with the sense of adventure brewing.

As I made my way down the stairs into the hallway, I could hear pots and pans clanging in the kitchen, no doubt Anna cooking supper. I exited the house and scanned the yard, it still looked as cluttered as before. Connor's car was gone and in its place was a battered old Land Rover which I assumed belonged to my dad. It was strange really as dad usually drove the fanciest of cars.

It was still a bright evening but was much cooler than I had anticipated. The farm was situated in a valley and I loved the countryside setting. I knew from dad's emails that the farm grew crops, kept sheep and pigs but made most of its money from trading cattle.

I plodded over and into the barn where a cluster of cows were housed and eyed the glossy black and white coats. There were tons of them; all fenced together, but they looked fairly healthy and content. I was surprised that the dung smell from earlier had disappeared and that the air was now quite sweet.

I stepped onto the metal fencing to peer further into the enclosure. A couple of furry heads lifted to peer at me, their mouths continuously chewing.

"Careful you don't fall in," a voice uttered from behind me. Startled I jerked my head around to see two men standing at the entrance of the barn. One was near my dad's age and the other my own I guessed. I released my death-grip from the fence and lowered myself to the hay strewn floor.

"Now you *must* be Harlow," the older of the two men began, moving forward with a hand raised towards me. He was tall and gangly with a mop of curly blonde hair and he was well spoken, not a hint of Yorkshire. I noticed he held a large bag in one hand.

I approached them, avoiding a smudge of what looked suspiciously like part of a cow pat and shook his hand with a bright smile.

"Yes, that's right," I admitted as my heart rate normalised, rising a 'hi there' hand at the younger guy. Shaking hands with a boy my age would surely be weird. It was definitely an old person's thing to do.

They both wore beige combats and green T shirts with a medical type logo on.

"I'm Marcus. I'm your dad's vet and this is my apprentice, Tom," the older chap introduced.

"Yeah, but we're vets to your dad's livestock, not to your dad," the boy Tom joked with a nervous chuckle. He transferred his weight from one foot to the other in a swaying motion as he spoke. I'd seen guys do this before. He was probably a bit shy in the company of girls. I grinned, not wanting him to feel silly.

Vets? That made sense considering the logo.

Tom had a genuine, friendly smile on his face and I felt thankful that at least there was one guy here near my age, who hadn't taken an immediate dislike to me.

"I was just admiring the cows; this is probably the closest I've been to one in my entire life." I laughed.

Marcus shifted the weight of the bag he carried to his other hand. I imagined it contained his medical tools.

"You haven't missed much. All they do is eat. Eat and crap of course," the vet added, chuckling at his own words. "When did you get here?"

Cocking my head thoughtfully I replied. "A couple of hours ago."

"Well, I bet Mike is relieved you're here at last, he's done nothing but talk about you for months."

Tom echoed his words. "Yeah, months."

Warmth bloomed in my tummy. I liked it that dad talked about me.

"It's great to finally see the place. I'd seen a few pictures, but it's nothing like I expected."

"That's the country for you. It isn't the same unless you experience it in person," Marcus said proudly, taking a swift glance around.

"Mike said something about you maybe going to Uni here? Tom is at Scarborough, so you'd have one friendly face."

I moved my focus to Tom who was still grinning widely. He was soaking up the banter, but his eyes were literally pinned to my face. It felt nice to have some good-looking boy attention again. And from a clever one too. He'd have to be super smart if he was training to be a vet.

"Yes, possibly," I replied, pushing my hands into the pockets of my dress. I felt extra feminine in their company. Country men, rough to my smooth.

Marcus nodded thoughtfully. "Cool. What do you fancy studying?"

"I'm interested in the Early Years course they offer. Maybe to go into teaching or something. Dad sent me the prospectus."

Marcus nodded thoughtfully. "I can imagine he did, he'd get to see you more then. Dad's and their ulterior movies."

"That'd be cool Harlow, you'll love the campus. Maybe I could take you on one of my afternoon's off?" Tom offered brightly. His expression had altered to a similar look the guy on the train had worn. He was now in contemplation mode.

"That would be great."

Marcus cast Tom a knowing smile before saying.

"Anyways, I'm sure we'll see lots of each other. We've just finished our rounds and I better get back to the Mrs. I'll be in bother if I'm late for supper." Marcus chimed, giving me one of those 'I'm a hen-pecked man and I love it' looks. He turned briefly to his apprentice with a meatier grin and patted him on the shoulder. "I'll see you at the car Tom. Bye Harlow."

I gave him a finger tipped wave. He looked like he belonged on the set of Emmerdale.

Tom straightened and watched Marcus depart before glancing back at me. I felt heat sneak into my cheeks as he shamelessly checked me out. I wasn't offended, not after the way Connor had treated me. I needed a bit of male attention to sooth those seriously ruffled feathers.

I pursed my lips, suddenly curious. "So, you're training to be a vet? That's cool," I said.

My words seemed to shake him out of his stupor and he had the intelligence to look embarrassed.

"Sorry—er—for staring. Yes, I'm trying to be. A vet that is. The hours are mind-numbingly long but it gets you out and about," he blurted in response. "When would you apply if you did decide on Scarborough?"

"I have one more year of A-Levels, so next year, ready for September I think."

Tom's face lit up further. "I'm in my second of five years at Scarborough, so I'll still be there. Probably ground down by stress, if I even make it that far," he explained with a boyish grin.

He had chocolate brown eyes and brown hair that looked like he ran his hands through it, a lot. He was cute in a boyish way but wore way too much aftershave, enough to down an otter I would guess.

As he spoke, he'd moved further towards me. He was still taller, but I would say of average height for a boy his age. He certainly didn't tower over me like Connor did. A cow mooed, almost drowning out my reply which made me grin and shoot a glance behind me.

"Cool," I answered.

"So, teaching? Don't you fancy following in your dad's footsteps".

I grinned as we both knew I was no farmer. "I don't know for definite, how are you supposed to know what you want to do with your life at sixteen. It's crazy really."

"I agree although it was easy for me. My dad's a vet and so it was kind of expected. Anyway, we'll see if I ever graduate, I must say I struggle with the paperwork side of things."

I imagined he was humouring me; his eyes were bright with intelligence. He was probably excellent at everything, especially as it was in his blood. Didn't you need loads of A-Levels to train to be a vet or something?

He leaned forward with a keen look on his face, dashing his hands across his thighs before asking. "So, sixteen?"

I paused for a moment, wondering whether to do the whole, 'how old do you think I am' thing but decided against it. I had briefly mentioned my age, but I knew I looked younger and if he said so, I wouldn't have liked it. I decided not to put myself in that position. I was slight in height and baby faced. It was another one of life's frustrations. I could never get in the bars and stuff when my friends went.

I cleared my throat. "Almost seventeen—you?

His eyes widened; it was a telling sign that he *had* thought me younger. "Twenty—twenty-one next month."

So, he was around the same age as Connor.

My shoulders slumped at the fact that I had misjudged his age. Was it wrong of me to feel disappointed that he was so much older than me? It would have been nice to have someone nearer my own age. I didn't want all the guys to view me like some type of kid.

He pushed a hand through his hair again, it was like a nervous tic but I grinned at the motion. "Do you have any brothers or sisters?"

"No, it's just me," I replied.

He scratched his perfectly shaven jaw; either that or he wasn't at that whisker stage yet. He also looked younger than his age. "Lucky you. I have a sister, Ella. She's eighteen and just plain annoying."

I raised my eyebrows in understanding and chuckled. Tom's eyes brightened. He was obviously pleased I found him funny.

"What are you up to tonight?" From the intonation of his question, I had a feeling he was about to ask me out. I inhaled and pretended to play tonight's plans in my head, it didn't take long.

"Well, nothing really—just dinner with my dad."

I was actually looking forward to a bit of quiet time and so I hoped he didn't push it.

"Why don't you come to the pub, I'll introduce you around?" There it was— as expected. His body language was very readable.

I faked thinking about it. It was a nice offer and one that I would probably have accepted, had it not been my first night at the farm.

I constructed my reply and let him down gently with my usual amount of tact. "Another time maybe? I just got here and need to see my dad really."

I didn't want to scare him off and never receive another invitation. As he digested my words, I remembered dad saying that Connor went to the pub on Thursdays. Knowledge of this would again have given me a second reason not to go; the thought of him putting me down in front of a pub full of people was not a pretty picture.

"No, that's fine and makes total sense," Tom replied jovially. As least I'd not burnt my bridges there.

"Tom!" a voice sounded in the distance.

"Ah, better go otherwise Marcus will shit a brick. Anyway, good to meet you at last and I'll see you soon Harlow." He dashed off with a fairly effeminate wave.

"I'll look forward to it," I threw out there. I sure hoped he was one of the nice ones. I could see he was interested in me and I quite liked it. He appeared to be a pleasant, intelligent guy with an OK face. He also had a good sense of humour and absolutely no demons, well none that I could see through a first impression anyway.

I grinned, pretty much, perfect boyfriend material, if maybe a little on the safe side.

I pondered that thought as it may be nice to have a little light flirtation. Build back the armour that had been smashed down by my step-monster Connor.

I spent the next half an hour, walking around the farm, peering into an assortment of nooks and crannies. I also paid a quick visit to the sheep in the fields and an even quicker trip to the pig pens, the smell there was eyebrow curling stuff.

After popping to the bathroom to wash my hands, I set off for dinner, thoroughly looking forward to spending some quality time with dad.

Four

I sank onto the bed *exhausted*. My limbs felt heavy and the make-up I still wore felt like a face mask. I leaned over to the bedside table to retrieve some baby wipes, my eyes were gritty and I needed to clean my skin.

Checking my phone, it was almost midnight and was now pitch-black outside, the fact that there were no streetlights in the area added to the darkness. There was just the glow of the moon and a slight beam from a security light.

Dinner had been perfection; a homemade quiche, jacket potato and loads of salad with lashings of dressing. Anna had prepared it beautifully before she went out.

Dad and I had chatted about this and that as we ate and then we went to chill out in his study. It was much messier than it had been earlier, with loads of unopened letters on the desk.

We spoke briefly about mum and he didn't go into any details about the divorce which I appreciated. No daughter wanted to participate in discussions about their parents' break up. It was hard enough when my mother brought it up.

It didn't matter now that he went off with another woman, if he'd been happy, he would have stayed. It was text book stuff really; most of my friend's folks were separated.

We spoke about my A-Levels and dad mentioned Uni again. I was good with young kids but did I really want to teach?

After talking about possible career options, we listened to music together. Dad even poured me a glass of red wine, which wasn't *totally* awful.

All in all, our first proper get together at the farm was a success. I even kissed him goodnight on the cheek and he wore the meatiest of smiles as I left for bed.

As I laid back, fully dressed, I allowed my eyes to drift closed. I was looking forward to the morning. I was an early riser and dad had said that he would give me the 'official' tour and introduce me to how things worked on the farm. Maybe I'd love it so much I'd would be a farmer? I imagined myself in baggy dungarees and a straw hat. It could work.

I rubbed my eyes and was about to slip under the covers when I heard the growl of an engine outside. I pushed up on my elbows, rolled off the bed and headed to the window.

Drawing back a curtain, I peeked outside to see who it was, aware that it was pretty late for visitors.

It was Connor. He climbed out of the Ranger and slammed the door; he must have just come in from the pub, although he didn't appear drunk. His steps were straight and determined, no swaying like Lisa when she was pissed. I pushed the thought of drink driving aside. Who cared, he could do what the hell he wanted; if he wished to drive his car into a tree; that was *his* business.

Although it was dark, I could see clearly enough and I watched as he strode around to the back to the car and riffled in the boot.

My curiosity was well and truly stoked and I moved the curtain wider for a better view, wondering what on earth he was doing. Did he have a body in there? I grinned at my own joke.

He appeared to be bandaging his knuckles which sent a shard of alarm into me. Had he hurt himself? Had he been fighting? My maternal instincts kicked in and I felt a moment of genuine concern that he may be hurt.

Wrinkling my nose, I pushed away the unearned loyalty, knowing that any offer of assistance would be vehemently rebuffed.

He wore clean jeans which hung low on his hips and a black T shirt which had the image of a scary looking rock band on it.

I watched as he made his way toward the hay barn with his hands wrapped in tape and caught the glimpse of the determination on his face. I drew away from the window. Whatever he was up too wasn't my business and if he knew I'd been watching him, I'd be mortified.

I climbed onto the bed and decided to push all thoughts and concerns about Connor Barratt from my head.

My phone pinged from the bedside table and I lifted it to my face, the light from the screen was bright. I had four texts from my mother, all saying the same thing.

`Hope you're havg fun. Love you x`
`Hope you're havg fun. Love you x`
`Hope you're havg fun. Love you x`

Hope you're havg fun. Love you x

As I anticipated. Mum was probably shit faced. No emojis this time thank goodness.

I knew she'd be fine, she always stopped when she knew she'd had enough and pretty much *never* had a hangover.

Pushing thoughts of everything aside, I closed my eyes and slept like the dead.

Having woken up in my crumpled clothes, bedhead hair and half of my face still made up, I decided to take a quick shower before breakfast.

I wasn't really sure where dad would take me, but I imagined dirt would be involved so I tugged on a black camisole top with spaghetti straps, blue skinny jeans and my pink converse. I checked myself in the mirror; I certainly smashed the farm girl look and I dragged my freshly washed hair into a ponytail without drying it.

As I entered the kitchen, it was empty but there was a bowl of freshly cooked croissants on the table and I tore a piece off one and popped it between my lips, the flavour causing my mouth to water.

As I heaved open the front door to search for dad, I welcomed the feel of the sunshine on my face and moved forward onto the stone steps. My eyes took their time to adjust and I inhaled the air which was surprisingly dung free today or maybe I was just getting used to it, like Connor had said.

A rustle at my feet caught my attention and I looked down to see a girl crouched on the floor. She was fiddling with the laces of her trainers.

"Er, hello?" I puffed as she raised her head. She had brown short pixie-like hair and eyes the colour of milk chocolate. She scrambled to her feet, uncurling what was actually a very long body. I shuffled back a step.

I raised my eyebrows in silent question and she looked me up and down.

"Can I help you?" I prompted in a friendly enough way, considering her semi-rude assessment, which I was of course used to receiving from members of my sex.

She shot me an uncomfortable look before finally finding her voice. "Sorry, I wasn't sure you'd be here. Anna thought you'd left with Mike. Harlow, is it?"

I nodded "That's me," taking in the unfeminine baggy jeans and overly large sweater she wore. She certainly didn't conform to the masses in respect of fashion.

"I'm Ella." Her accent wasn't easy to read, but sounded familiar.

"OK. Sorry, do you work here?" My question could have been taken as impolite but I said it in a super nice way.

She dealt me one of those smiles that are a bit too wide to be genuine.

"No, my brother does though. Well, sort of, when the need arises. He's training to be a Vet. You met him yesterday."

It took a moment to digest her words as they erupted from her lips like gunfire. So, *this* was the sister that Tom had mentioned. She certainly wasn't as friendly as her brother but I suppose that shouldn't surprise me. First introductions with other girls were never a straightforward operation for me.

"Yes, of course er—Tom... He isn't here though," I pointed out.

"Yes, I know." There was an awkward pause. "I just thought I'd pop by and check you out in person."

Now *that* reply was an odd one.

"Oh—OK," I stuttered. It was a strange situation. She'd come to see me but she didn't look very happy about it.

She exhaled noisily. "Sorry, I'll start again—Hi—I'm Ella—and you must be Harlow?" Her hand shot out in a gesture of greeting. "Good to meet you."

I smiled and took her hand. "Hi, yes. Good to meet you too." The whole situation screamed awkward, but I went with it.

She held my hand a little longer than was necessary. "Sorry," she cut in as my eyes creased, withdrawing her fingers. "I'm not usually so weird but, you surprised me."

I pursed my lips in realisation. I had almost *trodden* on the girl after all. "Sorry I didn't see you down there."

She shot me what I would now take as a genuine smile and it lit up her face, cancelling out that tetchy first impression. She was pretty in a tomboyish type of way.

43

She ran a hand through her short crown of hair. "No, I don't mean that. I mean, shocked because you do look *exactly* like Tom described. We all thought what he said was—well— you know—a bit over the top?"

I pursed my lips. "Oh, is that good or bad?" I quizzed her, uncertainty thrumming within me.

"I suppose it depends on who you are. Good for the boys, bad for us girls I suppose," she snorted.

I grimaced, struggling to decipher her code.

She strummed a fist across her nose before clarifying. "As in you *are gorgeous*. Stunning. Like a Barbie doll but shorter."

The Barbie doll comment again, *really*? An awkward silence loomed before I quickly cut in. "Thanks—I guess." I tried to be gracious with my response but if was difficult, I was so tired of everything being about my looks all the time. After the situation with Samantha, it had started to annoy me more. Beauty was not the be all and end all FFS!

I combed my fingers through my damp ponytail, suddenly feeling self-conscious.

"*Everyone* in the pub is *dying* to see you," she announced with a grin, her teeth were slightly crooked but not in a mega bad way.

"Great," I managed between tight lips.

I suppose I should have been happy that people wanted to get to know me, but her words created a sinking feeling in my stomach. I couldn't put my finger on it, but something was off. Maybe she viewed me as some type of competition?

Ella continued to smile at me and the situation got stranger. I felt a further twinge of discomfort and my body itched to leave. She eyed me as if I had something mildly contagious for a minute longer before saying. "Anyway, I just wanted to say hi," sensing the changed vibe between us.

"OK, cool."

There was another moments silence and I attempted to shake myself out of my stupor. I wasn't usually so poor at making conversation, but something about her arrival didn't sit right.

"Sorry for the weird intro, but I don't have any girlfriends in the village. I'm sort of one of the boys really.

You want to hang out for a bit?" she suddenly proposed brightly, a hopeful look on her face.

Every instinct inside me wanted to reject her offer. I hurriedly searched for excuses but then realised I didn't need to make anything up. I was waiting for my father.

"Sorry but I'm just waiting for my dad to come down. He's going to show me the farm. I only arrived yesterday," I pointed out with an attempt at being friendly, rather than being Mrs Rejection.

She nodded her head in silent understanding. "I thought he'd already left but OK—I'll wait with you. Gorgeous day for it."

Damn, she didn't get the message. I relented anyway and my palms also started to itch. A sign I was nervous.

"So, were your ears burning last night? Tom has it bad. Connor wasn't best pleased."

Great, so we were back to that again, I was hoping her comment about the weather had taken the conversation into a more comfortable zone. I could see I was the one who would have to try and steer the subject away from me.

I eyed her thoughtfully, wondering about her 'Connor wasn't best pleased' comment.

Ella wore a cheeky expression, like she'd just delivered the juiciest piece of gossip and my stomach knotted.

The cows in the barn behind us emitted the loudest of moos. Well said, I thought to myself.

She must have read my expression and realised that I felt slightly uncomfortable and she moved the conversation on. "How old are you anyway?" Her brow knotted.

Boy she was a nosy one, it was like I was being cross-examined. She was probably on a fact-finding mission.

"I'll be seventeen soon."

She clapped her hands together, excited by the news. "Oh wow, we have to have a party. Do you have a boyfriend?" she blurted; her dark eyes wide; her ability to jump from one subject to another was fairly impressive.

I tried to keep up and redirected the question back at her. Two could play that game. "No. You?"

She rubbed her hands down her jeans. "Not really, it's complicated?" She said briefly looking away. I noted her eyebrows met in the middle. What was it with village folk and grooming?

"Care to elaborate," I asked.

She looked at me shyly, which was strange considering she'd asked me the *exact* same question. Maybe she didn't have a boyfriend but wanted me to *think* she did so she'd appear more grown up. Girls used to do that at school. The imaginary boyfriend had always been a thing.

"Nah, not really. There is a guy that I like though." She paused for thought as if weighing up whether to say more. "I can't believe you don't have one, a boyfriend I mean. You're not one of those prudish types I hope."

I inwardly acknowledged that the conversation wasn't that odd really in the scheme of things. The main topic of discussion between my other friends was *always* boy related. Although considering this girl and I had *just* met, it all felt a bit forced. Maybe country girls were more direct? I thought fleetingly about the issues I'd had in the past with girls due to guys and this again prompted me to steer away from a potential, 'problem' topic.

Ella nudged my arm, shaking me out of my thoughts. "Want to sit whilst your dad comes back?" she questioned, pointing to the flaking iron bench in front of the house. Her previous 'hang out' comment was very American and I wondered if she'd spent time in the states.

I conceded defeat and moved to take a seat and she followed me. I silently willed my dad to appear.

"So, I'm probably breaking some type of brother-sister trust code, but don't be surprised if Tom asks you out. He's very much the smitten kitten." She said with a laugh. The sound rolled unpleasantly across my bones. I decided the way Ella sat grinning at me like the Cheshire cat was annoying, but I batted the mean comeback to one side.

"I don't really know what to say to that, he seems lovely but I'm not really after a summer fling or anything." My reply wasn't the total truth of course, but I wasn't going to show my cards too soon.

46

"Surely that's the perfect time for a fling, summer. Especially when you're pretty much surrounded by guys here. Some ancient. Although it depends on your type of course." She said elbowing me suggestively from her seated position on the bench.

Ella angled her body further towards me, her fingers threaded on her lap. "Sorry, I'm back to talking about guys again. Believe it or not, I do have *some* other interests." She promised.

I smiled, not wanting her to feel uncomfortable.

"What's *your* type?" I quizzed.

Her expression brightened. She was obviously relieved I'd met her half way with the guy chat.

"Tall and dark, the usual I suppose, but older guys definitely. I can't be doing with guys my age; immature and too wrapped up in the haze of their own self-righteous farts."

I smiled at the fart comment and agreed about the older guy thing, but how old were we talking. She'd mentioned the word ancient a minute ago. Maybe she was dating someone's dad on the quiet, hence the weirdness. I shook off the thought, her strange thought processes appeared to be contagious.

"How about you? What's your type?" she prompted.

I had the courtesy to look like I was thinking about it, but I felt quite bored with the conversation.

"I'm not sure really. I suppose tall, dark and handsome, the usual cliché."

My thoughts roamed to Connor who unfortunately ticked all those boxes before I quickly added. "But personality is key for me. So, someone nice and fun who listens and stuff. I can't do with all the moody bullshit." Boxes he most certainly did *not* tick!

She then pointed out the obvious. Which again proved that it was well documented that Connor was a grumpy sod and not just with me. Anna had said the same.

As if reading my thoughts, she chucked. "Connor's out of luck then. He can be a right moody twat."

My smile widened and I nodded. "He's also my stepbrother."

"So, you don't fancy Connor at all?"

And there it was as she finally cut to the chase.

That's why she'd come to see me, to grill the new girl to see if she had any intentions of making a move on her possible crush. She had a thing for Connor and felt threatened. That *had* to be it, hence the atmosphere.

Adrenalin fizzed through me. I hated that just the sound of Connor's name did something funny to my insides.

I cocked my head, constructing my reply carefully. It was the only obvious answer, she fancied Connor, *that's* why her behaviour was so weird.

"Totally not my thing," I almost choked the words out with a gruff voice. 'Act indifferent' my head instructed me. The words left my mouth like gunfire and therefore had the opposite effect.

"So, you *do* fancy Connor then?"

I bit back the long sigh and gritted my teeth.

My face must have been a picture and I babbled my reply again, with a bit too much force.

"Absolutely not."

Her eyes narrowed into slits as they assessed my face and she leaned forwards, her jean clad thigh brushing my own before commencing her interrogation. "You're kidding right? You have to be. He's fit as fuck." The look of disbelief on her face was laughable. "You *don't* think Connor Barratt is fit as fuck?"

She spoke like the thought of me not being attracted to my stepbrother was totally unpalatable.

I needed to do some damage control quickly or it would be all around the village that I fancied my own stepbrother. I had watched plenty of those small village-based TV shows and so I *knew* what these tight-knit communities were like for gossip. Proper curtain twitchers.

"He's OK looking, but he isn't my type at all," I lied.

She gave me a knowing look. No doubt every female in these parts found Connor attractive.

"If you say so," she deadpanned.

There was now a definite tone to her voice, which was interesting. She obviously didn't believe me. Surely if she was interested in my stepbrother, my news would have been welcomed. She probably knew I was lying.

Silence fell between us and I shooed my tongue out of its hiding place.

"We're supposed to be family," I pointed out, sounding like a broken record.

Ella crossed her legs and sat straighter, as if preparing herself for a serious discussion on the subject; a definite 'getting down to the nitty gritty' type of stance.

"Sure, but it's not like you're related by blood or anything."

I pursed my lips. She was right of course, but I needed to nip it in the bud. Our conversation was heading into strange waters.

I knew I couldn't totally lie and say I thought him a complete toad. She was shrewd, she'd see straight through that. "As I said, he isn't bad looking, but… well he could probably use a personality transplant."

There, I'd said it.

The truth of my comment made her smile widen but she had an odd look in her eye as she turned slowly away, staring vacantly out into the yard.

"Yeah, he can be a nasty bastard. I imagine you haven't seen half of it yet. You should see him work out though, it's *proper* intense; scary *and* sexy at the same time, like he has the devil in him, gives you full on fanny flutters."

The laugh left my body at light speed. Her comment was pretty disgusting but funny nonetheless.

Now the ice had well and truly been smashed to smithereens, I knew exactly what she meant, but it wasn't the type of language I would have chosen to use, especially in the company of someone I had literally *just* met.

I didn't want to appear like the prude she'd alluded to earlier and so I just smiled and moved the discussion on. "Anyway, I imagine he already has a girlfriend?" Again, I attempted to make myself sound disinterested, as if I was talking about the weather. I lifted my words at the end, to mould them into more of a question.

Her reply was amusing, even though I felt a twinge of jealousy.

"Oh, he has lots of girls. I'm not sure if any of them are his friends though." Ella smirked.

I decided to go for a counter-attack. "Anyway, why all the talk about Connor? Do *you* like him? If you do, its fine you know. I won't say anything."

I watched as she shrugged and kicked at a pebble with her foot. "It wouldn't do me any good if I did."

She spoke almost as if she were talking to herself, her voice reflective and before I could encourage her to elaborate, she changed the subject swiftly to fashion.

"Love your converse by the way."

"Thanks—I like your hoodie."

We spoke about the shops in the village and a new online clothing store that had recently launched before Ella pretty much tripped me up with an out of the blue comment. "You made up with your dad then?"

My mouth dropped open. Where had that come from?

She sent me a semi-apologetic look. "Sorry, I'm a nosy bitch. I just heard that you hadn't spoken in a while."

"No, it's fine. We're good. It's just been a busy time with school and stuff."

Ella asked me what A-Levels I had taken and then explained that she'd recently finished hers. Her grades had not been what she had hoped for and I got the feeling she was probably walking in the shadow of her older brother. Future veterinarian was a hard one to follow.

Ella said she was intending running her own gardening business one day and loved the outdoors. She spoke about how she had helped to re-landscape a few of the gardens in the village.

"Anyways, I had better head."

Ella clambered awkwardly to her feet and offered her hand to pull me up. Her fingers were cold.

"You're OK Harlow, thanks for our chat and sorry for the grilling about Connor but it's probably for the best that you don't fancy him. He's a complex guy." She said in a matter-of-fact way as she dusted off her jeans with her hands. "His dad pretty much fucked him up for life. Damaged goods and all that."

She didn't elaborate on her last comment. She was probably referring to his parents' divorce.

I straightened and pulled my top down which had rolled up slightly, revealing my stomach.

"You sound like you care about him. Maybe there's more there than you think?"

I decided to go in for the kill as she'd ignored me the first time and anyway, I imagined most girls in the village would fancy Connor. I hated the fact that I cared so much about that.

Her eyebrows crinkled.

"Not with him being friends with my brother. It's sort of not allowed. Funny what is and isn't allowed isn't it. Village life can be so restrictive."

Her stare was pensive and her shoulders slumped. I took this as a sign that I needed to remove myself from this situation. I was certainly no agony aunt.

"Well, if you ever need to talk. I'm a good listener," I offered, lying through my teeth.

My words seemed to sooth her mood and she brightened.

"Thanks. That'd be cool. Sorry for just dropping by and for all the questions, but I had strict instructions from the guys who are dying to meet you."

"Cool. Me too."

I wasn't really sure I was that bothered about meeting 'the guys.' They sounded like trouble. It sounded like the locals *were* all panting for female action and I hated players.

"It was Connor who called you Barbie by the way."

I hadn't really needed her to tell me that it was Connor who'd compared me to a doll. Rotten sod.

"I just didn't want you to think it was Tom. He wouldn't say something like that."

I nodded. "That's fine, Connor called me that the first time we met." I confessed, thinking back to the party.

"Nasty bastard," Ella said, grimacing. "Although is it actually an insult? I'd fricking love to look like Barbie, she's perfect," she pointed out upon reflection.

"Believe me, the way he said it, he meant it as one."

Her face almost contorted

"I wouldn't be so sure."

I frowned but before I could question her, she moved on. "Please don't tell Connor I was talking about him. He'd be pissed," Ella put in as we stopped by the front door of the house.

"I wouldn't worry about that. We aren't close."

Ella nodded her understanding.

"It's probably for the best. All guys are dicks. Especially the controlling type."

From her words I suspected she had experience but wasn't quite ready to share. We'd known each other all of twenty minutes and so this came as no shock.

"You sound like you know the type well?"

She flashed me a semi-pained look and I immediately regretted my words. There was something she wasn't saying. I could read a deep sadness in her. Maybe she and Connor *did* have a past. Now I felt like a bitch, but she wasn't beaten for long.

"Farm boys are not like other guys. It's so cut off here and there is so much competition, due to the lack of girls who live in the area," she stated and then briefly looked me up and down. "Well, girlie girls anyway. Honestly when the guys see you, they'll be all over you like a rash."

I suddenly had an image of hairy, weathered faced men in dungarees, waving pitch forks and panting heavily. It was comical really.

Ella now looked sad and I decided she needed a compliment. It was the prefect medicine for a girl who was feeling insecure and this girl *blatantly* was. I was used to it. I saw it all the time in my friends.

"OK, thanks for the warning I guess and anyway, what about you? You're not so bad looking yourself. If I were a guy I would," I grinned with raised eyebrows.

Her face creased in the semblance of a smile but it didn't quite reach her eyes and I was being fairly sincere. She wasn't *totally* unfortunate looking.

Ella shrugged me off with an air of polite indifference. "That's sweet and thank you I guess, but I've grown up here; to most of the boys in the village, I'm one of them."

Anna suddenly appeared in the doorway and began sweeping the gravel off the front step, looking her usual windswept self.

"Sorry Ladies." She chuckled as she showered us with a cloud of dust.

We moved to the side and I touched Ella's arm to try and show her that I wanted us to be friends. "Look, thanks for coming to see me and don't worry, I shall tread carefully with the farm boys." I reassured her with a pointed look. I was pleased I'd kept my cool.

One of Ella's bushy eyebrows curved and she tilted her jaw to deliver what I took as a pensive stare, her eyes roaming over my face. "It won't be easy. As I said, like a rash."

I felt a frisson of something heat my spine. I narrowed my eyes, cutting her a hard look. "I suppose we'll see."

"I suppose we will," she mirrored.

I decided to bury it. We exchanged numbers and said our goodbyes. I was relieved as the banter had been like being on a see-saw.

I watched her as she walked away, my eyes burning into the back of her head as Anna came to stand beside me. We stood in silence for a moment staring as Ella departed down the driveway.

"Poor girl. She's not had an easy ride that one."

Really? It sounded like farm life was much more interesting than I had once thought. I schooled my irritation at her empathy.

"Really, in what way?"

"There were whispers around the village that she got herself into trouble last year."

Her revelation didn't really need a footnote, but I wanted to shake the actual words out of her.

"No, sorry, what do you mean?"

She sighed and tucked a strand of frizzy hair back over her ear. "There was a horrible pregnancy rumour. It was probably just mean talk. It happens way out here too you know; silly girls and boys making up stories."

What the actual fuck? I almost choked. "Are you sure there wasn't any truth in it?" I questioned, uncertainty whooshing into me as I thought about Ella's 'complicated' comment.

Leaning on the broom, Anna pushed her free hand into the pocket of her dusty apron before she replied. "No, not really and if she did get pregnant, she must have got rid of it as no one ever saw a baby. She left town for a few months, went abroad to America and that's when the questions started. When she came back, she was a different girl. Less into the partying and more reserved. She'd grown up I suppose." And there was the reason for the occasional twang. She'd staying in the States.

A sick feeling hit my stomach. How awful! The poor girl being the brunt of such horrible gossip; if it *was* gossip.

But if it was true? It would explain her strange behaviour. My heart and my mind were momentarily paralysed as a surreal thought floated to the surface. I turned to Anna, getting straight to the point.

"Was there talk as to who the father was? I mean, if there were any truth to it?" I asked.

There was a beat or two before she answered; her expression now vacant.

"Anna?" I prompted and she shot me an apologetic look.

"Sorry, there was talk of course but that's all it was. It's died down now but it must have been horrible for her at the time," Anna replied at last, softly; her weathered face full of sympathy. Technically she hadn't answered my question and I wondered why.

A strange taste spilled into my mouth, like I'd been sucking on metal.

Could Connor have been the father of said alleged baby? That would surely explain her weirdness towards me. Maybe they they'd kept their affair a secret as she would be 'off limits' being the sister of a 'friend'.

Although, during our Connor related discussion, she'd seemed the most at ease. Wouldn't she have given *something* away at that point?

My brain had actually started to ache and I shooed away the thoughts. Who cared right? Connor Barratt and Ella Wade were not my business.

I released the breath I hadn't realised I'd been holding. To hell with the drama, I would certainly *not* be getting involved in it.

It was just annoying that I couldn't swallow that feeling of upset. Was this why my stepbrother had issues, because he'd knocked up his friend's sister? Surely that would be enough to mess with *anyone's* head.

My meanderings were interrupted when dad suddenly appeared from the house in his work clothes and I filed away the rest of the troublesome questions in my head. For now, thoughts about Connor Barratt could do one.

"You ready?" Dad piped in warmly, his weathered face now clean shaven. He looked so much younger without the bristle.

I swallowed down another one of those lumps, and constructed my reply.

"Absolutely." I grinned. All concerns of knocked up teenagers forgotten... for now.

Five

After I had been treated to a thorough introduction to farm life, we made our way back to the house. I'd had a preconception about driving around the open countryside staring at fields all day, thinking it would be fairly dull, but I'd enjoyed myself in the end. Dad appeared to be well into farming now and his attitude was infectious. It forced me to embrace my 'outdoor girl'.

The place was much larger than I had first anticipated and was set in around ten acres of grassland.

Depending on the season, each area would be ploughed before the crops were sown, cultivated and then eventually harvested. It was quite a lengthy process and of course much more complex than the carrots I had grown with mum in the garden back home.

As we rattled around in the Land Rover, I listened keenly as my father spoke about the pressures on farming, climate change, high input costs and his five-minute rant about unfeasible government policies for agriculture. I must admit to being guilty of zoning out at *that* point.

As we drove up the driveway and into the yard, I saw Connor by his Ranger. The bonnet was up, I could only see part of his head, but I knew it was him as the two farmhands I'd been introduced to that morning were a totally different build.

The Land Rover pulled up to the house and then dad apologised as he took a call from his phone. I clambered ungraciously from the vehicle, feeling hot and sweaty.

As dad disappeared, I started kicking a few stones at my feet, wondering if Connor would look up from what he was doing and actually talk to me. He must have heard the car but had decided to ignore me anyway. I couldn't understand why I suddenly felt the need to hover.

I shook my foot in an attempt to dislodge a trapped pebble from my shoe and moved closer, wondering how best to break the silence. I had toyed with the thought of saying something about Ella, curious to see how he'd react, but I had promised her I wouldn't say anything.

"So how was the pub?" I began breezily as I plonked myself at the front of the truck. He kept fiddling under the bonnet, looking fit even though he wore oil-stained jeans and a tank top. The muscles in his arms were bulging. In a word, he was mouth-watering. The tattoos on his arm appeared to be of all sorts of different images and wording which I didn't understand. By some miracle, I managed not to drool.

Connor glanced sideways at me and straightened, wiping his oily hands on a rag before gesturing for me to move out of the way with a flick of his fingers. I moved back, determined not to be put off. He reached past me and stuffed the rag into a gap between the engine and the wing.

"How was the pub?" he repeated slowly, almost tasting the words, now actually looking at me. I almost turned away but managed to stand my ground. I was here all summer, we'd have to speak at some point.

"Yes, dad says you go every week. Is there a quiz on or something?" I replied, feeling like a school girl again.

He gave me a pointed look and raised an eyebrow. "Do I look like I do quizzes?"

I gulped down a ball of frustration. Here we go again. "I'm just making conversation Connor. You could attempt to play nice. Don't you think we should try and get along?" I said, trying to reason with him.

His dark eyes narrowed as he turned fully towards me, placing one hand on the car near a section littered with tools. "Firstly, I don't play, and what's the point? After the summers over, you'll just fuck off back down South again. That's *if* you make it through the first week. You'll be bored to tears without all your fancy shops and stilly girlfriends to gossip with."

I smiled thinly. Same old shit, different day.

"So, you see me as one of those society girls," I snorted. "You've been watching too many dodgy American dramas. You're wrong, I may like nice clothes and stuff but I'm not like that at all."

"Really?" he grunted, doubt radiating from his pinned expression.

"Yes, really. Not that my life is any of your business." I curled my fingers into fists.

He nodded and agreed with me. But it still wasn't nice. "That's right. It isn't my business and I really couldn't give a shit."

I felt the urge to thump him and backed away a few steps. The closeness of our bodies was doing strange things to my pulse. The wall hit my back and I attempted to look casual as I leaned against it. Hopefully the stone support would make me appear more chilled out than I was feeling.

I eyed him warily beneath my lashes, recalling Ella's words about Connor and his issues with his dad. Maybe the punk brought it on himself, it wouldn't surprise me.

I felt momentarily deflated but powered on. "Look I'd like us to get on while I'm here. Why don't we call a truce?"

I sure hoped he took the offer. It was extremely gracious of me, bearing in mind his terrible behaviour so far.

Connor smirked and propped his backside against the car, leaning against it before folding his arms across his chest. A hot wave of lust crashed against my pelvis.

"I suppose I'm just a difficult kind of guy." He cocked his head to one side and regarded me.

I smiled, for once we agreed with each other. "Yes, one that doesn't do quizzes I hear." I pointed out with a half joking tone. He didn't return my smile. He was merely humouring me.

"That's me."

I chewed my lip and pushed my hands into the pockets of my shorts. His eyes followed the movement.

"So, what *did* you do at the pub?" I asked, regaining his attention. His eyes darkened as they drilled into me, talk about intense. I could see from his face that he thought my question moronic and I suppose it was, but I was trying to coax a response. "Drink." He replied in a 'dur' type of tone.

It made me smile. "Yes, I know that but what else? Do you play darts or something?"

Although he fought it, my words forced his lips into a grin and my pulse sky rocketed. Connor Barratt wore an actual smile and the fact that I had put it there felt like I'd created a miracle. It made him appear human, boyish even. It was the first proper smile I'd seen on his face.

I didn't know why I questioned him. I wanted to poke for answers but knew the chance of getting any true facts was probably slim to none.

Connor unfolded his arms and placed them behind his back on the truck, one winged brow arched in question. It was a very sexy eyebrow, if eyebrows could be deemed sexy of course. "Is that your idea of how a farmer spends his spare time, playing darts? Now who's been watching too many dodgy dramas?" The muscles on his shoulders bunched as he rocked his weight against the car, eyeing me thoughtfully. "It's the pub. I do what everyone else does in there. I drink, I hang out, relax; catch up with mates, that sort of thing."

I raised my freshly tweezed eyebrows, gaining confidence. We were now engaged in actual banter, it felt refreshing.

"You do have some friends then?" I cast him my best playful look. Usually when I used that expression, boys fell to their knees. Connor didn't of course but the atmosphere between us changed to a lighter tone.

He shot me one of those smiles. "Funny." He acknowledged grimly.

A few strands of hair had come loose from my ponytail and I pushed them back whilst powering on. "What did you talk about?" I asked, genuinely interested to know what farm boys discussed when getting pissed. Would they chat about girls or their opinion on the latest model of tractor? I'd put my money on the latter.

He eyed me thoughtfully. His reply shouldn't have surprised me after what Ella had said, but it did.

"*You* actually."

My brow threaded and I felt a whoosh of adrenalin hit me. The fact that he just laid it out there rattled me a little.

A mixture of raw emotions slapped me. Disbelief, frustration, distrust.

"Me?"

It was strange hearing Connor confess without a trace of embarrassment.

He pushed off the car and took a step towards me, his eyes scanning my face, like he was looking for something.

"Yep, *you* were the main topic of discussion. Thomas Wade believes he's found his future Mrs."

A smirk crossed his lips and he shot me a look I couldn't determine.

"Really?" My voice was way too squeaky.

He slowly nodded his head. "Yep. I imagine he'll start following you around like a fucking puppy."

I wrinkled my nose, not really sure how to respond. It now felt odd having a 'boys' discussion with this particular one. Discomfort snaked its way from my stomach to my chest.

Turning my face away slightly, I muttered, "I only spoke to him for five minutes," almost tripping over the words. I wasn't sure why I was suddenly feeling the need to defend myself.

Connor took another step forward into my space and I felt the fine hairs on my neck bristle. "Speak the hell up and stop mumbling." He said into my ear, drawing the words out slowly to highlight his point. I could feel his breath against my neck.

He was so close and considering he'd probably been working on the Ranger all morning, he smelled amazing. He was all male but free from aftershave and there was no hint of sweat, even though his top was slightly damp. Heady is the word I would go for.

"I said we only spoke for five minutes. But the banter was good".

Connor bent his head even closer, his eyes now intensely focused on my lips. "It doesn't matter, five minutes, one minute. I imagine it hit him the second he laid eyes on you. And I hate to break it to you but his attraction has *nothing* to do with what you spoke about."

I pulled my hands from my pockets and clasped them together in front of me, they were shaking. Was he steering the conversation to a place where he could be horrible to me? I felt so uncertain in my skin at that point.

"Sorry, I don't get you?"

Connor viewed me with a skewed type of fascination. It was unsettling. I sure hoped he didn't think I was fishing.

"You actually think he gives a shit about your sparkling personality?"

I gnawed on my answer, it was a simple enough question but there was an edge to his tone and I didn't know how to take it.

I squinted up at him. "He was actually interested in what I had to say thank you very much. He's really easy to talk to," I put out there.

My reply didn't seem to sit well with him and a darkness clouded his features. His eyes were now hooded as he continued to watch me.

"Is he? He's still a guy Harlow and guys think with their dicks. You should remember that."

I wrung my hands together, suddenly feeling pressure to provide the perfect reply. "I'll remember that the next time I give two shits about what you think. His is sister is nice too. Met her today."

There, I had said it. Boom! I had also gone back on my word to Ella, although I hadn't gone into any detail.

I needed to pop her name in there to gauge his reaction.

Connor cleared his throat but he gave nothing away. "So, I heard," he deadpanned in a bored voice.

Silence filled the space between us and I tilted my head and focused on a spot behind him in the yard, momentarily breaking eye contact. "Yes, she seemed really nice. She surprised me." I pointed out like it was no big deal.

His response was not one that I'd hoped for, although by now I should have expected it. Connor Barratt was a guarded guy and he wasn't about to spill the beans about getting it on with Ella. "I imagine she came to see what all the fuss was about." He drew out.

My face twisted. "To see what the fuss is about?" I shot back, puzzled at how easily he drew the subject back to me.

He stepped back and dashed a frustrated hand across his jaw. "Stop repeating my words, it's just plain annoying." His voice was raised.

I exhaled before putting in. "She's pretty."

"If you like that sort of thing," he said dispassionately.

"There's nothing *not* to like. Surely you find her attractive?"

"Not particularly," he replied before adding. "And if you think I'm going to gossip about relationships and boys you can think again."

I forced a sigh as if I was disappointed and he shot me one of *those* looks.

"Why not? 'Guys think with their dicks', don't they? It sounds like all village boys are panting for it. Ella said the same." I was on a roll. This was the most I had gotten out of him. "*You're* a guy." I pointed out with a winning smile.

"I think your heading into dangerous waters Harlow. You don't really want to discuss my sex life."

My heart surely skipped a beat as the word sex rolled from those perfect lips.

He quirked an eyebrow at me.

"Why not? I'll tell you about mine," I said in a luring voice, now copying his expression like for like.

He snorted at that one. "Whatever. You don't fucking have one."

He was right of course but I was now having too much fun. "How do you know?"

His expression was drawn and his look said that he was contemplating running me over with his Ranger. Maybe the thought of me with other boys annoyed him?

Connor dashed a hand across his jaw and then he laughed.

"Well, how would you know? I might be a right tart."

"And the fact that you used the word tart just reinforces the fact that you're the opposite."

I pursed my lips thoughtfully, considering his reply. "I'm that obvious?"

He slowly nodded his head whilst maintaining eye contact. "It's stamped all over you. Have you even *kissed* a boy?"

I grinned as he dashed the other hand through his hair, having realised that I had managed to trap him into talking about relationships and boys after all.

"You're clever, I'll give you that."

I was awarded with a half-smile which wasn't so bad and his face softened.

"So how about you? Have you even kissed a girl? You certainly don't know how to talk to one," I questioned rocking back on my heels to scrutinise his face.

He slowly shook his head. "I don't kiss and tell Harlow."

I sighed, not wanting to give in. "Or do you not want to say because your tastes run towards a certain type?" I was attempting playful but my next words were blatantly provocative. "What's the matter Connor, don't you like girls?" I regretted them as soon as they had tumbled out of my mouth.

Silence closed in around us and it was suddenly so quiet, considering we were outside. Even the cows seemed to be holding their breath. *'Don't you like girls?'* WTF had that come from?

Connor shoved off the car with an animal-like grace, rolling his shoulders and invading my space, a confident expression on his face. I straightened, my eyes raised to his and I could see his pupils had dilated. Like two dark pools, it was mesmerizing. It was only when I felt his hand slide around the side of my neck and grip my ponytail that snapped my attention back.

My lips parted and heat jetted into me. His body was so close to mine. He didn't yank my hair, he just held it and then gently pulled my head back, exposing my neck. I was trapped between the wall and his hard body and my blood felt thicker in my veins. His manner could have been considered slightly threatening, but I wasn't scared. I *wanted* him to touch me, wanted to see how my body would feel against his.

Dark eyes lingered on the skin of my throat before they lifted to my lips.

His voice dropped to a whisper and he lowered his head, placing his forehead against mine, his eyes closing. We were now skin to skin.

I was focused on his mouth and it curled slightly before he said. "I like girls just fine Harlow. But you're hardly ready for adult conversations about relationships on any level. You wanted to talk and we've talked. Now piss off and quit while you're ahead."

Connor drew back and opened his eyes before twisting my hair, angling my head to meet his penetrating gaze. "Don't poke the mean boy, you won't like the results," he said in a low voice, full of sensual warning. Pins and needles shot through my scalp but it didn't hurt, his grip was just firm.

That fight or flight thing Mr Cunningham always went on about in Psychology kicked in and it appeared fight won as I replied. "Is that a threat?"

He quirked his head to the side and shot me a give-me-a break expression before returning his gaze to my lips. They parted in response like an automatic invitation. My body appeared to have completely taken over and was responding as a woman does to an attractive man.

"Don't start with all that clichéd crap. You want me to say that's a promise, don't you? Maybe it is." He assured me in a raspy tone. My God, was it weird that I wanted to lick him?

His eyes glimmered, he was enjoying our banter, I could tell.

I probably should have listened to his warning, but being this close felt so natural, my arms seemed to rise of their own accord and I placed my palms face down against his chest. I heard his sharp intake of breath as my fingers touched his skin through his top.

I didn't push him away. I knew that I should but I just stood there, in silence, dazed. Did he too feel the electric type charge which appeared to be travelling up my body? I was sure I could feel his heart beating gently against my palm.

His expression was now thoughtful and he was breathing fairly deeply. He definitely wasn't as immune to me as he made out and the realisation of this gave me a burst of courage. I felt prepared to take anything he decided to dish out. So, I goaded him, on purpose.

"Whatever, now who's talking shit. You're all talk." My eyes widened as I watched him through my lashes, feeling the most feminine I ever had. We were so different in so many ways, but I felt the connection and he had to feel it too.

He realised my hair and slid his hand to curl around the back of my neck, smiling with a challenging light in his eyes. "That's just I you see Harlow, I don't make empty promises Harlow, I had too many of those growing up so I suggest you stop baiting me. As I said before, I never play, at *anything*. You wouldn't be able to handle me on any level virgin."

The attraction I felt at that moment was almost painful and my nipples tightened against the silk of my bra. I so wanted to lean up and put my mouth against his. My body and my mind were now completely aligned. This must have been what naked lust felt like.

I opened my mouth to speak but the sound of a vehicle dragged me out of my trance and I pulled back, pushing off his chest, panicked that someone would see us.

Connor released my hair as he stepped back, glancing over his shoulder as Marcus, the Vet I had met the other day drove into the yard, spraying pebbles.

I shakily brushed my hands against my hair to straighten back any unruly bits. Frustrated at the interruption. My ponytail must have been in tatters.

Connor turned back to face me, stroking his hand down his firm chin, like he was contemplating something.

His eyes met mine and my stomach knotted. "This isn't over," I told him, straight to his face. I now had his full attention as he dropped his arm and his fingers curled into fists.

That sweet, sensual connection which had bound us was broken and although he attempted to appear unaffected, I could see he was battling with himself.

"It never even started," his words were softly spoken but I recognised a hint of regret.

I opened my mouth to say something but what? Confusion and hurt raced around my head. He must have seen my upset as his face started to soften but then Marcus's voice broke in between us.

"Con, you have a heifer down in field four. Clive just called." Marcus's voice was business-like and Connor turned to face him. His back was broad and well-muscled and I threw a couple of invisible darts at it, now feeling totally mugged off.

I stood there for a few minutes and my eyes narrowed as I watched the two men talking about an issue with a cow. A cow for goodness's sake! It was like I wasn't even there.

I tutted and slid past them with a full-on pout, I needed to be alone to lick my wounds.

As I entered the house, I almost ran in to dad who was on his way out, concern etched into his face. No doubt to do with the cow. How I blamed that bloody cow.

He sidestepped me so we didn't bump into each other. "Sorry darling. Everything OK?" he said with concern. He could probably see from my body language that I was miffed.

I carried on walking and shot over my shoulder.

"Fine. Absolutely fine." My tone of course said the exact opposite.

"Good stuff," he chimed before marching out towards the other two men who were now walking determinedly to the car.

As I mounted the steps towards my room, I felt thoroughly pissed off at myself. Was I that mentally naïve? Had I totally read the situation wrong and just made a complete fool of myself, it certainly felt that way.

Maybe he was just toying with me, I already knew he was an asshole.

I exhaled, full on annoyed with myself now. I'd travelled here, hating the guy and planning on staying away from him and now appeared to be chasing him. WTF was wrong with me. My head needed to have a few words with my libido it seemed.

As I threw myself backwards onto my bed, I must have spent the next hour playing and replaying the whole bloody event in my head.

Eventually, I was finally given closure as I dozed off, my head at last free from thoughts of my desperate behaviour and annoying, unpredictable boys.

Six

It was a colossal relief that the rest of the week passed by without any major boy drama. I was still disappointed in myself for flirting with Connor.

During those awkward moments when we bumped into each other, we exchanged the occasional 'hi', or at least I did. Connor ejected more of a grunt than a word.

Over the last couple of days, I'd spent more alone time with my father, which was cool. Our relationship was becoming stronger all the time and I felt relaxed in his company.

On Saturday evening after supper, dad and I chilled out in his study again and listened to old David Bowie records.

The majority of our conversations were either about school or farm related, which was safe.

Dad also raised the point of my birthday and asked if there was anything specific which I would like. I had thought long and hard, but there was nothing I needed really. What did you buy the girl who had everything? Thinking about my birthday reminded me of what Connor had alluded to at the train station. Maybe he was right and I had been spoiled in the past.

After much thought, I asked my dad for a surprise and said that he wasn't to go too mad.

For the rest of that evening, when it was at last quiet outside, I managed to read my book. Considering it had been a weekend, the yard had been outrageously busy, with deliveries and tractors rolling in and out. I had found it difficult to concentrate on my Kindle.

On Sunday at supper, Anna joined us at the table for roast beef and the conversation flowed, even Connor made a rare appearance.

We all chipped in, speaking about a variety of general topics but discussions about our favourite movies was the highlight. To be honest, I was surprised by Connor's knowledge of films, considering there were no TVs in the house. I mean, what family doesn't have a TV? Part of me imagined it was probably in Connor's room, but there was no way I was venturing into the lion's den to check.

Whilst Connor was talking about the scene in Jaws when Quint dies and I was mesmerised, thoroughly enjoying the conversation. His voice was even more attractive when he wasn't growling.

On Monday, I decided to break the ice even more. Having had a thoroughly normal conversation with him at dinner, I had assumed that Connor and I would now have come to some type of truce. However, when I shouted hello, a little bit too keenly to him, he walked across the yard and totally blanked me. I pursed my lips, once again feeling that muggy vibe. The damn boy blew hot and cold at the drop of a hat.

My time on the farm was still enjoyable, irrespective of the odd atmosphere with Connor.

I now thoroughly had my bearings and the need for exploration had gradually fizzled away. I felt relaxed and content in my surroundings and so far, I had escaped from being dragged in to any type of unappealing farm work.

One evening, when dad came in from work looking utterly worn out; I started to feel guilty that I hadn't offered to help.

On Tuesday morning, dad and Connor had already left for work so I spent most of the day annoying Anna. I helped bake bread which wasn't a totally disaster, although my version of a loaf didn't appear to rise much.

I spent the rest of the day rattling around the house and playing Candy Crush on my phone. I had been stuck at level 146 for the last three months and was determined to get through it.

I made sure I kept myself busy most days, doing bits and bobs.

On the occasions I wanted to chat to my friends, I had to use the landline like I did when I called mum. There was only one corner in my bedroom where mobile signal was possible.

After decimating the ham sandwich which I made myself for lunch (purposefully out of Anna's bread and not my own), I decided to walk off the calories and see if I could find my father.

As I left the house, I noticed there was a Sky dish on the side of the roof which was strange considering the lack of TVs. Maybe I was right and Connor had the only set? His room was the only place I hadn't checked. What I wouldn't give for a bit of Netflix.

Connor's room was at the back of the house, two doors away from me; the sections in between us a main bathroom and a large airing cupboard which explained the noise of the pipes which rattled every night.

I eyed the satellite dish moodily. Maybe there was a separate outhouse which they used as a TV room or something?

As I got to the back of the house, I bumped into Nigel, one of the older farm hands who had been working in one of the barns. He explained that dad had popped into the village but wouldn't be long. I thanked him and moved away. He had one of those 'pushed for time' looks and I didn't want to be the one to keep him from his duties.

I started to make my way back towards the house, but raised voices coming from the other side of the barn told me I had company.

I followed the noise and rounded the corner where I was met by a group of teenagers who immediately stopped talking and turned to face me. I instantly recognised Tom but not any of the others.

"Hi you," Tom put in brightly, a huge smile plastered on his face. My goodness he was a keen bean. He obviously didn't know about the 'treat them mean keep them keen' thing. Not that I cared, it was refreshing that someone apart from my dad was pleased to see me. I had felt as if I was diseased or something and was definitely starting to suffer from a touch of cabin fever.

Tom was dressed in casual clothing, a pair of fitted black jeans and a green tee.

"Hi," I replied, raising a hand in greeting.

There were four of them.

"Hi yourself," a tall guy with jet black hair said with a dimpled grin. He was probably a similar height to Connor, but leaner and less intense from the expression he was wearing. His ear was pierced. It made me think of a pirate.

I approached the group whilst fanning out my hair, annoyed that I hadn't brushed it.

The other two guys were similar in appearance with messy brown locks. You could tell they were related. Tom introduced them as Kyle and Max, twins but not identical. The other guy was called Nathan Lane. He was extremely cocksure and a practiced flirt, a definite player I guessed.

Tom, the pirate and the twins all came to stand in a huddle around me. They were all from the village and seemed harmful enough. I surmised that this was 'the guys' who Ella had said were 'dying' to meet me. And possibly the men who Connor had warned me off.

As we completed our introductions in the usual way, I scanned the yard for a sign of Connor. It was strange as I was sure I'd heard his voice. It had been too long since we'd spoken and I didn't like it. I felt irritated by the lack of attention.

I could feel Tom's eyes drilling into me every time Nathan asked me a question. He definitely did the glancing back and forth thing, a hint of jealousy perhaps? I couldn't blame him really, I wasn't going out of my way to alienate anyone, but the banter between Nathan and I just flowed. It was less forced and quite fun and Nathan was certainly good looking with his dark looks and swarthy skin. Had had a scar running through one eyebrow, it gave him that bad boy look. The special ingredient nice girls crave in their man, even though they know it will end in tears.

"What have you been doing with your time whilst Connor has been hiding you away here?" Nathan suddenly asked in his northern drawl.

"I only arrived yesterday and why would Connor want to hide me?"

Nathan rocked towards me whilst Tom looked on. The twins had broken from the group and were now play fighting like a couple of high school kids. I internally rolled my eyes.

"Maybe to keep you safe from the wicked boys in the village?"

"What's that supposed to mean?" I laughed.

He winked playfully. "To stop them trying to get in your pants to start."

I laughed at his directness. "I'm sure I can handle myself just fine and who says they would all want to."

"Well now I've seen you, I haven't got a clue. Although I suppose you're not *that* bad looking," he shrugged with a cheeky grin. "For a southerner."

Tom snorted and looked uncomfortable with Nate's brand of flirtation but I kept grinning. I was glad Nate wasn't being overly complimentary, it felt refreshing from the pedestal Tom seemed to have placed me on.

Tom excused himself and took a call on his phone, leaving me, Nathan and the two boys, who stopped wrestling and joined us. Kyle and Max were funny, they actually *did* finish each other's sentences. We'd studied twins in Psychology and I had read that twins sometimes did this.

"So, are you going to come and live up here do you think?" Kyle asked after jabbing his brother on the arm.

I pondered a bit before I replied.

"Not sure. I may study here eventually, but I still have another year of A-Levels to finish."

Kyle looked impressed and shot his reply in his brother's direction. "So gorgeous and has brains. You hear that Max, A-Levels. Tell us how you did in yours last year?" He was blatantly goading his brother and so I imagined Max hadn't done so well.

Max flipped him the finger and they started play fighting again. The old me, would have turned her nose up at such immature behaviour, but their banter and cheap shots about each other were actually quite funny.

Tom circled back towards us super-fast as he ended his call. "What did I miss?"

Nathan winked at me. "Nothing, just Harlow agreeing to go out with me," he smirked, enjoying winding his friend up.

Tom looked like he'd been slapped, so I put in quickly. "He's kidding. He hasn't even asked me."

My face started to ache I was smiling so widely. It was nice being the centre of attention again.

"Is that an invitation?" Nate said suggestively. I was surprised he didn't wiggle his eyebrows. Corny sod.

Tom shifted uncomfortably on his feet and shoved his hands into his pockets as the twins came to his side.

"What's up T, Nathan after your girl again?" Max chuckled.

Tom suddenly looked like a kicked puppy and Nathan straightened. OMG had Nathan stolen Tom's girlfriend in the past? Awkward much.

It was Nathan who recovered first and replied. "Piss off. Anyway, I heard you two were part of triplets, but the other one died of laughing."

His joke lightened the atmosphere and a bit more flirting commenced with Tom stood there like a spare part. Like he felt unequipped to join in, like a proper square.

As we stood there chatting and putting the world to rights, the unmistakable throaty roar of Connor's truck sounded into the yard, drowning out my answer to Tom's question. Kyle also tried to speak over the noise and said something about a party. I didn't fully hear what he said and my attention was then dragged to Connor who was climbing out of his Ranger. He was filthy and looked tired and moody, like he'd possibly been working flat out all day. He still looked *extremely* edible of course.

Everyone turned to acknowledge both Connor and Clive, who climbed out of the passenger side.

"Missed you at Slater's last night man," Nathan boomed across the yard as Connor slammed the door of the truck and approached us. He was scowling which didn't surprise me; it seemed to be his signature look. Clive went into the house.

His gaze drifted across us, assessing the group before his eyes locked on mine with an accusatory element. Great. Now what had I done? I was starting to think the guy had major mental health issues.

His eyes skimmed over my body and I could see he was trying to control his dark mood.

All sets of eyes then darted between us and there was a definite tension in the air.

"What are you doing here? I said I'd meet you guys later," he shot at the boys, his brow knotted in disapproval. He obviously didn't like the fact that I was speaking to his friends. I felt like a third wheel and suddenly disregarded.

As Nathan spoke, he turned away but I saw Connor's jaw tic, the way it did when he was annoyed about something.

"Mike said you needed a hand attaching the press?" Nathan fired back, blatantly reacting to the definite tone in Connor's voice.

Connor shook his head, his forehead creasing. "No, it's sorted. Clive was here."

Kyle and Max exchanged semi-amused looks, probably due to the change in atmosphere. It was almost like one of those 'elephant in the room' scenarios.

Nathan raised his eyebrows and swayed back a step which put more of a gap in between the huddle. "OK, cool. We were just catching up with your new sister here," he said jokingly and looked at me with a mock brother fondness, like we'd known each other longer than those few minutes. If he ruffled my hair, I'd thump him.

71

There was a moment's pause before Connor replied. "She's not my sister." His tone was flat without any trace of humour and Nathan's face dropped. The grin he was wearing falling away.

"I know. It was a joke man," Nathan replied, half under his breath.

"What did you say?" Connor shot back. His head dipping aggressively. There was a steely element to his tone.

Nathan had the sense to look worried and he backtracked. There was definitely something missing in the equation.

"I said I was joking. Why so pissed today bruv?"

The atmosphere changed to one of those uncomfortable silences and I was about to break it, when Connor beat me to it.

Shaking his head, possibly at himself and his overreaction, he apologised. "Sorry man. Bad day."

Wow, that was a first. I almost swallowed my tongue. He actually knew the word existed! "Don't you have somewhere you need to be Harlow?" he said, now addressing me directly. His brisk tone made me flinch.

I worried my lip, threading a chunk of hair behind my ear as I met his stare. "No, not really. I was just talking to the guys." I didn't know why I felt the need to defend myself but his expression made me feel guilty.

"Yeah, I can see that and you're done now. Mike's looking for you anyway."

I was being dismissed and I just didn't have the energy to fight it, especially in front of his friends.

The added annoying thing was that I *knew* he was lying. There was no way dad could have been looking for me as Nigel had already told me he was in town. His car wasn't there either.

The next thing that came to mind was... absolute zero comeback.

"Fine, whatever," I replied dryly, focusing on the floor by his feet. "I'll see you guys later."

I flicked the group a shy smile. They said their goodbyes all over each other, it was all very odd and I could feel their eyes on my back as I headed for the house. It felt like the walk of shame and the branding on my skin would be Connor shaped.

What the *hell* was his problem? Did he think me some type of slut that would work her way through all his friends and make a name for herself? Or was he trying to protect me from them? It was all very bizarre. They came across as regular boys to me not sex starved lunatics.

I replayed the scenario in my head as I walked into the kitchen, the smell of bread still lingering.

"What did you mean, 'later'?"

I jumped, startled at Connor's voice. He must have ditched his friends and followed me into the house.

I turned to face him and folded my arms, conscious of my braless chest. Connor tilted his head to one side and eyed the motion curiously.

I blew out a breath, confused. "Nothing. I was just saying 'see you', you know, in the *usual* way."

His eyes narrowed. "So, they didn't invite you to the party?"

I was well and truly puzzled.

"Party?" I began. Ah, yes. Kyle *had* mentioned something, but his voice had been drowned out by the noise of the car. "Not sure about any party."

"Don't play dumb. The party tonight at Nathan's house."

He spoke to me like he would a five-year-old.

"I don't know what you're talking about Connor," I snapped. I so didn't want to argue with him, but I wasn't sure what to say to shut it down.

He shook his head and his expression twisted. "It doesn't matter as you won't be going."

His words wound me up, instantly grating on my nerves. Who they hell did he think he was telling me what I could and couldn't do? I remembered Ella's controlling comment. No shit.

I squared my shoulders and shook my hair away from my face before stating in a tone of my own. "I'm not? Oh, *please* dad," I mocked in my best fake begging voice. "Who the hell died and made you in charge?"

He didn't like that. "While Mike is out, I'm responsible for you."

His words were like a red flag to a bull. Ah ha, so he knew Mike was out, the lying sod.

"So, dad is out and therefore can't be '*looking* for me'. You're such a lying shit," I bit out, impressed by my willpower. I literally wanted to strangle him at that point.

He had the guts to look slightly uncomfortable as he replied. "You should thank me for helping you out of an awkward situation."

I wrinkled my nose. "*Awkward* situation? What awkward situation? Me surrounded by fit guys who were all giving me attention and being *nice* to me? *That* type?"

I was astounded that he had the balls to make himself out to be my saviour.

He didn't reply straight away and cleared his throat. I thought I was actually managing to back him into a corner for once, but of course he recovered.

"Lane is bad news. He isn't interested in conversation, just what you keep in your jeans," he drawled nastily.

I flinched. "It wasn't like that at all Connor, we were just having a conversation," I bit in, feeling thoroughly offended. Was he trying to gaslight me now?

He snorted. "Yeah, because that's why Nathan Lane, the biggest player in Yorkshire was drooling all over you, because of how amazing the banter is. That's up there with rocking horse shit Harlow."

"You're disgusting. Isn't he your friend?"

"We *tolerate* each other, there's little friendship there. It's a mutual feeling believe me. I mean it, if you go, I won't be happy and I can guarantee neither will you."

I itched to slap his face. Again, it was all about my looks, my mums warning about the downside of beauty again doing the rounds in my head. Connor me made feel like I had nothing to say for myself and that I was some type of easy lay that would jump at the chance to shag anyone that showed me interest. How I wished I could really hate him.

"It's a fact. And you know it. The guys have been panting to meet you after Tom's fucking revelation about you the other night. They'll be making bets next. The twins are also fuckers when it comes to girls."

"Making bets? How *dare* you say that to me? Even if that's the case, don't you think I have a say in the matter?" I shot out, uncrossing my arms and dropping them to my sides. My nails were digging into my palms so much, I would surely have a mark for days. "One minute you're calling me a buttoned-up virgin and the next I'm an easy lay that would drop her knickers at the first sign of interest."

"Bottom line. Stay the fuck away from Nathan Lane. You know fuck all about the guy. Even his parents thinks he's a tool. As I said, he's bad news."

I almost yelled, 'and you're not' but changed my tack. "What if I don't? What do you think you can do about it? You're not my brother and you're *certainly* not my dad."

He was unimpressed and he took a menacing step towards me, getting in my face.

"I mean it. Do as I fucking tell you!" His breath fanned my skin and I felt goose bumps skitter up my arms.

I swallowed, slightly intimidated before releasing a breath of exasperation. "You're impossible. There is no talking to you. Do you *ever* lose an argument?"

His lip curled. "Fuck no. Not anymore." He said it with such force that I believed him.

Out of every party I had ever 'not' been invited to, this was the one I'd now trade a kidney to attend. My dear stepbrother obviously wasn't aware of the story of Pandora's Box.

I searched his features for any sign that he was joking. He wasn't. Surely, he didn't think he could tell me what to do? I seriously didn't get his attitude. My neck started to ache from trying to retain eye contact. The boy was like a giant.

"If you think for—" I started to argue.

"—Mike won't let you go, so accept it and spare us both the drama," Connor interjected with a derisive lilt, annoyance still plain on his face.

I almost laughed out loud. "So, you're pulling the 'I'm telling daddy card on me now?" I pointed out. My eyebrows were sky high. "You're so full of shit. You're no grass."

Connor scowled before taking me roughly by the upper arm and almost stuffing me into dad's study. A frisson shot up my spine at the contact. His fingers were firm but gentle.

He basically manhandled me into the room and then swung me around to face him. Releasing me, he glared down into my face. "Nate's parties always end in trouble and Mike would flip if you went." His voice was uneven and slightly breathless. "I thought you wanted to build on your relationship with your dad and learn more about the farm. Going to Lane's house is *not* the way to do that. You should stay here tonight, stay out of trouble. I won't be going and you're *definitely* not either."

Curiosity bubbled within me. Wasn't he barefaced lying again now? He'd said to the guys that he'd expected to see them later.

I paused and pretended to consider his words before replying. Was he really concerned about me? Had our normal on and off conversations made him actually care about my welfare, or did he just enjoy being a bossy dick?

"I see. And this is all about looking out for me, is it? You care all of a suddenly?" I said in a cynical voice.

He rolled his eyes before shooting me an unwavering dark gaze.

"I care about Mike yes. He wouldn't want you there. Nate is a proper pisshead. The police have been involved in the past. To be honest, I'm surprised Sally and Adam have left Nathan in the house without Ryan to keep an eye on him. At least *he* has a brain."

I shrugged not bothering to ask who Ryan was. "Look whatever, I'm going to my room so move out of my way please."

I made an attempt to pass him but he stepped sideways to block my path.

I swallowed, feeling intimidated again, he was so strong, a tower of male aggression. That feeling of fear was also a turn on. A strange combination I know.

I took a deep breath, silent for a moment as if trying to calm himself down. "I mean it Harlow. You're to stay here tonight," his voice was now super serious and his eyes were searching my face, probably for a sign that he'd weakened me.

He meant it. He *really* didn't want me to go to the party, which as you can imagine made me more determine to do the opposite. It was strange behaviour for me really, when did I become such a rebel?

I decided to play ball, purely for his benefit, knowing that as soon as I walked away, I'd text Tom to find out more about this stupid party. If anything, at least it got me Connor's attention. I had *hated* being ignored and if Connor could lie, so could I.

"Well, I can hardly go when a) I wasn't invited and b) I haven't got a clue where he lives can I?" I pointed out like he was stupid. I was now an Oscar winning actress it appeared.

He pursed his lips whilst watching me and I felt a slight twinge of guilt, although it was very slight. Miniscule really.

"That's the right decision," he said stepping out of my way before adding. "Honestly, I'm not saying it to be a dick."

Whatever, 'over the top control freak' I thought, as I breezed past him with my head held high. I almost didn't grace his bullshit with a response. "Whatever you say *brother*." I bet he didn't like that.

I exited the study and headed for the stairs without looking back.

Tom had called and I rang him back, standing in that special corner of my room to ensure my phone didn't cut in and out. I asked him about the party and he instantly offered to take me. Irrespective of my desire to mess with Connor, I suddenly really fancied going; it pulled me away from the house for few hours. I could actually start to feel that farm smell on my skin and not just my clothes. Something seriously had to give.

Tom said that he'd pick me up at six and I spent the next hour contemplating what to wear, feeling like an evil genius.

Seven

Dad seemed fine when I told him about the call from Tom, he even said what a nice lad he was and how he was 'going places.' I had decided to take this as a father seal of approval. I'd left the bit out about the party of course.

I made the finishing touches to my make-up and grabbed my bag. I'd shed the cut offs I seemed to have lived in since my arrival and went for fresh and feminine in a purple strapless maxi dress with a denim jacket.

I'd left my hair loose and after some careful coercion, it fell in a sculptured wave over one shoulder.

Glancing in the mirror once last time, I felt very much like the old me.

As I headed for the stairs, part of me hoped I'd bump into Connor, so that he could see me at my best. As usual, he was nowhere to be seen. He only ever seemed to appear when I looked like shit and was totally unprepared.

To be honest, it was probably for the best. If he saw me dressed up, my lie about not going to the party would be exposed.

I stood on the steps of the house, wondering whether to go back inside. I didn't want to appear too keen but as I turned, Tom's car pulled into the yard. It was a Volvo which was typical I thought, reliable and straightforward and the total the opposite of Connor's beat up piece of crap.

Waving, I scooted forward towards the passenger door but Tom burst from the vehicle and skipped around to open it for me. I grinned. It was a bit on the cringe side but I appreciated the gentleman-like gesture nonetheless.

"You look amazing," he puffed, as he joined me in the front and turned on the ignition.

I smiled my thanks and commenced with the usual small talk, feeling relaxed and back on my throne again, for the time being anyway.

I had found life on the farm to be unpredictable and things could change in a split second, especially if Connor Barratt was involved.

As Tom steered the car, we spoke about my mum and more about Uni. The conversation flowed and it felt nice and normal. I wasn't alive with pleasure or anything but at least the exchange wasn't strained or dramatic.

I didn't mention Connor or ask about the troubles he'd mentioned from past parties. I'd see when I got there, so why be nosy and spoil the surprise?

I wondered whether to question Tom about Ella, but didn't want to sound like a gossip. She was his sister after all.

Tom changed the CD to one of my favourite Cold Play albums which ticked another box, at least he had good taste in music. Connor seemed to prefer Radio Head or music by shit aggressive rock bands.

As Tom pulled the car in through the gates of what had to be Nathan's house, I felt a strange pulling in my chest and a jet of adrenalin darted into me. I wasn't sure if it was excitement or worry.

Everything inside me suddenly screamed 'don't do it'! Don't cause yourself unnecessary grief! *This* is the party you have been barred from by your overbearing stepbrother and he'll probably grass you up the first chance he gets!

Tom parked the car, switched off the engine and turned towards me with a puzzled look.

"What's wrong?"

I could feel my heart pumping in my chest. "Oh—erm, nothing. I was just thinking."

He grinned, understanding slowly wiping away each curious grove on his face.

"If you're nervous don't be. We can just drop by for a couple. I'm not sure if Connor said anything but Nate's parties can get a bit wild. Do you drink?"

His question phased me momentarily as I didn't drink that much really due to what I saw the stuff do to my mother. The occasional glass at Christmas and that was it.

"Not really. I don't mind a couple though." Two would be fine surely. I didn't want to look like a total prude.

"Cool, I don't drink much either and especially not at Nate's dos. Need to keep a level head, plus I'm driving." His cautionary words had started to put me off the idea. Would the party be wild with people making out everywhere like at Mathew Mason's place? Anything like that, totally wasn't my scene.

He paused for thought before replying. "It's usually fine but a huge fight broke out last year, Nathan was going through something and behaved like a proper dick." Tom replied with a hitch in his voice.

"Really? Why were they fighting?"

"They were pissed, it's what happens when people can't take their booze. Not sure what they were arguing about, but Ella got elbowed in the face by accident. She never comes to these parties now. Anyway, that's the locals for you. They get bored with close knit village life. That's why we go clubbing in Scarborough every month. A change in scene is always a good thing. Resets the balance."

My eyebrows crinkled. "Did *you* fight?"

He shook his head, suddenly looking horrified. "Absolutely not. I need all my fingers to do my job," he laughed.

I smirked but in a warm way. "Of course."

The moment was broken as my phone pinged to say I had a text and I briefly checked it before opening my door.

It's was from an unknown number. **"Where the fuck are you!"**

From the tone of the text, I guessed it must have been from Connor and my body tingled with nerves.

Grimacing, I swiped off the screen. I didn't even realise that we'd exchanged numbers. I deleted the message without replying.

We climbed out of the car and Tom offered me his arm. We approached the front door and Tom explained that Nathan's' family sold farming equipment. He pointed out three large warehouses which peeked out behind the main house, it was a mansion similar to the size of mine back home.

Several cars were already park messily around the yard and music was booming from inside.

My stomach seemed to be sending my brain mixed messages. I bobbed my head thoughtfully at what Tom was saying, pretending to listen to the last bit of his earlier story about hoof rot, eyeing his profile.

He was good looking guy in a cute boyish way and had been nothing but lovely to me but I wasn't really attracted to him and some things shouldn't be forced.

Tom was in the process of laughing at his own joke as we let ourselves in through the front entrance. A couple brushed past us in the doorway, lighting their cigarettes.

As we entered the house, there were people *everywhere* and only a small amount of light. The place was pretty trashed. It was hot and loud and totally uncivilised and yet a jet of excitement fizzled into me at the thought of being somewhere I shouldn't be.

I checked my watch and noted it was just after eight.

Tom shepherded me into the kitchen whilst I attempted to bump into as few of the bodies as possible. A few party goers nodded to Tom as we passed, but I couldn't hear exactly what was being said over the music and loud voices.

The kitchen was quite large and was strewn with abandoned red solo cups, like the ones you saw at frat parties on American TV shows. Guys and girls were huddled in clusters and I noted a few exchanged smiles as they glanced vacantly in our direction.

Tom washed one of the solo cups out in one of the sinks, the other was full of ice and bottled beers. He uncapped one and poured it for me. I took the drink with a smile, suddenly feeling adventurous.

We made our way, drinks in hand to a conservatory at the back of the house which was littered with a handful of people. Nathan carelessly uncurled the redhead who had been draped across hi and pushed himself to his feet. Yup, he was a player alright. I felt a frisson of discomfort but batted it away.

"You guys made it. Fucking awesome!" he slurred, moving towards us.

He leaned forward and pecked my cheek which felt odd, considering I had known him all of fifteen minutes. I could smell alcohol on his breath and it wasn't attractive.

"No Ella then?" he questioned hopefully, glancing behind us.

Tom looked uncomfortable and shrugged, which was an interesting reaction. "She didn't want to come Nate." I caught a flash of something in Nathan's expression before he masked it, taking another slug from the bottle of spirits he was holding.

The atmosphere between them was weird again. Maybe Nate was the one who knocked her up and it was nothing to do with Connor after all? Hope clawed at my chest. Getting elbowed in the head at one of his parties was also another reason for the strange feeling between them. I decided that one was more plausible. I tucked both thoughts away.

"Come join us. The party is just getting started." Nathan slurred again, taking my arm and pulling me into the glassed conservatory. He started to introduce me to the room full of half inebriated people.

I held my smile and nodded my hellos, suddenly feeling uncomfortable when Tom slid a protective arm around me. I took a sip of beer; it was rank as usual and tasted like it had something else in it too. I saw him uncap the bottle and so wasn't overly concerned about the date rape shit. It was probably one of those beers which was infused with spirits.

We must have been there for over an hour. Stood in one group, chatting about this and that with the music blaring in the background and a scream from an over excited girl or two, thrown into the mix.

Nathan had started getting gradually louder and more, touchy feely and I slowly started to regret my decision to come. It was so different from the tame high school house parties I'd been to where everyone was a similar age. From the look of the people in the house, there was a variety of ages present, some of whom should surely know better. A couple of guys who were stood smoking in the garden, eyed me suggestively through the glass. They had to be well into their twenties. I felt like jail bait.

After a shrill girl called Natalie swayed past me and almost knocked what was now my third drink from my hand, I knew it was time to leave.

I moved over to Tom, he was stood in front of the conservatory doors which were open, allowing the cool breeze into the sticky room. Nathan, who had left earlier for a smoke came back in through the doors and approached us, his body swaying. He darted a glance between us standing way too close to me. I was almost wearing the guy.

"So, you guy's together then?" he drawled, a stupid look on his face as he started rubbing his hand up and down my arm. I wondered how I had ever thought him attractive. He did not look good plastered, but then again, who did?

"Tom's not the guy for you Harlow. He's too much of a vagina. You look like the type of girl who likes a bit of rough. A real man." Out of the blue, Nathan switched onto full blown come-on mode. His bullshit grafting attempt with the 'real man' comment so cringe.

Tom and I exchanged an embarrassed look and I conjured up a fun reply but held it when Nathan's entire face dropped. The playful grin he had been wearing bleeding away. He looked past me and I turned just in time to see Connor moving toward us through the crowd of people.

I stiffened. He was wearing a padded bomber jacket and looked twice his usual size. From the expression he was wearing, he was less than happy. I felt a jet of guilty adrenaline. The shit was about to hit the fan. I twisted back to Tom who only shook his head as if signalling for me to do and say nothing.

Connor levelled with us and he pulled me to one side away from Nathan, his fingers angry against my elbow. The beer in my hand sloshed and I teetered in my sandals slightly. Narrowed eyes suspiciously caught the movement, he obviously thought I was pissed. I opened my mouth to correct him and say that everything was fine, but the look he shot me drowned out any coherent reply. I wasn't surprised to see the don't-fuck-with me-look stamped across his face.

Nathan sobered slightly and moved forward a step, somehow making him appear larger. I recognised it as one of those squaring-up types of gestures. His eyes were pinned to Connor's hold on me. He didn't like it, which was strange considering we hardly knew each other.

My chest tightened at the thought of trouble.

"What's up man? I thought you said you weren't coming. I get it, you *sick* puppy. You're stalking your *sister*?" Nathan sneered, glancing back up at Connor, uncurling his body in an attempt to match their heights. He was obviously prepared for trouble. I recalled Connor's words about them tolerating each other. Yeah, well the 'tolerance' levels between them had just hit zero.

A low chorus of mutters circled around us, the atmosphere was tense.

Tom stepped forward and made a gesture for me to pull away and join him, which caused Connor to tug me further to his side. I certainly wasn't ready for an elbow in the face and I welcomed Tom's concern.

Connor held my arm firmly, his silence scary.

Nathan wasn't having it, his eyes narrowing at Connor's actions.

"Chill man, grab a beer. Har's having a great time." I cringed at the shortening of my name. I so wasn't a 'Har'.

My stepbrother's expression turned to distaste.

"She's sixteen you fucking retard!" he shot out at Nathan, bellowing against the music, thoroughly unimpressed as he briefly scanned the crowded area. It felt like the air had been sucked from the room and from the look of anticipation on the faces of those surrounding us; everyone was happily soaking up the drama.

Considering the look on Connor's face, Nathan made the unwise decision of remaining exactly where he was.

"*So*? She has a mind of her own, doesn't she? No one's forced her to come. Calm the hell down," he snapped back, his face rigid.

Someone in the room behind me whistled, as if to say, *not* a good idea as Nathan put a hand on Connor's shoulder. Was it to warn him off or appease, you couldn't really tell?

My stepbrother eyed where his friend had touched him, blatantly not happy that he had made physical contact and he released his grip on my elbow. The skin burned from where his fingers had been. And not in a bad way.

Adrenalin bubbled in my stomach as I helplessly watched the scene unfold before me, not really knowing if any interference from me would help or make things worse.

The two men stood squared up to each other, their body language fierce. I recalled what Tom had said about fighting as my eyes grazed the cluster of people who were now gathered around us, like coyotes waiting for the scraps. *Wasted* coyotes of course.

Connor shrugged Nathan's hand from his shoulder, his words dripping with menace. "You want me to calm down?" he repeated with an arched eyebrow, disbelief radiating from him in waves. "I *warned* you at The Crown that she's off limits. You *should* have sent her home."

The situation was fast escalating to full on aggressive action. These boys were about to come to blows and it was all my fault.

Butterflies fluttered in my chest and I started to feel like I was floating. At least my legs did, which was odd considering the incident about explode in front of me.

That annoying Natalie girl drifted past us, blatantly eyeing up Connor as if one of her ovaries was about to burst and I wanted to grab her by the hair. Yeah, that's right, *keep on walking bitch* I thought, shocking myself. The alcohol appeared to be making me meaner.

I refocused my attention. Nathan seemed to be weighing up his response to Connor's comment, a stubborn angle to his jaw. I imagined it was the booze that gave him courage as Connor's stance was foreboding.

"We were talking, *that's* it! You don't have to act like a fucking psycho. You get me? Or shall I shout it in your good ear?" Nathan almost sang theatrically, a strange smirk on his face. I tried to register what he meant by 'good ear'.

Fury twisted Connor's features and he took a menacing step forward into Nathan's space, getting in his face. My arm was now free and I stood slightly behind him. Was the room spinning?

Tom shuffled towards the two men, attempting to calm the situation, which was brave and so not the actions of a 'vagina' as Nate had called him. His face was a picture of panic that would have been comical under any other circumstances.

"Come on guys, let's not do this. It's my fault Connor, I brought her."

I heard someone behind me say something about Connor and his 'meds?' What the hell? What kind of meds were they talking about? I'd never seen Connor take anything.

"He's going to lose his shit." A guy to the left of me said.

"I know, this is fucking awesome." Another chimed, clearly relishing the entertainment. There were a couple of girls to my left who were giggling, apparently excited by the thought of these two guys laying into each other. I couldn't think of anything worse.

My mouth opened and closed in a fish-like motion and my twitchy eye kicked in. Genuine horror at the thought of it getting ugly faced me like a rabid dog. Panic beat behind my ribcage.

I took this as my moment to speak, "Connor?" I began with a croak but he cut me off.

"Get in the car," he bit back at me before shoving Nathan in the chest, *hard*. Thank God the guy had the sense to step back, and he did so with both arms raised in a gesture of surrender.

"That's what I thought you *pussy*," Connor spat as the other guy backed down. "Now I suggest you walk away before I knock you the fuck out." That tone held no idle threat. Connor's low voice growled promise.

Nathan eyeballed him, weighing up his options. I sure hoped he made the right decision to walk the hell away.

"Whatever man, don't lose your shit over fuck all."

There was a split second where I thought it may kick off again as they stood squared up in silence for a moment longer. Nathan was obviously battling with his emotions about what he should do. I imagine our audience had something to do with that. He wouldn't want to look like a wimp. But between the two men, there was no comparison, it could in no way be considered a fair fight. Yes, Nathan was tall and broad but he wasn't packed with shoulders like steel girders and a body honed with solid muscle like his adversary. An angry Connor was a *scary* Connor, I knew that now.

"This is bullshit!" Nathan yelled back suddenly, spinning away and storming out into the garden. I heard a smashing noise as he threw his bottle of beer onto the patio seething with rage.

Tom let out a huge sigh of relief that he must have been holding for ages.

"Fuck me man!" A spectator behind me said in an amused voice, obviously having enjoyed the scene.

The chatter about the incident was instant and then people started to drift away, now 'the show' was over.

Relief swept through me like a tsunami.

Connor shot me a look, dragging back my attention, his dark eyes drilling into mine with another 'don't fuck with me' message written there.

"Look, I'm sorry, I don't…" I stuttered shying my gaze away from that look.

"I said get in the car. For once, do what I fucking tell you to do!" His jaw tightened as he glared at me and I knew that unless I did exactly as he said, the situation would become even more embarrassing. If the guy tried to put me over his shoulder like you saw in the movies, I would die on the spot.

I turned and pushed the beer into Tom's hands, heat stinging my cheeks before retrieving my bag and jacket. It felt like I was getting told off by the teacher in front of the whole class. "Fine," my tone was unbelievably firm, considering the shit storm stood in front of me.

Tom shot me a reassuring smile before saying. "I'm sorry Harlow, I shouldn't have brought you."

I fanned back my hair and straightened my dress, composing myself for my exit.

"I'll see you later. I'm sorry, I didn't mean to cause so much trouble."

He nodded in silent understand but didn't reply, all too aware of Connor looming beside us, his hands at his side fisted.

"And *you* should have known better after what happened with Ella," Connor said accusingly to Tom.

He looked thoroughly ashamed.

"I know, I'm sorry, Connor I—."

"Save it," Connor shot out dismissively before grabbing me by the top of my arm, his grip angry. All eyes were on us as he literally dragged me through the throng of people. "Walk," his voice was full of warning and in spite of myself, I felt slightly turned on by his harsh treatment of me.

His chest pressed into my back and he ushered me through the front door and into the yard. The fresh air hit me full in the face and made me wobble again. Connor's hand tightened to the point where I'd surely have bruises.

"You're actually hurting my arm Connor," I complained as I tried to free myself. His touch wasn't *that* painful, but it was certainly generating a significant amount of chaos against my skin.

He ignored me and only released his grip after he'd manhandled me to the passenger side of the Ranger.

Once free, I hit him on the chest but it was like slapping stone, he didn't move a muscle. Just stood there like a tower of rock, *glaring* down at me.

"*What the hell* Connor, are you mad! You know what, forget that, of course you are, you're *completely insane!*" I practically snarled.

He pinned me with an unimpressed look and leaned behind me to *yank* open the door.

"Get in," he instructed harshly with a nod of his head. Heat fizzed through me and a strange giddy sensation vibrated through my limbs. He was so bossy.

I didn't jump to it as he expected me to and I folded my arms across my chest and eyed him moodily. He'd just literally dragged me from the party, my face must have been like a beetroot.

"*Do it* Harlow. Don't make me put you in there, I *won't* be gentle about it."

His stern threat turned my anger into something else. Molten hot desire flooded my insides. I batted down my impressive stubborn streak and moved to do as he'd commanded. I certainly didn't want to be wrestled into the car with half of the house watching. I could see people at the window, holding the curtain back clearly enjoying the show. We'd probably be the talk of the village. Great.

As I awkwardly clambered up into the cab of the car, Connor slammed the door and circled the vehicle, his eyes never leaving mine through the windscreen.

Climbing up into the vehicle, he moodily started the engine, his shoulders jerking as he jammed the gear stick backwards. The Ranger revved and jolted and Connor placed his arm around the back of my seat as he reversed.

"I can't believe you caused such a scene." I bit out between clenched teeth.

He didn't like that and literally yelled back at me. "*You* caused the scene by *fucking being there*! I *told* you not to go."

As the vehicle lurched, I saw Tom standing in the doorway, his face unreadable in the shadows. Part of me wanted to cry and the other part to laugh which was odd. The emotions I was experiencing were off the chart. I wasn't totally stupid, I knew the booze was to blame.

Connor slammed the car into another gear and we shot forward down the driveway.

I placed the flat of my hand against the dashboard to steady myself. He was driving like a maniac.

He shot Tom a glower as we shot past him. "It appears *that* pain in the arse has got balls, having the guts bringing you here."

Connor was breathing heavily, obviously struggling to get his temper under control and I remained silent until we'd pulled out on the road and he started to calm down.

"What the hell was that about? Tom and I *literally* arrived an hour ago and we weren't staying," I defended, partly annoyed that he'd come to fetch me and partly turned on that he had. There appeared to be serious things going on with my body as we sat there. We were so close and I had an urge to feel his strong thigh through his jeans against my fingers.

He shot me a look whilst negotiating the car around what appeared to be an abandoned vehicle.

It was dark outside and there were no streetlights. The light of the moon danced shadows across his face and I saw his jaw was set at a determined angle.

"An hour is long enough," he replied, his voice much calmer now, but still gruff.

I wrinkled my nose. "For what? What the hell are you talking about?"

Connor swore and the vehicle lurched, his eyes snapping back at me.

"I can't decide whether you're just extremely reckless or incredibly stupid. You don't know these people and obviously have no fucking idea about village mentality."

My mind was racing and the realisation that I had probably drunk more than I should, rattled me like a steam train. Was this pissed? I bit back a giggle at the thought as Connor twisted his head to glare back at me, his eyes narrowing suspiciously.

"Plain fucking stupidity." He said, shaking his head and redirecting his eyes back to the road.

"Maybe I know more than you think? About village boys I mean. You're all the same. All sex starved buffoons." For some reason I felt myself grinning like an idiot, 'buffoon' would not have been one of my usual choice of words. It tickled me.

Connor didn't miss my expression. Bright, furious eyes glared at me.

"You find this funny?" he questioned, blatantly astonished, looking from my lap to the road. "And put your bloody seatbelt on! Do you have a fucking death wish?"

God he was a moody bastard. I begrudgingly clicked my belt on, but I liked it. I was suddenly enjoying myself; the booze having given me a boost of confidence.

Connor Barratt had come to fetch me from the party purely because he fancied me. That *must* have been the reason. He was jealous and was worried I'd get off with another guy. I had given him no option but to fetch me, kicking and screaming if necessary. The 'over the shoulder' image snuck in there and caused me to catch my breath.

Connor and Harlow sitting in a tree and all that...

At least that's what my incoherent mind was trying to convince me of.

The look he had shot Nathan when he'd first stormed into the room was text book stuff surely? I'd seen that jealous boyfriend vibe before.

I cleared my throat and patted at the wrinkles in my dress.

My grin became much meatier and I giggled again. It was weird, my voice didn't sound like me.

'You're wasted," Connor accused, shaking his head again, as he aggressively steered the car in through the gates of the farm.

His muscles flexed as he drove and I savoured the picture of him with his top off which suddenly popped into my head. Where the hell did *that* come from? I hadn't even seen him without his shirt yet. But that was certainly something I was looking forward to.

"Were you worried about me? Is that why you came to get me?"

Connor didn't reply as he parked the car at an awkward angle and then turned the engine off. He pushed back into his seat and stared forward through the front windshield, rolling his shoulders.

We sat in silence for a moment before he unstrapped his belt and twisted towards me.

There was only a small space between our two bodies, the atmosphere thick and yet I felt as light as a feather.

"Well?" I questioned; my voice hoarse. Connor's eyes flickered to my lips and my nipples pebbled again against my strapless bra. I imagined how it would feel if he placed his mouth there.

"Well—what?" His voice had thickened slightly, his eyes now hooded as they moved around my face. "You lied to me. You actually had the guts to lie to my face."

"I didn't lie exactly, I said I hadn't been invited, they're not the same thing."

His nostrils flared at that one, like a bull before it attacked and my head suddenly started feeling heavier.

"Your drink could have been spiked. It's happened before."

He carried on balling me out like a naughty school girl. "You led me to believe you wouldn't go and then went to spite me. I didn't tell you not to because I get off on ordering you around for fucks sake. It was for your own good. You're new here and you don't know the people. They're bored fuckers with very little entertainment and boredom encourages bad fucking decisions."

He moved forward resting one hand on the dash, his eyes piercing into me. He *had* been worried. It was plain to see in his expression.

A cocktail of excitement and anxiety swirled in my stomach. If I took the initiative and leaned forward, would he back away or meet me half way? It was strange, I had never made the first move with a boy before, but then again, I had never been so thoroughly attracted to one that I had wanted to.

This was more than an itch I needed to scratch, more than girlish curiosity. Something was happening here and had been since the day by his car. I was right, this thing whatever it was, wasn't over.

I twisted my body into a position on the seat that allowed me to face him fully, the leather creaking under my bottom. The lights from the house allowed a soft glow into the vehicle. His face was so perfect and I raised my hand to touch it but he caught my wrist.

Panic jetted into me at the thought of rejection but he transferred his grip to my hand and threaded his fingers through my own, his eyes never leaving my face. I felt thoroughly confused, out of my comfort zone and I opened my mouth to speak but no words left my throat.

"You can stop it with the seduction attempt. I don't hit on plastered females. You need to stop. Whatever the fuck it is, you need to deal with it." Connor's voice slid into the silence. To be honest, I found it difficult to concentrate with our fingers curled together, the skin-to-skin contact felt amazing, my whole body was singing.

"What do you mean, I don't understand? What would you like me to deal with Connor?" I asked shyly with a pout, feeling a little uncertain which way it was going to go. He'd been so mean to me over the last few days, there was no way of knowing if he really was interested or playing some type of cruel sick game. Like boys did in the playground when they pulled the hair of the girl they fancied and pushed her to the ground.

"Well, why don't you enlighten me? Tell me what you want," I repeated, wanting, no *needing* him to tell me how he felt, that familiar ache pumping in my veins.

And then suddenly, it felt like I'd been hit by a bucket of ice-cold water.

"You need to lose it. Whatever this thing of yours is; this *fucking* girlish crush."

And BOOM, my usually none existent temper, exploded!

What made it worse was that everything about his face was composed and icy.

It felt too hot to breath in the car and I yanked my hand away, disappointment smashed away with fury.

91

"Girlish crush!? What am I, ten?" I snapped out, a rush of annoyance shooting up my spine. I almost plastered my back against the door in order to put more space between our two bodies.

Connor wrapped the hand that had held mine around the steering wheel as if he needed something safe to do with it.

I almost choked on the atmosphere, watching him from my retreated position.

He released a frustrated breath and jammed his fingers through his hair, before pushing back into his seat and staring out of the front windscreen again.

Crush!? *Crush* was such a *childish* word, it appeared I had more of an obsession than a fucking crush.

Connor took a deep breath and shot me a look. "You know what I mean? I've seen the way you look at me, but *nothing* can happen. I won't allow it. You've been here two minutes and you're already fucking trouble," he bit out.

"*I'm* trouble? I haven't even done *anything*, and as for the way I look at you, you obviously don't know *flagrant contempt* when you see it. You've been nothing but a dick to me since I got here. I'd have to be a sadist to be interested in you." I yelled with a sob.

He shook his head and turned to look at me again, his face a mask and it forced my temper up into the next gear. How dare he appear so calm and unaffected, as if he didn't feel that strange pull between us!

Yes, I was young and inexperienced, having only kissed a couple of guys but I wasn't stupid, I *knew* when someone was attracted to me. The way he'd watched me at the table that night when we'd spoken about all our favourite movies was proof. The way I caught him looking at me, *stealing* glances. I knew *want* when I saw it.

"I think I hate you," my voice came out a whisper.

"Good, you *need* to hate me. I don't fuck around with inexperienced girls. Can you imagine what Mike would say? He *knows* me and the nightmare in my past and it isn't all roses Harlow. It's majorly fucked up and so am I. So *back the fuck off* with the blatant come-ons."

My breath whooshed through my teeth as I fumbled for my bag and grabbed my jacket from the foot-well. I had to get out of there and quick, the risk of bursting into tears at any second was approaching like a race car.

"*You* back the fuck off. You *want* me to hate you? How f-fucked up is that?" I almost stuttered as I fumbled with the handle on the door.

"You aren't even my type farm boy! I prefer a guy who knows how to behave around girls. Someone who treats me nice and who I can talk to. Not one that avoids conversation like the plague. Did you even go to school?" God knows where that one came from.

"Now you're being childish," he said quietly. "I mean it Harlow, stick to your safe little high school boys who like to fumble around and stay away me and the fucking Nate's of this world. You saw where the party was heading. Take my point?" Connor growled.

His words were like a lash against my senses. "It was a party so what, I've been to parties before and you can shove your point up your arse Connor Barratt."

I heaved open the door and jumped down before turning back to shoot him a look of pure contempt. To say the guy rubbed me up the wrong way was the understatement of the year.

I slammed the door as Connor shouted my name, drowning out his reply. Tears started to stream from my eyes. If he came after me I'd hit him.

I held my shoulders back and lifted my chin high, moving towards the house, my heart thumping in my chest.

I refused to let him see how upset I felt and I struggled for coherence, the desire to find my bed and hide beneath the duvet, the only clear thought I could process.

Eight

Over the next couple of days, Connor was notably absent which was a colossal relief. He didn't even show for my birthday meal which didn't bother me. I was mortified by what had happened after the party and his vanishing act allowed me an appropriate amount of time for some essential wound licking.

It turned out that dad had bought me a car, a fucking car! Who does that? I was grateful of course, until I caught Connor's expression when he saw it. He shot me one of those looks that made me feel like an overindulged brat again. I couldn't even drive the thing and still had to apply for my provisional licence.

"Connor can teach you." Dad had suggested at breakfast. Yeah right, I'd rather chew my own fingers off.

On Thursday morning, I watched Connor glumly from my room. He was in the yard in all his male glory. My new mini also sat there, gleaming and new and un-driven with its perfect shiny paintwork. It even had go-faster stripes! I'd sat in it a few times of course, not wanting to appear ungracious but in the dusty surroundings, it stood out like a sore thumb, an example of two different worlds almost. I so wished dad hadn't gone for such a big gesture. Mum had sent me a necklace from Pandora and a card.

I stood ogling Connor from my window like a proper sad case. He was working on one of the main barns which housed the cows, his now shirtless body taunting me as I appraised every chiselled angle. He made me think of that scene in Top Gun where the guys are playing volley ball on the beach half naked. Every girl's wet dream I imagined.

I had tried my hardest to keep my distance, but dad had put an end to that at breakfast when he hinted that I could give Connor a hand with some 'light' repairs he'd been working on. A black eye was my preference.

The thought of Connor ordering me about without bringing up what had happened in the car was going to be tough, but I was determined to appear unaffected and under *no circumstances* would I give him *any* ammunition to throw back in my face. Longing looks were now out of the question and if he was still shirtless when I got downstairs, I'd pinch myself as a distraction if necessary.

I pulled on baggy sweats and a tee and left my room, the air was muggy, hence the probable reason for Connor stripping off in the first place. The body I had expected beneath his clothes was definitely worth the wait, wash board abs and everything and those tattoos could make a girl foam at the mouth.

I chewed the inside of my cheek as I waited in front of the barn like a spare part, wondering where the hell he'd suddenly disappeared to. I ran my hands across my pink joggers feeling like a first-class loser. I'd chosen the baggiest T shirt I'd brought which fell off one shoulder and revealed my bra strap. It was comfortable but still sexy I supposed, in a *voluminous* kind of way. I'd strategically opted for a black bra, again suggestive but also the perfect shade to match my mood.

My body tensed as he appeared at last, striding out from around the side the house with that determined expression on his face, a look that I had now become so accustomed to. He still wore the jeans he'd had on earlier but thankfully had pulled on a snug fitting black button down with paint marks on it. At least I could refrain from foaming at the mouth now. He also wore a tool belt which sat low on his hips.

The mundane thing carried hammers and spanners FFS but my libido still decided it added to the hotness. Let the nipping commence.

Connor Barratt looked very much the part of your typical contractor but less weathered, more like the models you saw in the ads, who were too perfect to be true and had probably never picked up a spanner in their lives.

"Mike said you'd offered to help?" He put in cynically, a blatant 'as if' message underpinning his words.

I felt like flipping him the finger but thankfully restrained myself. "Yes well, I had nothing better to do so—." I did a fluttery thing with my hand. WTF was *that*?

Connor cleared his throat. "Let's crack on then. I see you've dressed the part." He smirked as his eyes shot up and down my body.

It took effort but I smiled. Not a genuine one of course, I was annoyed that he'd made a point of commenting on my shapeless clothing. Spawn of Satan.

I winkled my nose. "What did you imagine I'd wear; a tight dress and heels?" I drawled sarcastically.

He chuckled which knocked me and an actual smile followed, if the cruel curve to his mouth could be called that of course.

95

His gaze roamed over me again, this time quite provocatively. "You don't want to know what I imagine you wearing Harlow."

I blushed; yup, an *actually* blush, staggered by his veiled compliment. I then exhaled nosily and bit back my retort. What the *actual* hell? Talk about split personality. The guy could give Jackal/Hyde a run for his/their money.

Connor raised his perfect eyebrows as he moved past me, lips twisted, motioning for me to follow with a flick of his head. "Get a shift on."

His hair was mussed, like he'd not long since crawled out of bed and I quickly shook off my growing contemplation of what *that* would look like. Imagining Connor in bed? When the hell had I become such a pervert?

"So, I'll patch the roof and you hold the ladder. I may need you to pass me stuff. I take it you're alright with heights?"

I nodded my head without giving his question any actual thought. The number of ladders I'd climbed would be around the zero mark and so who knew right?

"You're a bit on the scrawny side, but you should be able to stop it from sliding?"

He spoke to me like you would a five-year old and I gave him another tight-lipped nod as we stopped beside the bottom of said scary-ass ladders. I batted his scrawny comment to one side as I peered up; they were *huge* and were already extended to what surely had to be their full height. My stomach turned over. At least he didn't expect me to go up there, or did he? I narrowed my eyes.

"I need to finish the section I was working on this morning. You put your feet here and here to hold the ladder in place and then grip it with both hands. It shouldn't go anywhere really, the grounds fairly even, so you can lose the terrified expression."

'Yes, *Mein Fuhrer!*' I thought, watching the display of where I should stand through squinted eyes.

Connor shot me a condescending look before twisting away and darting up the ladder with admirable speed, the muscles of his perfect backside flexing. I so wanted to bite it.

As he got to the top, I did as he instructed and straddled the metal with my feet, wrapping my fingers around the cold steel. I sure hoped it *didn't* slide anywhere as I seriously doubted that I'd be able to stop it anyway. Connor was right, my arms had always been on the thin side, no matter how much resistance training I did.

"OK?" he shouted down and I nodded to alleviate any concern. My tongue had decided to abandon me it appeared. I probably resembled one of those nodding dogs from the Churchill advert. It was like I couldn't get my throat to work.

As Connor pulled tools out of his belt and started working, my eyes were creased against the sun. It was impossible not to notice how his muscles moved with each movement and the sight of his denim encased backside was a picture that would probably be carved into my memory for a very long time. The thing could sell postcards!

I dragged my head away, disgusted with myself and tried to concentrate on my duty, purposefully glaring at one of the rungs of the ladder.

I was still pissed off after the way he'd mugged me off in the car. He'd had the perfect opportunity to kiss me and I'd been certain that he'd wanted to. I saw that type of expression on guys all the time.

I replayed the scene in my head, wondering if I had imagined it again and that maybe I would have to deal with the fact that here was one guy that just didn't really fancy me. It was a hard pill to swallow. It felt so strange. I'd lived through my teens with boys literally throwing themselves at me like starved animals. I'd even checked myself out naked in the mirror last night wondering if everything was going droopy. I'd soon dragged my robe on of course, annoyed with myself for my superficial thoughts. I cringed thinking back to my original intention of staying away from Connor whilst staying here. Look how good *that* was going.

The ladder suddenly vibrated with Connor's weight as he started to climb back down, his booted feet appearing level with my face. Thank goodness whatever he'd had to do was quick. I stepped back to allow him space to climb off and he turned to face me, I noted again how my head barely reached his shoulder.

It was then that it happened. I made that foolish decision to glance up at him through my lashes; it was the oldest girlie trick in the book, but it happened on impulse. Our eyes locked and I held my breath, again those fireworks vibrating through my chest. Connor's face was unreadable but he *had* to feel it, that pull, that chemistry. Every muscle in my body screamed for attention.

He scratched his jaw before quickly unclipped the tool-belt without looking away and dropped it to the floor with clunk. I didn't follow the movement; it felt physically impossible to avert my eyes.

"Stop it," He cautioned in a low voice heavy with emotion, but he didn't move away and that gave me my answer.

Giddiness swamped me as he raised his hand and pushed a stray strand of my hair behind my ear, warmth blossoming in my belly. Our bodies were so close, but who knew who'd moved to reduce that small space between us. The sun caressed my cheeks as Connor continued to stare down at me, into me even, and my temperature soared

And then my control snapped.

I took the advantage, pushing up onto my tiptoes and fusing my mouth against his. I heard his breath hitch, startled by my actions as I cushioned myself against him; fingers clutching at his biceps for balance.

My pulse took off as Connor reacted and his arms slid around my waist pulling me further against him, our legs together, my chest flush against the lower part of his. I felt the muscles in his arms flex with the movement and it turned me on even more. Closing my eyes, I gently slid my tongue against his lips, unsure, hoping he'd take the lead.

And he did. His mouth opened and he took control.

His tongue swept into my mouth, thick and demanding and it felt fricking *amazing*. My entire body was on fire and I surrendered myself wholeheartedly to that feeling, greedily savouring everything he had to give.

Just when I thought it couldn't get any more deliciously insane, he deepened the kiss further; the thrust of his tongue moving determinedly against my own, stroking and coaxing as I attempted to match his technique, revelling in his experience. It felt so right, heat throbbed between my legs and I wished at that moment that he would reach down and touch me there.

I inhaled his masculine scent which pushed my breasts further against the hardness of his chest, his hands now cupping my face as he angled my head to where he wanted it to go; leading me, branding me.

Desire like I'd never experienced was raging and I felt a tremor run through my body as Connor growled against my mouth. I felt him hard against my stomach.

So, *this* is what sexual excitement was like. It was shocking and exhilarating at the same time and my response was out of control. I didn't give a damn that anyone could walk by and see us; all I cared about was feeding the hunger that had throbbed within me since that first moment I had seen him. That split second when our eyes had connected and that strange something had rushed through me.

A car engine revved up the driveway, rudely smashing into my consciousness and tore us apart. He pulled away first and I felt like someone had torn a limb off. I was trembling and touched my lips with my fingers, trying to calm the hell down. Connor was quicker to recover and moved back, setting me away from him, splitting that special connection which had bound us. My own body was too affected by the feelings I was experiencing and I stumbled forward but Connor shot out a hand to steady me.

"Easy," he whispered, as I tried to regain my balance.

My face was on fire as we maintained eye contact, irrespective of the interruption and a silent message passed between us. It was almost painful, but I pulled my gaze away to see my dad parking the car. Rachel was with him waving frantically. Of all the bloody times!

We both turned to face them, putting an even more respectable distance between our two bodies.

Connor's fists clenched and unclenched by his sides and guilt and embarrassment started to bleed into me. OMG, I had just *kissed* my stepbrother like some type of high school slut. I *never* made the first move and worse than that, had my father and Rachel *seen* it? The thought cast a proper frantic cat among my pigeons and my gaze narrowed as they approached us. I attempted to weight up the possibility and repercussions in my head.

Both Dad and Rachel's faces were fairly impassive. If they *had* seen us, they didn't appear fazed by it. Heat continued to steal into my cheeks and I smoothed back my hair in fear that there was a tell-tale sign of what we had just been doing.

They trotted towards us and I continued to assess their expressions but still didn't see anything to be too concerned about. That would certainly be an embarrassing conversation to have with Rachel on what would be the first time I'd seen her since the anniversary party.

"You kid's alright? All OK today?" Dad put in, doing that looking from one to the other thing which made my heart skip a beat. Shit, one of us had to speak soon or it just looked plain weird. Maybe he thought we'd been rowing again? Yes, fighting, that would be better!

I struggled to peel my tongue away from the roof of my mouth as Connor moved towards his mother, his composure now firmly back in place. I couldn't think straight and was afraid my tongue would trip me up.

"Dad, Rachel!" I blurted out in a high-pitched squeak. It was one of those tones that surely only dogs could hear and I added insult to it by making another weird fluttery gesture with my hand. What the hell was with the hand thing? That was new.

Connor shot me a pointed look and I clamped my mouth closed, obeying his silent message to shut the fuck up, running my hands through my hair again to halt the hand thing.

"How's Gran?" he asked, begrudgingly accepting the hug from his mother in an 'if I show any emotion, it makes me weak' way. A typical misguided boy thought.

My lips were still throbbing from our kiss but I tried my hardest to concentrate and look normal. Were they the same size or would they appear swollen? Swollen with lust. Slut, slut, slut!

"She's OK, on the mend. I'll tell you all about it all later sweetie," Rachel replied as she kissed his cheek.

"So, Harlow. What do you think of the farm; you settling in OK?" she questioned, with a warm smile.

I reigned in the desire to laugh hysterically and managed to deliver a semi-normal smile. "Yes thanks. It's cool," I said. She beamed at my words and dad put his arm around her shoulders in a loving gesture. I suppose it should have bothered me but weirdly it didn't. It was blatantly obvious that he was happier now and to be honest, I had my own shit to deal with. My stomach dipped with a bit of sympathy for my mother back in London and I realised how I hadn't heard from since my birthday.

The conversation flowed around me and I attempted to join in but they were mainly discussing Rita, Rachel's mother and her current health scare.

"Anyways, I have to unpack. I have washing coming out of my ears. I'll catch you both later at supper," Rachel said with a parting shot.

Dad did another glance between Connor and I before following her into the house, muttering something about an overdue gas bill.

I pursed my lips.

There it was again, that tense silence. We stood there, side by side, the murmur of farm equipment in the distance. I hated awkward silences.

Finally, Connor broke the quiet. "It never happened," he stated flatly.

His words ruffled me.

Coward, my insides screamed and I moved to look up at him. He didn't turn to face me and remained looking across at the house. I felt like screaming, not wanting to believe that he was doing that denial thing—again! I was now past hiding.

"Really Connor? Now who's being childish?" I hated to admit it but his words had driven a stake of pain through my heart.

A rush of crimson flashed across his God-like cheekbones. Good, I thought, you deserved it.

I gave it a couple of beats before I left, giving him the chance to take it back and admit that he'd wanted it too.

Unfortunately, I made an unintentional pig-like noise before strutting away towards the house, now desperate to shed the silly clothes I had decided to wear. After I'd taken a few steps, I stopped and turned. Connor was still standing in the same place, watching me with a guarded expression.

"Oh and Connor?" I said, raising my voice to ensure he heard me. Our eyes were locked again and he angled his head slightly which was the only sign that I had his attention.

"I can assure you that it did—*happen* that is."

His jaw tightened and I blew him a pantomime style kiss.

He'd kissed me back and he *knew* it, it was written in every regretful contour on his face.

My sense of victory was immense and I twisted away, biting back the desire to taunt him further.

He wanted me, *just* like all the others. The rules were mine and the outcome, if I wanted it, was inevitable. I walked away with a triumphant smile.

As I made my way to my room, I truly understood the saying of the cat that got the cream as I thought about the magic of Connor's mouth against mine.

I had him. He may not like it but there was no doubt about it that Connor Barratt was as hot for me as all the others.

I entered my room and pulled the baggy top over my head, meeting my face in the mirror. I paused with my fingers in the waistband of my sweat pants, eyeing the girl in the glass. She seemed different, like something had changed. Like the little lost girl was gone and the confident seventeen-year-old that I was, had finally risen.

After showering, I padded back into my room from the bathroom, brushing my freshly conditioned hair. As I threw the hairbrush onto my bed, I turned towards the dressing table to see a small bunch of flowers on the side.

I approached with a frown, had they been there when I'd come in?

They were laid over a postcard of a seaside setting and I pulled the card out to see handwriting on the back.

'Happy Belated Birthday', Con x.

The ache that came with thoughts of Connor returned and my face lit up.

The flowers were tied together with a piece of string and had obviously been handpicked. They were also wild flowers which of course immediately made me think of Connor.

I allowed the wave of pleasure to wash over me as I re-read the card and then another thought popped in there. Connor must have entered my room, whilst I was in the shower. That sent another shard of excitement into me.

Trotting over to the window, with the card held lovingly against my chest, I searched for Connor in the yard below. He was in the process of attaching some machinery to the back of the tractor and he froze suddenly, as if sensing he was being watched.

My eyes ate him up, his broad shoulders flexed as he stopped fiddling with the attachment. He wore thick leather gloves that only added to my excitement. The tats on his arm screaming bad boy.

I bit my lip as he turned his head and looked up towards my window. Our eyes met and I smiled back at him, flicking the card towards him in a thank you gesture. He returned my smile with a nod of his dark head before turning back to his task.

I literally danced away from the window and collected the flowers so I could pop them in some water, grinning ear to ear. Pleasure fizzed through me, his gesture had been so romantic and so not what I had expected, which only made it more special.

After popping downstairs for a vase to display the flowers in, I must have sat back on my bed admiring them for ages.

My first bunch of flowers and just like the pleasure and feeling pumping through my body, I hope they and it never died.

I spent the next couple of hours reading in my room and then dropped my mother a call. It was still fairly early in the evening and so she wouldn't have cracked open the bottle just yet. The conversation was positive and more coherent than usual which was good. Thankfully, my time away from home seemed to have changed my mother's usual routine.

She said she was feeling really good about herself and that she was actually enjoying having some space.

I wasn't sure how to take that at first, if I went home and she'd turned my room into a gym the shit would hit it. She also explained that Phil from the supermarket was due to come over and that they would share a pizza and then watch the British Bake Off together. I held back my grim reply, Phil had a bit of a body odour issue but he was pleasant enough for an old person. I batted the spiteful thought aside and we said our goodbyes. When had I become such a bitch?

My phone pinged and I swiped the screen to see I had a message from Tom. He was apologising again for the party and asked how I was. I ignored his question and decided to use this as an opportunity to raise a few questions of my own.

Everything is fine. By the way, do you know if Connor is on any medication?

I dropped onto the bed as I awaited his reply.

Why do you ask?

It appeared he was still a 'typical guy', answering a question with a question. I batted down my annoyance.

Someone at the party said something about him 'not taking his meds', I'm just being nosey. It would explain a lot is all.

I popped a LOL emoji at the end, so I didn't appear overly concerned.

I didn't hear that, good job Connor didn't either.

I frowned before keying in. **Why?** My curiosity was bubbling towards the boil.

It seemed like forever before he responded and I moodily eyed the 'Tom is Typing' icon. Of course, he was answering me in boy time.

`He's really private about stuff like that.`

I went in for the kill and repeated my question.

`So, he is on medication?`

I pulled my phone guiltily into my chest and eyed the door as footsteps passed my room. Connor's door banged shut and his usual shit music started up.

I glanced back at my iPhone. `Yeah, for three years now, I think?` Tom had responded.

'Tom is Typing' appeared again and I held off my reply. `I shouldn't really say anymore to be honest. I don't want him to go crazy on my ass. You haven't seen him when he loses his shit.`

The next conversation was a bit back and forth and I found it incredibly frustrating.

What are they for? I texted without shame, I needed to know.

`You can't say anything if I tell you.`

I chewed the inside of my cheek as I typed in my reply.

`I won't say a word. We don't have a close type of relationship so why would I? Spill it Wade.`

Eventually he caved.

`They're to chill him out, calm him down. Surely, you've noticed he has serious anger management issues.`

The penny still didn't drop. I thought about the harsh conversations I'd had with him and yes, he'd been a mean bastard but apart from the party, I hadn't actually seen him lose his temper at all. Even at the anniversary do, when he had been downright rude, he'd been calm and controlled the whole time.

I thumbed in my reply.

`Nope. Not really. Nathan's was the first time I'd seen him kick off and it wasn't that bad. He's a shit to me most of the time, but he doesn't seem overly aggressive.`

I shuffled across the bed and plugged my charger in as the phone beeped to notify me that the battery was low.

Tom messaged again.

Please delete this conversation. If Connor found out I'd been talking about him, he'd kick my face in.

He added a worried looking emoji which made me smile.

Will do and don't worry. Thanks for the Intel. Speak later.

I was running the meds thing through my mind and was just about to place my phone on the bedside table as another message beeped in from Tom.

A group of us are going into Scarborough Friday night for drinks, you brave enough?

I pondered my answer for a couple of minutes before responding.

Pub crawl type of thing?

Yes. Tom responded. **Maybe a club?**

My nose wrinkled of its own accord.

I fingered my reply. **I don't think they'll let me in and I don't have any fake ID or anything.**

My phone buffered again and I moved it around the room, attempting to find signal.

Well, we can play it by ear. If you don't get in, you and me can go for food or something. Dirty kebabs?

I grinned, Lisa used to go on about dirty meat and how it helped with the hang over process.

I'll think about it. I responded.

He sent me an eye rolling emoji and two kisses. I was pleased with the level of 'safe' banter with Tom and I hoped that this was a sign that any romantic notions he'd originally felt, would eventually dry up altogether. One could only hope so. Tom being interested in me would only complicate things. It was hard enough dealing with Connor, let alone anyone else. I definitely wasn't a triangle girl.

I shuffled further back onto the bed and closed my eyes for a while.

Fashioning a fresh pair of skinny jeans and a cream lightweight blouse, I made my way to look for dad and hopefully find some dinner. I'd been asleep for the last two hours and my stomach felt hollow. Anna usually served up around now, but the kitchen was empty and there was no sign of cooking. As I grabbed an apple from the fruit bowl on the table, I glanced out of the back window into the garden. Dad was standing in front of a BBQ with smoke billowing out around him. I pulled a face and popped back the apple. He'd never been the best of cooks, if he was the chef, it was probably going to be rank. My God, how I would have killed for a Big Mac and fries right then.

I moved towards the back door, but low voices stopped me in my tracks. I strained to listen. Great, now I was a nosy bitch as well as a slut. Life on the farm appeared to be moulding a whole new me.

My brain seemed to be supplying my feet with mixed messages but I persevered, shuffling forward, wincing at the tap-tap from my sandals. The thought of being caught eavesdropping was not one I relished and I felt a sick sensation pool in the pit of my stomach.

I pursed my lips and circled around, cocking my head, trying to establish where the voices were coming from.

It was Rachel and Connor and it sounded like they were in Dad's study. I fought against going to listen, but curiosity got the better of me as the exchange started to get heated. OMG, what if Rachel had seen the kiss and were talking about me? I cursed myself and added 'self-involved' to the personality traits of the new me.

"—need to be more careful—knows where Gran lives and could easily have followed you from there. I thought you were coming back last week when he was still inside?" Connor's voice was stern as usual.

"I couldn't leave her, she looked shocking," Rachel replied, her voice paper thin. "And will you *stop* worrying. He doesn't even know she's been ill."

Who the hell were they talking about? Inside what?

"Bullshit. You usually visit the first weekend of every month. You need to change it. You know what we were told about regular patterns of behaviour."

I could hear every word clearly and any guilt I may have felt in the first instance vanished as I saw they'd left the office door wide open. It surely couldn't be *that* top secret if they hadn't closed themselves in there?

I folded my arms and stood on the inside of the kitchen. Rachel and Connor's voices were now being clearly carried down the corridor and from my new position, I could make a quick escape if the need arose.

"I'd rather you not use that language Connor and we need to talk about this later, Mike's making supper."

"Screw supper. I think this conversation is a little more important than fucking food."

I heard Rachel pause as a moments silence dripped down the corridor and I shuffled back slightly, ensuring they wouldn't see me half sticking out of the kitchen if they left the room.

"I don't think we have anything to worry about. I took a different route on the way back and stopped several times. Just as I said I would."

"You should have come back when you said you would. What if Martha's spoken to him, you know she's a fucking busybody."

I heard shuffled footsteps as they made their way around the room and poised myself for flight, just in case.

My mind raced as I tried to process everything they were saying. They were talking about a man and one that they were hiding from for some reason?

I heard the patio doors in the study being opened.

Rachel's voice became quieter as she moved away. "Please Connor, just let it go. We're safe. You've nothing to worry about. He's out but he will have moved on by now, he's let us both go."

Another silence followed. Were they talking about Connor's father?

Connor's voice was strained and angry, the pitch not at all pleasant and I felt a wave of worry. This wasn't good.

"Safe, that's an interesting word. We will never be safe now the fuckers free and if I ever see him again, I'll wipe the floor with the fucker."

Rachel's voice shot up an octave and I started to regret my decision to eavesdrop. Now afraid of what I was hearing. "You need to see Doctor Mitchell again Connor, please. Mike said that you've been struggling."

I was now certain that Connor's father *was* the person they were discussing. I stored the word 'safe' into my memory, deciding to deal with that piece of information later. A new and unsettling realisation that I might have misjudged his situation, needled away at me.

"Fuck that, I've had enough of that shit and feeling half asleep all the time. I'm doing things my way now."

107

So, Connor *had* stopped taking his 'chill out' medication. Fuck! My hands started sweating.

"Rachel, Connor!" Dad's voice cut in, immediately ending their conversation and I panicked.

"Coming," Rachel shouted.

"Look we'll discuss this later. I'm your mother and you'll do as I say."

I'd never heard Rachel use that tone before and I was glued to the spot as I awaited Connor's response.

His voice was low and nasty. He was close to losing his temper; I recognised the tone from Nate's party.

"Really, so *that's* what you are. I'm out of here." His voice was so cold a chill rippled through me.

As I realised it was Connor leaving the room, I jumped forward to move away.

I must have caught a pan or something as I swung around and the metal fell to the floor, with the loudest clatter ever.

Adrenalin burst in my chest like a mushroom cloud as my red-faced stepbrother strode out of the study, his eyes searching the source of noise. Those dark eyes met mine from my crouched position. I was in mid-retrieval of what was actually a baking tray from the floor and his face went from neutral to livid, he *knew* I'd been listening. I wanted to curl up inside myself and die.

That special moment between us from my bedroom window was lost.

Connor moved towards me shooting black daggers and I shoved the tray on the side with nervous hands, my mouth opening and closing as I fought for an excuse. My twitchy eye kicked in.

He was almost upon me when my focus was pulled past him as Rachel appeared, a flushed look on her face. She paused momentarily when she saw me, her recovery swift, her expression showing no trace of concern.

"Harlow, sweetie. I was just coming to get you for dinner." She said with a catch in her voice, which I couldn't determine.

Connor stopped advancing, his fists clenched at his sides, he looked larger than life, a tight black T shirt hugging his huge shoulders. His eyes never left my face and he didn't turn to his mother at the sound of her voice. Talk about awkward.

His expression glittered in a way that made the air thump from my lungs. He was angry. Even his tattooed arm seemed to bristle.

Rachel brushed past her son. "Con was just about to take over from your father. He isn't the best cook your dad, as I imagine you're more than aware of." She smiled, but I could tell she was uncomfortable. Probably because Connor just continued to stand there in silence glaring at me.

He was as still as a statue and I took a step forward and recovered myself, craning my head to Rachel.

"Cool. I'm starving," I replied breezily, not wanting to cause a further scene. Rachel trotted over to me. She was also slight in build but still taller than I was.

She squinted at Connor as we made our way towards the backdoor. "Connor, are you coming?"

I turned back to meet his eyes again, but he dragged his gaze away and shot his mother a look that could have melted glass. My heart leapt in my chest.

Temper oozed from him and his mouth had thinned. "I've lost my appetite," he drawled before turning around and heading through the hallway with determined steps. The front door slammed angrily, shaking the windows in the kitchen and my heart sank.

I worried my lip as I glanced nervously up at Rachel but she had gathered herself again and she ushered me through the back door, muttering something about kids.

I needed to shelve the chaos in my head for now and play nice to get through supper.

The smell in the air was divine. I had always loved that BBQ smell that came with summer. That and cut grass. Rachel and I went over to dad who appeared to be wearing a woman's apron, but I didn't smile. I was too worried about Connor. There were way too many thoughts swimming around my head.

My father was also wielding BBQ tools and looked completely out of his comfort zone. Weren't all men supposed to be born with the ability to BBQ?

He twisted his head as we approached and his face was flushed red, either from the heat of the grill or from the stress of attempting to cook. "There you are. You look nice love," Dad said as he briefly glanced over before focusing on the overdone burger he was cremating. "Both my girls do," he beamed.

Rachel and I exchanged glances with knowing smiles.

"Need a hand there?" she laughed as she unhooked her arm from mine and retrieved the BBQ tongues from my father.

"I thought you'd never ask. Did you speak to Connor?"

I saw Rachel's shoulders stiffen and sucked in a ragged breath. Guilt dug in between my ribs.

"Yes, and It's fine. He isn't eating though, so more for us!" She joked, but you could tell from the tremor in her voice that she was upset.

"Who's for a burger?" Dad asked, swiftly changing the subject. I raised my hand and gave him a nod before heading over to take a seat on one of the patio chairs. The table was laid with various salads and what I imagined were tin foiled jacket potatoes and an array of sauces.

"I hope you like them well done?" Rachel put in. Of course, we all laughed, but it felt kind of forced.

Rachel and dad buzzed around the BBQ, flipping burgers and turning sausages. I started picking at a burger bun as dad took my plate.

My mind was a myriad of questions. I was no Nancy Drew but it was obvious from what they had discussed that Connor's dad was the main focus and it wasn't good. I knew from my father that Rachel's relationship with her last husband had been hard, but the word safe had rocketed my conclusions up to the next level. Had he been an aggressive wife beating type? Was *that* why they were hiding? The thought made me sick to my stomach. Rachel was such a sweet lady and the thought of any physical abuse towards her made me angry. It was a deep-rooted anger, something I rarely experienced. My family life had been plain sailing compared to this, even with my mum and her drinking problems.

I thanked dad as he handed me back my plate and feigned interest as he and Rachel joined me and started to speak about the timings of the cattle show on Saturday.

I pushed my summations to the back of my mind as there was no point in dwelling on it or jumping to conclusions. I would speak with dad about it when we next had our chill out time together, but maybe not straight away. I wanted my dad to be with Rachel that evening as no doubt she needed to update him on her quarrel with Connor.

I took a bite of burger, it luckily tasted better than it looked and I added another blob of ketchup to an extra charred edge, my eyes flicking back and forth between my dad and his wife.

Whatever Connor thought of me, whatever his pain, I was part of this family now and I needed to know what was going on. I refused to be left in the dark, like when my parents were struggling yet 'pretending' to be happy. I was now a young adult and it was *my* duty to help and protect the family where I could. I'd get the truth out of my father one way or another and if that failed, I'd go to Connor.

We all ate our body weight in burnt burgers and sausage and I helped Rachel wash the dishes. We spoke about the usual stuff, although she did bring up 'boys' at one point, a topic I steered her away from, taking into account I'd had her son's tongue in my mouth earlier that day.

Rachel and dad had decided on an early night which should have freaked me out but didn't. I imagine they had a fairly healthy sex life. They still had that newlywed's vibe and were still very touchy feely in front of me. To be honest, I had too much on my mind to worry about that, as long as I didn't hear any sex noises, I could cope.

I slipped my sandals back on and walked down the side of the house to the front to sit on the bench by the door; the place where I'd had my first conversation with Ella Wade. Another jigsaw piece in what was fast becoming a slightly clearer puzzle. I still had to learn about her story and whether or not it was intertwined with Connor. I now had my doubts. Her shit was definitely directed another way. At least I hoped so.

I checked my phone and saw that it was almost ten, Connor would have been gone who knew where, for the past *two* hours. I realised I didn't even have his number and so couldn't message him to check he was OK. I'd deleted his text the night of the party. Not like he'd appreciate me texting him if I did.

I text my mother to say that I loved her as one thing was clear to me now, the breakup between my parents had been so much more straightforward compared to Connor's parents. I kicked myself for my past judgements.

There was a reason Connor was the person he was; moody, unpredictable, difficult with everyone and not just me. I should have felt relieved but I didn't. The thought of him hurting somewhere was causing me actual discomfort.

I closed my eyes and recalled what I had learned so far.

Rachel was estranged from her husband as was her son, and either their divorce or living conditions whilst they were together had been corrosive enough to mould Connor into a person who had anger issues. From Connor's reaction to his father finding Rachel, it had sounded like the guy was one nasty dude. The discussion also suggested that he was possibly abusive when they were married or as a result of her leaving him? Either way it was pretty toxic shit.

I continued to think about the possibilities. Maybe due to what had happened between his parents, Connor had been put on medication but had stopped taking them against his mother's wishes, hence the mood swings.

There was still so much more I needed to know. Suddenly, a night out in town on Friday was more appealing. It would also give me the chance to grill his friends to see what they knew.

Nine

It felt like I'd been laid in bed for hours, staring up at the Artext ceiling with abstract thoughts about how dated it looked and the possibility of the presence of asbestos. Strange how those weird obscure thoughts pop in there when you are trying not to think about the obvious. I was having a lot of those lately. I'd replayed the conversation Connor had with his mother that many times, that I could probably have written a play about it. What if I was wrong and it was more straightforward? I blamed the amount of drama I used to watch on TV.

Releasing a weary sigh, I pulled the covers up and continued to stare into the silence.

My feelings towards Connor seemed to be growing all the time which was annoying, considering my initial intention to keep my distance.

The fact that I wanted to be in his company twenty-four seven was now impossible to escape from, a bit like a non-swimmer in the middle of the sea.

My thoughts flickered back to my mother and I fleetingly wondered how things were going with Phil. He was probably the right guy for her, nice, quiet and uptight. Definitely a keeper and not the type to stray. I think if my mum lost another man to another women, it would probably finish her off.

I felt a rush of irritation that I couldn't sleep and blamed my stepbrother entirely. He'd still not come home and it worried the hell out of me. What if he'd driven into a ditch or something?

The house was quiet which suggested dad and Rachel had gone to bed. I mean, who did that, who allowed a not even twenty-two-year-old to storm off after an argument and then go to bed before he was safely home?

I rolled my eyes, maybe this wasn't so unusual for him? Maybe he did it all the time. How would I know, I had only known him a few weeks and yet for some reason, he'd still managed to work his voodoo shit on me? I couldn't stop thinking about him and now as I looked back, I acknowledged that he'd probably played on my mind since the anniversary party. Maybe it was due to him being so indifferent to me, as indifference was something I rarely experienced. Isn't there a saying that we all want what we can't have? The unattainable?

My mind skittered back to those last few weeks at school and how pathetic and immature the other boys were next to Connor.

Feeling fried, I screwed my eyes shut, willing myself to sleep for several minutes before I started to drift off.

An engine cut into my slumber as Connor's car pulled up to the house. The sound of gravel crunched against tyres. My bedroom was in darkness and I twisted to the bedside table to check my iPhone, scrunching my eyes against the offending light. It was well past midnight. Where the *hell* had he been?

The relief that spiralled in me was soon replaced with the feeling that something was wrong. He slammed the car door forcefully and I felt even more worried.

Sliding out from under the bedcovers, I readjusted my shorty pyjamas which had become twisted and padded barefoot over to the window to peel back the curtain.

Connor was closing the boot of the Ranger and I observed him through drowsy eyes as he strode off towards the hay barn, a swirling riptide of curiosity within me. This would be the fourth occasion I had caught him going in there at night, although this was certainly the latest that I had witnessed it. What on God's earth was he doing in there? Working? Smoking weed? *Meeting someone*? I struck the last thought off my list as it made me want to bleach my brain.

As he disappeared from sight, without thinking twice about what I was doing, I shot over to grab my robe, securing it tightly around my shivering body. The temperature in the house was so much cooler at night and no matter how much I'd tinkered with the radiator thermostat, it *never* helped. It was either boiling hot or too cold, there was no in between.

My thoughts shifted back to Connor. It was grating on me, I *had* to find out what the hell he did in there.

Listening for a sign that my dad and Rachel were still up, I pulled on my UGGs, weighing up my options. The house was still deathly quiet, signalling that the adults were probably fast asleep in bed, which fuelled my bravery. I had never been very successful in my two attempts to sneak out of the house back home but then again, mum usually stayed up late at night and didn't always pass out on the sofa. It was now or never.

One way or another I was going to get to the bottom of what was going on with my volatile, unreadable stepbrother. I had to find a way to reach him, to make him open up to me and share the burden, before he did something *really* stupid.

As I crept carefully down the poorly lit staircase, I toyed with several ideas on how to tackle the situation and how not to antagonise him. Calling Connor unpredictable was an understatement. If I said the wrong thing, he'd simply seize up or vent his spleen. Both of which were not outcomes I was not aiming to achieve on this particular trip.

The night air was chilly against my skin and I carefully closed the front door behind me so as not to alert those inside. It was a crisp fresh night with only the faint sounds of animals shuffling in the main barn and a rustling of trees. I pursed my lips as I made my way towards the hayloft where I saw a tell-tale faint glow of light.

I eyed Connor's car as I passed. It reminded me of that first day when he'd picked me up from the station and what a dick he had been. It was strange really. I had thought I'd despised him at that point. Now I didn't know how I felt, but it certainly wasn't hatred. Somehow in spite of his harsh treatment of me, he'd gotten under my skin and to the point where I *needed* to know more. I was desperate to fill in the gaps about what had happened to him and how that had affected his life with my father. It was all very mysterious and after all the years of keeping my head down, it was odd to think that since I'd arrived here, I'd done anything but. It appeared there was a bit of the adventurous in me after all.

I rubbed the gooseflesh from my arms and shook a curtain of hair back from my face. I usually slept with my hair in plaits but had left it loose and it was now creating chaos in the night breeze. As I approached the opening into the barn, I peered through and heard a strange repetitive thumping noise, pounding into the silence.

Turning the corner, I spied Connor and crept steadily forward, glancing briefly at my surroundings. He was alone apart from floor to ceiling stacks of hay bales and a couple of rusty bits of farm equipment.

Nervous knots were twisting in my stomach as I greedily eyed the scene before me. He looked sensational and I thought back to that first electric touch of his mouth.

The amber glow from the lamps illuminated his perfectly sculptured torso as he threw violent punches at what appeared to be a large sack of grain that was hanging from a beam with rope. It was like one of those workout bags you see at the gym.

His jabs were hard and fast, the material straining with each contact, like it could split at any minute. I bit back my knowing smile. So, *this* was how he'd replaced his medication. He dealt with his anger issues by beating the crap out of stuff. I was partly relieved to be honest, as the thought of him meeting someone in here for a midnight shag, was not an image I relished.

I could have groaned at how unbelievable he looked. Ripped blue jeans sat low on his hips. He had the best bum I had ever seen on a guy.

I ran my gaze up his back. His tee rippled over his shoulder muscles, but that wasn't the only thing that caught my eye, his knuckles were smeared with blood. So that's why they looked pretty mashed up all the time. I had assumed it was from farm work.

My hand reached out to notify him of my presence, but I stopped myself and tucked it behind my back.

It was then that he became still, like he'd sensed someone watching and he pulled his fists from the sack, slowly turning towards me.

Connor's eyes fell hard on mine and tension swelled. His breathing was heavy and I silently cursed my crazy idea to come now that it was way too late to retreat. Bad ass testosterone radiated from him.

My mouth went dry and I licked my lips, his predatory gaze lingering on the movement.

He didn't speak straight away, but I saw a muscle in his jaw tic and felt exposed in my scantily clad pyjamas, which the short silk robe barely covered. I should have pulled on my jeans. I had come here to talk, to find out if he was OK, not for anything else I'd told myself as I left the house.

Connor's gaze continued to roam over my body. It felt like he was physically touching me. He had obviously registered that I was wearing next to nothing and the aggressive passion he'd been directing into the seed bag, had now transferred to me.

He whistled in a sexy way. "Curiosity killed the kitty," he began with a wolfish look.

"So they say," I deadpanned, arching an eyebrow. I had to remain firm, this was about business, a fact-finding mission only.

There was a moment's pause before he continued, casting a glance at the thick watch he wore on his wrist. My tone must have got his attention.

"What are you doing here Harlow? Surely little girls should be tucked up in bed at this hour." His face was partially shadowed, but I could see his discontent.

At the word little girl, I felt my anger levels bubble. "What do you think I'm doing here? I've been worried. I wanted to check you're OK." I shot out, my heart galloping in my chest.

His eyes narrowed as if he didn't buy it. "Really?"

I scrunched my face up in disbelief. "Yes, fuckwit *really*!"

He cocked a brow, blatantly surprised by my language.

I told myself to relax before demanding in a typical fishwife type of tone. "Where have you been?"

Connor rolled his eyes. He wasn't going to tell me and I placed my hands on my hips, showing I meant business.

"Your hands are bleeding," I pointed out crossly in a 'matter of fact' way with a flick of my head. Like a mother telling a child off for ripping his jeans.

He didn't bat an eyelid. My comment was a dumb thing to say really, as if he didn't know that his hands were all messed up. His knuckles looked angry and my fingers twitched with the urge to sooth his injuries.

"And what, you've come to kiss them better?" he drawled mockingly, his lips curling as he moved towards me with determined, but slow steps. I stayed exactly where I was, equally resolute that I would not back away. I dropped my arms to my sides.

My reply surprised me. "Maybe?" I taunted. I was playing with fire but was past caring.

My directness was obviously unexpected by Connor as he came close and stared down at me with an all-seeing expression; like he was reaching into me, searching for the truth, stealing my secrets.

His eyes probed mine and he stopped around a couple of metres away before slowly withdrawing a rag from his jeans pocket. He wiped his knuckles without breaking eye contact.

Connor's lips curled slowly. "So, you've come for another taste?" he said as he twisted his head momentarily to throw the rag on a bale of hay.

He turned back to face me, he was baiting me back and I knew it, but I didn't care. Two could play that game.

I was stood with my heart in my mouth. "What if I have? What do you think about that?"

His mouth curled. "I think you're on dangerous ground." He was like a predatory animal on the verge of pouncing and I was the prey.

I folded my arms. "Why? You scared?" I tilted my head and shot him a provocative stare.

Considering I was so tired, I was on fire tonight, I usually hated any type of conflict, even when there was an undercurrent of attraction; a love/hate vibe, but I couldn't stop. I didn't want to.

Excitement flared in my chest at our banter. There was a definite battle of wills and I revelled in it. This guy brought out the worst in me, or maybe this was the best of me?

Connor exhaled sharply before he countered. "Not at all, but *you* should be. Maybe I'll take more than just a kiss."

I cursed my blush; the bubble of emotions swirling in my stomach coming to the boil, but in a good way.

I wanted this boy, *needed* to feed this hunger for him.

If only Lisa could see me now. Gone was the scared little girl and in her place was a, strong, confident young woman.

It was my turn to roll my eyes. "So, you're threatening me now?" I questioned with a twist to my lips, baiting him further, totally unfazed by what he was suggesting. I noted how he used the word 'take' instead of 'want', like it was his choice alone. That excited me more.

"You know I don't make threats. We've had this conversation before," he shook off the comment and contemplated his answer. "Just promises." He paused and gave me a pointed look. "Then you can't say I didn't try to warn you," he added using his 'serious' voice.

It was a blatant 'hit you between the eyes' challenge. The gauntlet was down and it poured fuel onto an already raging fire. My whole body was simmering and another trickle of excitement coursed through me.

I would not be the one to back down!

"I see. I think I'll stay. You need to learn that you can't boss me around like you can everyone else."

I saw a flash of something across his expression, like maybe he was impressed or relieved even, that I hadn't run away and taken the easy way out.

"Suit yourself," he replied before moving away towards a hay bale as if distance was the safest bet. I was surprised he hadn't reacted how I'd expected him to, considering I had challenged him.

He positioned himself a safe distance against a bale of hay but undeterred, I followed him so I was again stood before him, allowing him no means of escape.

I uncrossed my arms in order to appear less defensive and more open.

"You know I heard you and Rachel today, I didn't mean to listen but the door was open."

His eyes narrowed further, maybe he *hadn't* realised I'd been eavesdropping after all. "And what do you *think* you heard Harlow?" he said, searching my face.

I cleared my throat and banged a hand against my chest. Here goes. "I know you were talking about your dad and that you're both in hiding from him?"

Connor snorted rudely in a 'you know nothing' type of manner and I felt an unexpected twinge of sympathy.

"You heard wrong. My *mother* is hiding. I can't wait to meet the bastard face to face."

He tried to hide it but I heard the tremor in his voice, he wasn't as cocksure as he put out there.

His sentence confirmed that at last I appeared to be getting somewhere and I pushed my hands into my robe pockets to hide their trembling. I had a feeling that what I was about to hear may not be easy to digest and I needed to appear relaxed in order to encourage him to offload. I was certain he'd shut down in a heartbeat if he knew how stressed and out of my element I was really feeling.

"What did he do? Did he hurt your mother?" I asked quietly and tactfully. If that was the case as I suspected, it must have been terrible for him.

The directness of my question verbally knocked him back a step.

He cleared his throat. "Not physically. But it really isn't any of your fucking business."

I looked away for a moment. "No, but it could be. Have you never heard the saying of a problem shared is a problem halved?" I was desperate to awaken that thing inside him which he had obviously long buried. The ability to trust in someone else.

At my words, Connor smirked, searching my face. "Have you ever heard the phrase, don't stick your nose into things you could *never* understand?" he bit back.

I rocked forward as I battled with my reply. "Really, and *why* wouldn't I understand; because my life has been so perfect?" I spat sarcastically.

"You said it," he shot back.

I withdrew my hands but warded off the need to fold them again. Did he really think I'd had it easy with no problems of my own? Everyone has problems.

"That's rubbish and you know it," I growled, my knuckles curling into fists as I thought about my parent's divorce and the torture of my last few weeks at school.

He pushed himself off the hay bale and took a step closer, his breath against my face. His top was stuck to the hard planes of his chest with sweat but his scent was still heady.

I craned my neck to look up at him, determined not to be intimidated as he towered over me. He was so tall and strong. I was like a wilted flower in his presence.

"Everyone has problems Connor," I pointed out gently.

He turned his perfectly straight nose up. "Yes; and your biggest one will be me if you don't go, while I *let* you."

My pulse fluttered and I felt a momentary swirl of giddy panic rise in my chest. The latter part of the sentence was harsher, as if my determination to carry on the conversation had started to grind away his control.

I swallowed nervously but managed to hold my ground. I couldn't stop now. I wasn't afraid even though he was trying to be intimidating. I knew he'd never hurt me or force me to do anything, not really.

"No," I said, my bottom lip quivering slightly. His eyes darted to my mouth and his dark brows were knitted together. I couldn't believe the words that were coming out of me, it was totally surreal.

Connor's mouth twisted "No?" with one eyebrow arched.

I wrung my hands together before pushing a clump of hair off my shoulder. "Yes, as in no, I'm not going anywhere. I want to help and I'm a good listener."

I managed to maintain a passive expression, even though my body was coiled tight and rigid.

He looked up at the ceiling in a 'God give me strength' type of way before dropping his head to shoot me a stare. "Is that right?"

"Yep. Ask any of my girlfriends. I'm forever putting out fires," I put in brightly and I purposefully raised my eyebrows defiantly.

He wasn't impressed and his expression turned even more dark and brooding. "I just bet you are," he began, before dropping his voice to a whisper. He bent his head down towards me. "But you see, there's a different type of fire in me right now, and it has *nothing* to do with my parents," he added.

"OK," I replied, a pinch of uncertainty drizzling through me.

I was just about to move around him to sit on a hale bale and say 'I'm all ears' before he whispered. "Let me show you."

Connor drawled out his last sentence slowly, his eyes darkening, his expression altering to one of pure challenge. He was stood so close, I saw his pupils dilate and my heart fluttered like a wild bird against my ribcage, awareness pooling into me and then...I nearly died.

His eyes roamed over my body which was partly concealed in the short silk robe. His hands lifted to the belt and he pulled the ties. It slid open, revealing my camisole and shorts beneath it.

"Like opening a present," he murmured, his voice thickening.

Another jet of excitement shot into me as he took in the shape of my body before pushing the robe off my shoulders with his thumbs. I felt they were slightly calloused, probably from all the work he did on the farm. The silk puddled at our feet, totally forgotten.

My next words were swallowed as his arms shot out to grab my hips, dragging me against his body. I fell forward, plastered against him, my breasts crushed against his hard chest and my hands clutching at his arms for balance. He threaded a hand through my hair, dragging my head back, my eyes smarting from the sudden tug against my scalp and I gasped in surprise as he lowered his head.

I ignited and my heartbeat accelerated.

His mouth ground down against mine. The kiss was hard and demanding, intended as punishment, but the feel of his lips produced a sexual frenzy inside me and moisture flooded between my legs. He drove his tongue into my mouth and my own rose to greet it, I was so turned on and I leaned further into him, accepting everything he had to give. Lust, hot and insistent pulsated through my limbs, it was mind-blowing.

Connor moaned against my mouth as his onslaught continued, licking, nibbling, tasting. It was wild and I slid my arms around his neck pushing upwards, providing deeper access to my mouth.

I didn't realise he was walking me backwards until I felt the barn wall against my back, the cold seeping through my nightclothes. I was caged in and Connor released my head and ran his hands back down my spine before cupping my bottom and pulling me further against him. I could feel he was rock hard against my stomach and I longed to feel him between my legs. The thumping in my chest was almost painful.

I moaned in pleasure against his mouth, he was blowing my mind in more ways than one and I surrendered myself to him as my tongue fenced with his.

Sliding my hands across his broad shoulders, my fingertips gently traced the muscles on his arms. I faintly noted how the skin under his tattoos felt quite rough compared to the other side, but I filed away the thought, too wrapped up in the excitement being generated by his sensual attack.

Some type of skirmish occurred in the barn next to us which broke into my thoughts and alarm bells sounded in my head as Connor pulled away and abruptly ended the kiss. Reality crashing back into my senses like a cruel wave and my hands dropped to curl into his t-shirt, holding on to him as if my life depended on it. He was breathing hard and fast and my body shuddered.

An evil mixture of disappointment and shame crushed my chest. Had I really just behaved in such a way? Connor had kissed me as a punishment to warn me off him and I had *liked* it? My behaviour was all kinds of messed up. I needed to get a grip.

I took a step back and pressed a hand to my mouth, shaking, slightly confused but still uplifted.

Connor hissed out a sharp breath as he pulled further away, putting more distance between our bodies and I recognised his anger was battling against his arousal.

"You should go," he rasped as he turned back to face me, his face partially shadowed again.

I remained silent, allowing myself time to recover my composure. If Connor had not pulled away, I wouldn't have stopped him and the truth of that laid between us unspoken, but blatantly there. I wanted to have sex with him, needed him to be my first.

"It doesn't have to be this way. We could be friends you know. I'm not a bad person," I whispered, unable to hide the sadness in my voice.

His expression softened and he walked back to me, running his fingertips up and down my arms, but not actually holding me. It was a tender, affectionate thing to do and it felt so good. My spirits lifted slightly.

I inhaled him in as he closed his eyes and placed his forehead against my own, his body tense. My back was still pushed against the barn wall.

"No, I am and you *need* to keep your distance. You're too sweet, too young, to fucking perfect. You should experience this shit with a boy your own age, a good guy. Fuck me, maybe even Tom. Experiment, although just thinking about you doing that with anyone else, makes me want to hit stuff."

I was about to reply but he lifted his head and placed a finger to my lips. "Not you of course, you know I'd never do that," he promised.

I believed him. "I know that. I'm not afraid of you. Not at all, even when you're at your meanest."

His eyes drilled into me as he replied. "That's just it Harlow, you *haven't* seen me at my meanest, and I *never* want you to."

I raised an eyebrow at that one. "You came close at Nate's party."

Connor smiled but it was grim. "Not really. I wouldn't have hit him. Not unless he had his hands all over you. I'd probably have broken his nose then."

I pushed at his chest but he was like a rock. I gave him a pointed look. "So, you don't want me but you don't want others to have me, and then telling me I should 'experiment' with guys my age? Talk about mixed messages Connor."

He signed. "That's my point. At times I feel like I'm two different people, one good, one bad. Mixed. Do you *really* want to be close to someone like that Harlow? Someone unpredictable and so completely fucked up," he stated through a tortured voice.

The muscles in his arms shifted and tensed. His words pulled my chest tight.

"Give up on me."

I didn't even need to give my reply any thought as the word burst from my lips.

"No."

It was that 'no' that seemed to tether us together and his gaze roamed over my features as if looking for a different way to break me down.

He moved back a step our eyes still locked together.

"It's your funeral," he put in with a slight smile, that hint of misery fading from his eyes.

It was like there was a silent understanding between us at that moment and the tension lifted. Like Connor had surrendered slightly.

I moved forward and pushed gently against his body and he stepped back further to give me more space, his expression guarded.

"A few of us are going into Scarborough on Friday, why don't you come?"

This got his attention and he raised his eyebrows and shot me a pointed look.

"So now you're seventeen, you think it's safe to go clubbing? Town is a complete dive Harlow. You won't enjoy it."

"Maybe I will, maybe I won't. But it's a change. I'd enjoy it if you're there."

"Do I look like I'm the type to go clubbing?"

"Yes actually. You're a young, attractive guy. Why shouldn't you go and enjoy yourself. You have it all really Connor, you're just missing one element."

"I see, and what's that since you suddenly know me so well."

"Fun."

"Ah, that strange word that everyone goes on about."

"Yes. It's something that you appear to have forgotten how to have it."

"I can think of a lot more ways of having fun than getting shit faced and going clubbing Harlow."

"Well, me too but still. Why not? Give it a go. Come with us. I promise I won't force you to dance or anything."

"You couldn't if you tried Harlow."

I smiled. "Please at least think about it. I'd love it if you came but it's up to you of course."

I delivered what would be my last words that evening. Connor did open his mouth to speak but I held up my hand warding him off. "I suggest you soak your hands before bed Connor," I instructed, taking control. "I'll see you tomorrow."

I gave him one last meaningful look with my hand flat against my chest, hoping, no praying that he'd get the message that I was there for him. That I had some type of feelings for him even if I wasn't sure what kind they were yet. I wanted him to know he wasn't alone. So much had happened in such a short space of time, I felt thoroughly railroaded

As I walked away, I knew he was watching me leave and I hoped he'd call me back but of course he didn't. I felt an overwhelming urge to cry but managed to restrain myself.

As I arrived back in my room without waking anyone, my eyes were drawn to the faint trace of blood on one of my shoulders. Blood from Connor's hands, I traced it with my finger before an overwhelming feeling gripped me.

I threw myself onto the bed and allowed that evening's events to pour out of me into my pillow. I felt tightness in my throat, like I was nervous and at that point, I realised the barefaced truth of the matter.

Connor Barratt had the power to ruin me.

Ten

I didn't see him again for the next couple of days. Dad said that Connor had gone to the village to trade some cattle, but I had my suspicions that this was probably bullshit, he was still trying to avoid me. There may have been *some* truth in there of course but I imagined Connor had *offered* to go to market in order to escape from whatever this 'thing' was between us. I knew from my father that he usually took the cows to market himself.

August was rapidly passing by but the weather had started to turn, the skies were bleak and there was a chill in the air, which was strange for what was usually the hot point of the summer.

I had spent the last few hours pottering around and helping dad with bits and bobs, I'd even managed to sort out the nightmare that was his study. There were books, paperwork and unopened letter piles on his desk, not to mention an old cup which had who knew what growing in it, but I'd eventually managed to coordinate the chaos.

As I was in the process of wiping a space I'd cleared, the phone rang but I left it, believing that Anna would pick it up. After around a minute of listening to its shrill sound, I grabbed the receiver and a pen in case I needed to take a message.

As I answered, I was greeted by silence and I repeated my 'hello', surmising that it was probably a call centre and I was waiting to be connected. I'd cottoned onto to these types of call. There was always a delay, mum usually just hung up as she was sick to death of taking PPI and 'were you recently involved in an accident' calls.

"Mrs Williams?" a deep, scratchy male voice questioned. I winkled my nose, before I realised that he meant Rachel, and *not* my mother.

"No sorry, she isn't here right now, can I help?" I questioned, tucking the phone into the crook of my neck as I pulled a bit of paper towards me.

"Sorry, who am I speaking to? Are you're a relation to Mrs Williams?"

I checked the pen worked by starting to doodle my version of a plant pot on the corner of the notepaper. "I suppose, I'm her stepdaughter," I replied.

I was greeted with another silence and I exhaled, partly wishing I'd ignored the call, get on with it!

"I see. Look, I can only speak to members of the family. My name is David Smith and I'm calling from the bank. I have an urgent message for Mrs Williams. Could you just confirm your address, so I can check it against my system?"

I pursed my lips, already weary of the call and was just about to say that I didn't actually know the full address, but I spotted one of dad's unopened letters on the desk and pulled it towards me.

I reeled off the details, including the postcode and then waited with my pen poised; concerned that a call from the bank may be quite important.

Then the line went dead.

Odd.

My brow furrowed and I replaced the receiver. We'd obviously been cut off. The farm *was* in the middle of nowhere. I waited a minute or two for him to call back but when no call came, I wrote a quick message to say that the bank had called and took it into the kitchen. The chance of Rachel or my dad seeing it was more likely there and I popped it under one of the magnets on the fridge. Better than it being buried by papers in dad's office.

As I turned to leave the kitchen, Rachel came in through the front door holding something.

"Harlow, is this yours?" she began, approaching me with a peculiar expression.

I dipped my head to see what she was holding and then panic burst from my chest. What the actual F!

My stepmother was clutching my robe. My silky little number. The one I had worn that had been personally peeled away by her son hands during our 'encounter'. If 'encounter' was the right word, it felt like such a dull way to describe that amazing heated moment between us.

Rachel gave me a guarded look, as you would do I suppose if you found part of someone's sexy nightwear in the fricking barn of all places. Why the hell hadn't Connor picked it up? He must have been as lost in the moment as I was to have missed it.

I was sure my eyes were bulging from their sockets and I gave myself a mental kick, speak! "Oh, yes. Thanks. Been looking for that," I spluttered on a semi-stutter.

She then shot me what I took to be one of those 'woman to woman' looks. A knowing, 'I know that there is more to this that you are letting on' type of vibe. And of course, she was right. I can just imagine her face if she was aware of the whole truth and who was actually involved in my loss of attire. I could have been out there sneaking around with any of the farm hands. Gross but true. Either that or one of the other boys from the village, as far as Rachel knew, Connor and I didn't get along.

I took it, thanking her again and redirected her thoughts by saying. "Oh, you had a call from the bank."

Her brow furrowed before she replied. "Really? When?"

I pointed towards the fridge. "Just now, I made a note but they didn't leave a number."

She pursed her lips, as if suddenly in deep contemplation.

"That's odd. I didn't even realise they had this number. They called on the landline?" she questioned, looking thoroughly confused.

I nodded my head. "Yes," also feeling perplexed.

After a moment of silence where it just felt plain weird, Rachel smiled, tightly. "OK, thank you. I'm sure it's nothing to worry about."

As she drifted past me into the kitchen, her body language said the complete opposite.

Breaking me out of my train of thought, my own phone vibrated in the pocket of my jeans. It was from Tom detailing the arrangements for where I was to meet everyone that evening. I couldn't believe Friday had come so soon.

Over the last few days, I'd been carefully plotting what to wear. I knew I'd need to dress carefully to give the illusion that I was older. If they didn't let me in the club, I'd be mortified in front of the others. Anticipation punched my gut. I'd only ever gotten in a club once before and on that occasion the bouncer has been pretty shit faced.

I had been completely honest with dad and told him I was going into Scarborough with a group of friends. He gave me the usual safety talk and said that I could go, as long as he dropped me off and picked me up. I was also to keep my phone on me at all times.

As I stood in my bedroom, I told myself it was time to let my hair down and do what most girls my age did, minus the getting pissed and falling around like a loon of course.

Critically eying my reflection in the full-length mirror, my brow furrowed. I didn't look like me and I certainly didn't feel like me.

The dress I had chosen was figure hugging and made from laced material. As I'd dragged the garment over my head, I was relieved to see that it wasn't as transparent as I'd first assumed, the dress possessed a nude body liner which thankfully concealed my underwear.

I thoroughly appraised my appearance. The outfit clung to my body and was not overly short in length, but the sweetheart neckline was dangerously low and revealed pretty much most of my cleavage. It certainly 'enhanced my femininity in all the right' (or wrong) places.

Nervous knots started to work themselves loose within me. Was I comfortable enough to wear this in public? It certainly didn't fall in line with my usual sense of style. Goodness only knows what dad may say when he saw me. I did look older though, which was of course the point.

I smoothed my perfectly painted fingers over my hair, the red nails an afterthought and scanned the blonde silky paleness against the deep tone of the dress. I had purposefully left my hair loose and it fell past my shoulders in waves.

The more I appraised my appearance, the better I felt. I looked OK, a little on the slutty side but so what. It wasn't like we were going to church or anything.

I texted Tom to confirm I'd received his message and that my dad was going to drop me off outside the bar where we were due to meet.

Dad's eyes almost popped out of his head when he saw me coming down the stairs, but he didn't comment.

Thanking him for the lift, we agreed I'd message him later to arrange a time for pick up. He delivered yet another safety speech and told me not to put my drink down anywhere so it couldn't be spiked. I smiled at his concern as I was a little more streetwise than he was giving me credit for.

Pecking him on the cheek, I climbed down from the car feeling a little uneasy.

The town centre was alive with people, a variety of ages. Some dressed for a night out, others more student like in jeans and T shirts.

Two bouncers opened the doors to the pub and wished me a good night. I could see from their expressions that they were appreciative of what they saw and this gave me a boost of confidence, I'd never walked into a bar alone before.

As I entered the room, it was fairly busy with the low beat of music and plenty of noisy voices. Tom and the others were huddled around a booth at the back of the main room and I casually walked over to greet them.

All eyes were upon me and Ella was there with another girl, which took me by surprise.

She was sat opposite Kyle, Max and Nathan and looked pretty in what appeared to be a black dress. It was hard to tell as she was sitting.

"Hey." I greeted them. My heart dipped as I noted that Connor was a no show. Why I had even bothered hoping he'd come was beyond me. He probably didn't even have clothes that fit in with the dress code for a nightclub. Even at the engagement he'd worn jeans.

They all said hi over each other and the lads rose to greet me. I had hugs and air kisses. Kyle, Max and Nate were all dressed in trousers and shirts and all scrubbed up rather well, for country boys.

Ella introduced me to Natalie. A girl that I fleetingly remembered from Nate's party. She had long black hair, deep brown eyes and dark naturally tanned skin. She was beautiful and exotic and was dressed in tight black trousers and a floaty blouse that's print would make you feel nauseous if you stared at it for too long. Her lashes were also ridiculously long, but natural I guessed. It was explained briefly that the twins knew her from school.

Tom went to the bar to fetch me a beer and Ella moved over so I could sit in between her and Natalie. The three girls faced the three boys and when Tom came back, he pulled up a stool and positioned himself at the end of the table.

I sipped my beer. Tom wouldn't take the money I offered him for the beer which was nice.

The conversation flowed and I scanned the pub and soaked up the charged atmosphere. A guy and girl were holding hands by the bar and my heart squeezed, they looked so besotted with each other. I wondered fleetingly what it would be like to stand with Connor like that and hold hands.

"So how does it feel to be staying in the country Harlow, Ella tells me you live in London," Natalie asked. She spoke with a faint Yorkshire accent.

"Yes, it's cool. I'm sort of used to it now and everyone was so welcoming."

Her plump lips turned down at my response and she look surprised.

"Really, everyone? Even Connor?"

I swallowed the looming lump, here we go again I thought. There was a bitchy note to her voice, which hadn't been there at first.

"He was a bit standoffish at first but I suppose we didn't really know each other," I responded keeping it light. I wasn't going to get into another discussion about Connor when he wasn't there. I hated the behind the back approach.

Natalie grinned showing perfect, overly white teeth. She reminded me of one of those bull terrier dogs. "He's a tough one to crack alright."

Her comment seemed to drag Nate's attention away from what the boys were discussing.

"He's not the only one." Nathan put in with a grin at Ella.

"Don't start," she replied, kicking him under the table and rolling her eyes.

Interesting. Who was he referring to?

Shaking off the thought I simply replied. "It's fine. We're good."

Natalie took a drink from her glass, twisting sideways, eyeing me over the rim. "Tom was saying you want to be a teacher?" I knew her attempt at small talk was leading to something else.

I nodded before taking a sip of my beer. She so wasn't really interested. "Yes, I'm thinking about it." I could tell she was sizing me up with every syllable that left her lips.

She screwed her face up, it wasn't a nice look. "Doesn't your dad own shit loads of land and stuff? Surely you don't have to work at all."

I stared at her with a coolly impersonal smile. Both her words and tone were quite rude and I was surprised that no one commented on it. Was she generally a rude bitch and they were used to it or did they all see me as some type of overindulged brat? Even Tom hadn't said anything, although he was listening intently to something Nate was saying about the girls on the next table.

I chose my words carefully. I didn't want her to think she'd won any points with her snide remark. "My dad's OK off I suppose but that's not me. I still want to do my own thing."

Natalie full out scoffed at that one. "Bollocks," she put in waving her beer about.

Her use of language gave me an even lower opinion of her. Stupid bimbo.

At last, Nathan jumped to my defence. Better late than never I supposed.

"Shut it Nat, you're just jealous and bricking it that you'll end up as a hairdresser like your mother. Dying old ladies' hair pink and shit."

She shot him a dirty look. "Fuck you, Nathan. You can talk! You *absolute* leach. When are you going to get a job and stop sponging off *your* parents? You know, follow in Golden Boy's footsteps."

Upon Golden Boy being thrown into the mix, Tom shot a glance at Ella and she rapidly pushed to her feet, saying she needed to pee. I asked her if she wanted me to come, the whole 'girls go to the loo in twos' and all that, but she declined.

I shuffled in my seat now I had more room and Natalie nudged me with her elbow, her eyes roaming over my face.

"So where is Mr Moody tonight?" she asked with a pointed look, like I was his fucking keeper.

I shrugged. "Probably working."

Natalie shook her hair back and I was met with a waft of perfume: had the girl bathed in it? There was a definite uniqueness about the smell, it wasn't one that I would have worn. Bit pungent, like her attitude.

I shook off the thought upon realising she was still speaking. "Thought it was going to kick off at yours Nate."

To be honest, it was a shame she was there. Within the space of an hour, she had definitely soured my experience.

Nathan rolled his shoulders and then took another swig of beer. Boy the guy drank fast. "Nah, he's a fucking nutter at times but we've known each other too long to fall out over a chick."

"I see, and what chick are we talking about?" Natalie fished with eyes so narrow they had reduced to slits.

There was a pause and I felt like they were talking about something way above my head.

Nathan cleared his throat awkwardly before replying. "Harlow of course." Pointing his beer bottle at me with an 'aren't you a lucky girl' nod, like I'd just won a fucking Brit award.

OMG, I was mortified that he just came out with it. His reply was strange considering I hadn't actually felt that type of vibe coming from him at all. Maybe slightly at the party when he was pissed.

I laughed it off. "So, I'm a chick now, great."

Kyle cracked a sexist joke which cleared the air and everyone laughed. I had to force myself of course, it wasn't actually *that* funny.

"Another round here, then onto The Brewers Tap?" Tom piped up, necking his beer.

Yup, he was certainly trying to play the cool guy. I felt a bit sorry for him.

After another string of bars, everyone was starting to feel the effects of the booze and I decided I needed to pace myself. Especially considering my father was due to pick me up. He'd probably never trust me again if I passed out in the car on the way home.

After around an hour in the next pub, I popped to the loo.

"You look amazing in that dress. You're so tiny and cute." Natalie said, appearing beside me, meeting my gaze in the mirrored glass above the sinks. She too was redoing her lips. Her comment was so patronising and my palms itched. Smug cow.

I didn't smile, but returned her compliment, I wasn't a total bitch of course.

"I love that top." My voice still sounded insincere.

She started fluffing her hair. "So, Nate reckons there's something going on with you and Connor."

I paused as I ran the lip gloss over my lips, which were suddenly quite dry.

"Really?" I replied, attempting to feign innocence.

"Yeah, especially after he went crazy on your ass?"

I gave her a half-assed reply, which she totally didn't buy of course.

"I hadn't thought about it. He said I wasn't to go and I think I pissed him off by doing the opposite."

Her next words almost made my head explode.

"You must admit, he's as fit as fuck."

I put my lipstick away and broke eye contact.

"Yes, he's good looking." My reply sounded so wooden and as I raised my eyes back to her annoying reflection, her grin widened. I wanted to smack her in the face.

She tilted her head and considered me thoughtfully.

"You can be open with me you know, if you've done stuff. Maybe we could compare notes?"

Again, another exploding head moment occurred. What the actual fuck?

"What do you mean?" I shot out, a frown creasing my face. I turned to face her; my mind spinning with questions.

Natalie also twisted from her own annoying reflection and peered down at me with a fake trace of pity in her tone. She moistened her mouth with her tongue.

"Surely Connor's told you about us?"

My insides started to hurt. She was about to share gory details; I could sense it. And she *knew* I had feelings for Connor, it must have been etched into every crease of pain on my face. My stomach felt like it had a large nest of ants in it.

"I don't know, you used to go out?" I guessed tartly. Knowing there would be more to it than that.

Her overdone lips curled and I wasn't sure why I'd thought her petty before.

"Connor doesn't do relationships. We just fuck from time to time."

The word imploded from her lips and I suddenly wanted to be anywhere but there. Maybe at home, burrowing my head into my pillow.

There was a sinking feeling in my gut. Is that where he went when he was feeling stressed, like when he'd stormed off after his argument with Rachel? To shag this hoe? I felt like emptying the contents of my stomach all over her psychedelic top.

I managed to compose myself. I was now fully feeling the jealousy vibe which was pouring out of her like lava. This I was used to and this I could deal with, couldn't I? I saw it in girls all the time.

"Cool. Whatever, it's not my business."

She prodded me playfully in the arm and it made me want to snap her finger. Her nails were as garish as her outfit.

"You don't have to be jealous. It's just sex, there's nothing in it." Natalie piped in, with a forced giggle. She was thoroughly enjoying herself.

I pretended not to be bothered, unease continuing to pound my stomach.

"I think we should find the others."

I turned to leave the toilets. I still held the door for her for some strange reason.

"I hope I haven't upset you? I'm surprised he doesn't talk about me. He got a bit obsessed at one point. Couldn't get enough." She said in a spiteful voice, knowing she was wounding me with every word. I walked away, quickening my speed.

"Good for you." I muttered under my breath.

I saw the group and made a beeline, not waiting to see if Natalie had caught up to me.

"Hi, are you OK? You look upset? What's Natalie said?" Ella put in as she appeared suddenly at my side. She must have noticed the strange tension.

"She was just telling me how good my stepbrother is in bed," I deadpanned, my thoughts still spinning. Why was I even letting the bitch get to me? So, they *used* to shag, it wasn't like he was my boyfriend or anything. My God, if he really had been with that tart, there was a massive chance he'd be riddled. I attempted to use the thought to like him less, but it didn't work.

Natalie joined the twins who were walking ahead of us, the damage well and truly done and she knew it. You could tell from the way she trotted next to them that it was some type of victory walk. She irritated the hell out of me. I decided she was like one of those fancy, overindulged dogs that were dressed in clothes; cute to look at but useless.

Ella slid an arm around me which was a surprise.

"Ignore her, she's jealous of you because you're hotter than her and you have Connor's attention. She's been after him for years."

Her revelation needled me.

"Why are you friends with someone like that Ella?" I questioned, moving away slightly so her arm slipped off my shoulders. I didn't really want her poor attempt at comfort.

She looked uncomfortable at my words and shrugged.

"I don't know. Maybe because they aren't many girls to share stuff with in the village."

I felt a twinge of remorse for my comment and thought back to when I'd first me her. There had definitely been something she had wanted off her chest. Maybe she had stored it all up. I couldn't imagine anyone wanting to share anything of importance with the overly colourful Natalie.

"So, she isn't lying." I said, still feeling miserable. I blinked away a sting of tears, accepting that they were probably partly drink induced.

"Oh yes, they were definitely shagging at one point but it wasn't serious. Just a bit of fun."

I thought back to my comment to Connor about having fun. I certainly hadn't meant that sort of fun, at least not with anyone else anyway.

"Are you sure you don't have something going with Connor?" Ella's tone was accusatory again and it wound me up.

"Are you sure *you* don't?" I sniped back, still not sure if that ship had sailed.

Nate appeared between us.

"What the actual fuck was taking you girls so long, how long does it take to take a piss?"

His speech was slurred. I now felt angry at my self-pity and his appearance made me pull myself together.

"Nathan you're gross. You don't say that to the Ladies," Ella chided, elbowing him in the side as he pushed between us and placed his arms around both sets of shoulders.

"If I see some, I'll make sure I watch what I say." His smile was cheeky and his dimples appeared.

"You're such a dick. And if you get any more shit face, I'm going home." Ella replied with a serious edge.

"You love it."

I wasn't sure whether I'd misread the look they exchanged, was there a flirty vibe or had I just imagined it?

Eleven

I exhaled heavily. There was a strange throbbing sensation inside me. My body was floaty and warm and the material of my dress felt cool against my skin, but I wasn't that drunk. I was at that nice point where the alcohol relaxes you, but not so much so you make a tit of yourself. Natalie and Nate were pretty much three sheets to the wind and were now walking ahead of the group, wobbling all over the place.

The nightclub Josephine's had a huge queue and as we approached the tall glass fronted building, we immediately drew attention. Two guys I recognised who had been watching us in the first bar jogged up to us, one bumming a light from Natalie. One of the bouncers was staring straight at me, he didn't even attempt to hide his ogle. A pretty sleazy move considering he was supposed to be there for our protection?

I watched and listened in as Natalie spoke with the two younger guys in the queue whilst lighting 'Mark's' cigarette. Yet another surprise, I hadn't realised she smoked. She was probably giving them her number and telling them what slot they could have. She was definitely a slag.

Mark's friend was speaking to me, asking me my name, but just as I was about to reply, Ella grabbed my hand and tugged me along beside her. I couldn't do anything but follow mid-sentence and I stumbled along, my heels wobbling against the tarmac.

"We've got to go guys, places to be… people to see!" She yelled behind her, offering no apology for blatantly blowing them off.

The others fell in behind us.

We all negotiated our way through the glass entrance into the club, our heels clicking in succession against the flooring. We didn't need to pay an entry fee which was cool and they let me in with no questions which was a relief.

"Hey, where's the fire?" I puffed as Ella steered me along.

"Sorry, but I want to get to the bar before happy hour ends."

I managed to stop myself from tripping over a variety of feet. Of course, 'happy hour', silly me! What the hell was 'happy hour'?

The bar area was mashed and flustered staff were franticly taking orders.

It was a fairly classy looking place. The floors were solid wood and the walls a mixture of mahogany panelling and maroon paint. The disco lights flashed in time to the music. There was a distinctive 'the place to be' vibe and I felt my stomach muscles relax. I sure hoped Natalie didn't try and speak with me again, Mark was welcome to her. She'd wound me up that much and the thought of her and Connor together made me want to gouge her eyes out.

People were scattered across the dance floor and were chatting in groups. Not many people were dancing at that point.

Ella ordered two drinks a piece and it all was revealed that 'happy hour' was basically 'buy one get one free'. Needing to reign myself in a bit, I opted for a mock-tail. I eyed the tall glass of neon coloured liquid suspiciously.

I could feel appreciative eyes upon me from all directions and it felt good. I even allowed myself to return a few smiles.

As we approached the seating area, where the others were sat, a half-inebriated Nathan waved us towards two empty chairs. I was relieved as my feet were already killing me, the heat from the base of my foot threatening to melt the glue from the soles of my shoes.

Ella grabbed a chair and plonked herself in it, crossing her long legs, looking every bit at home. I still felt a bit conscious myself, considering my underage status. Natalie had obviously gone off with Mark thank goodness.

As I made myself more comfortable in my seat, Tom's carefree blue eyes ran over me and I felt heat sting my cheeks by his barefaced appraisal.

He pulled out the stool opposite and straddled it, leaning forward, resting his beer against one knee.

"So, are you enjoying yourself?" he began. He took a swig from his bottle of beer, his eyes never leaving my face. Alcohol had obviously given him courage but Ella nipped that in the bud pretty quickly.

"OK Tom, give the girl some breathing room."

Her comment embarrassed him and he backed off which I was thankful for, I was too busy scanning the club, willing Connor to appear.

I bent forward carefully, not wanting to hit him with an abundance of cleavage.

"Yes Tom, I am. It's great to be out. You should relax."

My words gave him back his glow and he grinned at me. Now being the true Tom.

My eyes scanned the room again as everyone carried on with their own bits of conversation.

"You won't see him you know," Ella's voice bit into my thoughts.

"I'm that easy to read?" I returned drily, no longer caring if I exposed how I felt about Connor. Ella was fairly astute.

She rolled her eyes in response.

"Sorry. Maybe not to the others. But I've seen that look before."

My focus was redirected as Kyle and Max started arguing. The banter between them competitive but playful and fairly funny to watch.

I smiled at her and squeezed her knee in silent understanding. The girl also had demons to share.

After an hour or so, Ella and I went to dance. The boys joined in on and off, although Tom looked really uncomfortable and did that shuffling from one foot to the other thing. Kyle, Max and Nathan just jumped around with each other to the music. Natalie and Mark join us briefly. She was all over the place and danced like you did when you thought no one was watching.

The DJ bled slow music into one of the more kicking tunes, changing the atmosphere on the dance floor into more of a smooch zone and everyone in our group left to sit down.

I excused myself and went to get some water. The queue at the main bar was huge so I went through the back of the club into an area which had a small, more intimate dance floor and bar which only had one person waiting.

After quenching my thirst, I walked over to stand at the edge of the dance floor and watched the people gathered there who were slow dancing. Couples, holding each other and swaying to the music and I wondered how it would feel to dance in Connor's arms.

One of my favourite songs suddenly fed into the current track, it was Halo by Beyoncé.

I closed my eyes, allowing the music to wash over me. There were a couple of groups of guys and girls sat around the edges of the floor but I didn't care. I was too lost in the moment.

As I opened my eyes, my heart swelled against my ribcage and excitement licked up my spine.

Connor stood at the other edge of the dancefloor, watching me intently. I wanted to run to him but my legs wouldn't move. I trembled, shocked into a trance by his presence, my lower body starting to pulse.

I drank in the sight of him as he moved through the swaying couples towards me, his expression intense, purposeful. His eyes remained connected to mine the whole time, like we were fused together. Connor's confident posture screamed that there was nothing he couldn't do if he put his mind to it. Controlled and powerful. Very much the confident alpha male.

As he came to stand in front of me so tall and strong, I raised my head to retain eye contact, feeling alive with pleasure. His sensual lips curled at the edge in silent greeting and I could see he was pleased to see me. It was written on every part of his face. He had a smile that could melt stone and a gaze that could heat blood.

He motioned down towards his clothes with a flick of his wrists, as if asking for my approval. He looked amazing and I nodded with a grin, confirming how gorgeous he looked.

His eyes appraised my dress, arching one eyebrow and I knew he too was pleased with what he saw. My heart began to thump irregularly again.

Connor wore black tailored trousers and a grey shirt which was open at the neck, exposing the strong line of his throat. I wanted to put my mouth there.

Suddenly running his hands down my shoulders, he entwined his fingers into mine before turning me and walking me backwards on to the dance floor.

Following him, my breath caught in my throat as he lifted my arms and draped them around his neck. My breasts were pushed flat above his chest.

Pleasure was surely going to burst from my chest at the contact of our bodies. He was so hard against my softness, the muscles of his abdomen, a reminder of his strength.

Closing my eyes, I placed my head against his chest and I could feel his breath in my hair. He moved his hands down to my hips and we moved slowly to the music.

Contentment throbbed inside me; I felt so safe, so protected and cherished. My body was trembling as his fingers slid further around my waist, resting just above my backside.

I was almost floored, but happy to continue to enjoy the moment. The scent of his body was making me light-headed and I clung onto him.

He was silent as his body pushed against mine, the song playing all around us. This wasn't just any song; this was *our* song.

I felt like I was floating and just when I thought it couldn't get any better, he curled his fingers around my wrists and gently pulled my arms to my sides. I raised my head and our eyes locked.

Connor's arms moved to capture my face and he lowered his head to kiss me, at first placing small kisses at each corner of my mouth, before fully covering my lips with his own.

My eyes flared as his mouth met mine and I grabbed his biceps which flexed against my fingers.

The kiss was unreal, so much hotter than anything we have shared so far and I was lost. It was as if there were only the two of us, no music, no other couples, time stood still.

He took my mouth with an uncompromising demand and I opened my lips as his tongue pushed inside. The kiss became quite fierce and I moaned into his mouth, excitement and need rushing into my body.

Connor came to his senses before I did. I was dazed at the new level of intimacy we have just shared. He slowly pulled away and his hands curved around my jaw as he stared down into my eyes.

"We need to stop before this gets out of hand. Public place and all that." He whispered directly in my ear in a gruff voice. I smiled and closed my eyes, feeling dreamy, revelling in the hottest sexual encountered I had experienced.

He released my face and caught me by the elbows, gently shaking me from my passion induced stupor.

"Harlow. Earth to Harlow."

I slowly opened my eyes and stared up at him dreamily.

"And you can wipe the silly girl lost look off your face." He had to speak into my ear as the volume of the music hit a crescendo.

My grin just became larger and he chuckled before tucking me into his side. As he led me off the dancefloor by my hand, he stopped at the entrance into the main club area.

He smiled again and then put a finger to his lips and I immediately knew what his message was. We were about to approach the others and they weren't to know.

I felt slightly disappointed as I actually wanted them to know. Especially Ella who I was still unsure about and of course Natalie, if she wasn't actually straddling Mark at that moment down some back alley.

Nodding my understanding, he released my hand. I felt like I imagined a drowning person felt without their life jacket.

We walked together over to our friends who were all pretty well mashed. It probably couldn't get any messier. The table by the seating area where jackets and bottles were strewn was rather chaotic.

Ella seemed the most coherent one and was sat with a bottle of beer in her hand, a glazed look on her face. Nathan was asleep with his head on her shoulder.

I took in the chaos and said with a grin. "How long was I gone?" Dragging up Ella's attention.

Connor instantly took control. His voice firm and clear over the music and chatter of the club.

"I think it's time to call it a night folks."

Relief pooled into Ella's expression. I felt a twinge of annoyance, she was obviously relieved at Connor's intervention. The girl must have some type of feeling for him, God only knew why she appeared to be hiding it from me.

I helped to stand a couple of bottles up on the table and Ella shook her shoulder to dislodge Nathan, telling him to wake up.

He did and sat up glassy-eyed as he took in his surroundings.

"Connor!" He cheered with a schoolboy type of glee, like a fucking celebrity had just turned up. Obviously pleased to see him, the old tension between them now firmly in the past.

"You need to get up man, Kyle and Max are taking a taxi. I suggest you share it."

Kyle and Max appeared on cue and helped Nathan to his feet. Nathan opened his mouth to refuse but Connor put in. "I'll drop Ella off on my way past."

He looked almost ready to argue but then nodded.

We all said our goodbyes and Connor and I waited by the door whist Ella went to the cloakroom to fetch her jacket.

We stood in silence. I did feel slightly woolly headed, but not a total lost cause.

"I take it dad sent you to get me?" I questioned breezily.

"No, not this time. I offered actually."

I lit up at his words and grinned and he shot me a pointed look before glancing to look for Ella's approach.

"Behave," he warned in a warm voice and I held my hands up in mock surrender.

Ella joined us, muttering something about her jacket smelling like fags and we all left the club together.

On the journey back to the farm, Ella chuntered about this and that. She put in a bit about boys and why they were all a nightmare and I couldn't stop that feeling of worry of something going on between her and Connor. Part of me wanted to interrogate him when she left the car but I felt so snoozy

I dozed off with my hand on Connor's strong warn thigh, replaying our kiss over and over until the nothingness kicked in.

The next morning, I woke up in bed, fully dressed. I hazily remember Connor carrying me upstairs and me making jokes about him tucking me in and that was about it. I didn't feel embarrassed though. After what we had shared, I felt confident in his company.

It was Saturday morning and Connor had gone into the village, dad explained over breakfast.

As I was reading my Kindle, Tom texted to say that they usually went to the pub in the village for the quiz on a Saturday and did I want to go. I thought about it for a while and then decided why not. Connor had been a no show all day and he hadn't even attempted to text me. I knew he had my number. I appeared to have spent the entire day pining after him like a silly school girl. Did last night even mean anything? Had I again, misjudged it due to the booze?

It appeared I was turning into a bit of a party animal, going out two nights in a row but it was just the local pub and a quiz at that.

Whilst I was getting ready, I still hadn't seen or heard anything from Connor and I felt annoyed. Like I was being ignored again, or was I just the neediest bitch on the planet?

Clothing wise, I'd chosen tight black jeans with rips in the knees and flat strappy sandals.

A definite dress down occasion, nice and casual.

The alarm went off on my iPhone to notify me of the time. Tom had said he'd come get me and was due to arrive any minute. I grabbed my clutch, pulled on my cropped leather jacket and set off downstairs. As I rounded the corner in the hallway, I met dad as he was going into his study.

He did a double take. "Wowzer! Where are you going? You look amazing, again," he announced proudly and I blushed. He looked me up and down with an appreciative grin. "My God you're growing up fast. And two nights on the trot," he pointed out through raised eyebrows.

"Thanks, I'm going to the pub for drinks with Tom."

He nodded. "I see, well enjoy yourself."

I smiled reassuringly. "Will do." I batted off the need to ask about Connor. I realised that a bit of space was probably for the best. Considering I hadn't got that much longer before I'd have to go home. The thought hung like a heavy chain around my neck, dragging my mood down.

He pulled me in for a hug. "Do you have enough money?"

"Yes, thanks. I've got a tenner. That will do," I replied.

Lights came in through the window as a car pulled up, which I guessed would be my ride.

"Have a good time then. Back by 11pm please. Rachel and I are also out but we'll probably be back before you. Do you have your phone?"

I nodded and brushed past him to open the front door.

As I left the house, I was pleased I'd chosen to wear my jacket, as it was much colder than it had been earlier.

I was in the process of double checking I had my phone when what I had thought was Tom appeared in front of me. I looked up, all smiles. Of course, it wasn't Tom, it was Connor.

I closed my clutch bag and looked up at him, thoughts of my phone forgotten. He held that brooding expression that I knew so well and it made my heart swell in my chest.

"Harlow," he began in a quiet voice, his eyes running over me.

"Connor."

He dropped the gym bag he'd been holding at his feet and motioned to my attire with one hand. "Off out again?"

I pursed my lips before replying. "Yes, just the pub though. I'm waiting for Tom."

Connor's mouth hardened.

Why did it feel wrong to say Tom's name? I suddenly felt guilty.

I wasn't sure what emotions flickered across my face but Connor seemed to be absorbing them all. He didn't press the matter. "You look nice."

My mouth fell open and I almost stuttered. *'Where the heck have you been all day'* I wanted to shout, instead I said. "I do?"

His mouth twisted and he cocked an eyebrow. "You know you do."

I paused before replying, wondering whether now was the right time to speak about last night's kiss. "Connor, I think…"

Again, the bloody burr of an engine cut me off and Tom's car drew into the yard.

I exhaled sharply. "I'd better go, I'll see you later."

He turned his head to take in the approaching vehicle. "Which pub?" he said again. This time his voice was soft.

"The Crown, in the village. You should come, it isn't a date with Tom," I added.

His frown told me he wasn't on board with that suggestion. He took a moment to answer before retrieving his bag and brushing past me. "We'll see."

I felt torn. I so wanted to talk about what was going on between us but Tom had already ejected himself out of the car.

He looked smart in black jeans and a button down top.

"Everything OK?" he began as he watched Connor leave. "He didn't look too impressed."

I rolled my eyes in a God give me strength manner before reassuring him. "It's fine, don't worry."

Tom pursed his lips, looking me up and down appreciatively. "You look amazing. Shall we go?"

We walked to the car with Tom shadowing me and then helping me into the vehicle like I was a member of the royal family. I sure hoped Connor wasn't watching from the house, no doubt he'd find Tom's chivalrous behaviour totally unnecessary.

I settled myself into the seat and put my belt on with a gargantuan lump in my throat, not really clear as to why I suddenly felt so sad.

Tom climbed in beside me and I tilted my head and asked. "What did you mean that Connor didn't look impressed?"

After starting the engine, he reversed the car.

"Well, I did speak to him about you. Explained that I was determined to see if we got on. He didn't really say much, just that if I hurt you, he'd break all of my fingers. I've decided to make my move in spite of his warning."

His words annoyed me. Connor had kissed me and yet was giving other guys the green light? I felt my usual calm attitude bubble to boiling point. To hell with bloody boys.

I cocked an eyebrow, pushing thoughts of Connor to the side for a second. "So, you taking me to the pub is 'making your move' right?" I said in a light tone.

Tom beamed at me, thoroughly proud of himself. "That's right. And anyway, if Connor does fancy you, it isn't like he'd ever do anything about it. You're family now. It's against the code."

If only he knew.

I decided encourage more conversation about Connor to try and establish some more of his background. There had to be a reason he had such a split personality. It couldn't be just the fact that he was a guy. It had to be inherited from his dad surely.

Tom was saying something about Connor's family.

My ears pricked up. "Do you think his parents screwed him up?"

Tom steered the car into the road slowly, he really did drive like an old lady. He'd also over done it with the aftershave again, you could almost taste it.

"To be honest, I was going to tell you the other night, but I thought it best to talk in person. I don't trust texts, they always get into the wrong hands."

"OK." Butterflies started fluttering in my tummy as I waited for him to spill it.

I felt a frisson of frustration as he took an age to answer and I wanted to physically shake it from him.

"Look, you're not telling me anything which is going to come as a total shock. I know Connor has issues with his dad." I said twisting toward him. My words had the desired affect and seemed to reassure him.

What he said of course was much worse than I had anticipated.

"So, rumour has it, Connor was mistreated by his dad," Tom exclaimed, darting me a difficult look.

I felt like I'd been physically slapped and the sadness I'd first felt minutes ago after leaving Connor, swelled to the surface. Of course, I'd imagined it had to be *something* like that but my guess had been wife beating, not child beating. I imagine they were both as bad as each other in reality but the latter felt worse. How could a parent put their hands on their own child?

Clearing my throat, I prompted. "As in, like, physical abuse?" Another jet of horror shot into me like an arrow.

Tom paused before he replied. "Yeah."

"That's awful. How do you know?" I replied in a shaky voice as he negotiated a tight bend. It was impossible to consider a guy like Connor being a victim of physical abuse. He was so tough and macho looking. But of course, he wouldn't always have been that way.

"Well, you know he hates his dad, right?"

I worried my lip. "So, that doesn't necessarily mean he was abused."

Tom pursed his lips before shooting me a look. "He confided in Ella one night. They were both pissed at the time. He probably doesn't even remember."

I tried to digest everything he was saying without losing my shit in front of him and demanding he take me back.

"Well, if it's true. That kind of explains a lot." I swallowed hard.

He nodded. "Absolutely and Ella wouldn't lie about something like that."

I paused with a painful feeling in my chest. It felt like a fist was crushing my heart. The fact that Connor had confided in Ella fricking Wade and not me stung, like really stung.

A thought occurred to me. "I wonder if my dad knows. Connor alluded that he does."

"I would imagine he does. Even if Connor doesn't easily speak about it. Rachel would have told him surely?"

Pausing for thought, I realised that I agreed with him. "Well, you'd think so. Dad never said anything to me though. Just that Rachel's ex isn't allowed anywhere near her. I thought he was spouting jealous boyfriend stuff. I remember him mentioning him before they were married."

We were in the village now and I could see the sign for the The Crown and knowing that we wouldn't be able to continue the conversation in public, I hurried him up.

"Is that all, do you know anything else. Did he used to beat him up and stuff?"

He shot me a cornered look.

"At first it was more sophisticated, if you can use that word to describe it. For instance, have you noticed that there are no TVs in your house?" he began.

My eyes narrowed, but I didn't think about my answer. I'd established there were no TVs on day one.

"So? What's that got to do with anything?"

Tom pulled the car into the car park. "Ella said that Connor's father used to turn the volume up on the TV and hold Connor's head against the speaker when he was a kid, as a punishment."

I screwed up my face in disgust as the impact of his comment hit me. "That's horrendous. How old was he?"

Tom parked the car and turned off the ignition.

"I don't know exactly, but young, like a toddler. As he got older, he also used to smack him around the head. That's why he struggles with his hearing in one of his ears and why your dad *must* know, otherwise why no TVs?"

The comment about Connor's hearing made me sit up straight in my seat

"What do you mean he *struggles with his hearing*?" I blasted.

"Ella reckons it's due to ear drum damage caused by his dad. You must have noticed?" He shot me a searching look before he reached around to the back seat to grab his jacket.

I shook my head. "Not really, although I suppose so now that you mention it, but I just put it down to him being ignorant."

I tried to recall all the instances when I'd spoken and he'd either blanked me or misheard what I'd said and a flood of emotion hit me. I had been such a bitch.

"This is majorly messed up. I've probably said stuff I shouldn't have but how the *hell* was I to know?" I confessed. "He doesn't wear a hearing aid or anything".

Tom slipped his coat on. "I know. It's obviously not *that* bad but he does ask you to repeat stuff quite a lot."

I folded my arms across my chest and pursed my lips. It was a struggle to digest everything he was saying. I closed my eyes and pushed my head back against the headrest.

"God, this is a shit storm isn't it. Now I understand Nate's cruel comment about his 'good ear'."

Tom twisted towards me. "I thought you should know. And that's only part of the abuse, as he got older and started to retaliate, it got a lot worse so I heard. Ella didn't tell me everything and he's covered up the scars on his arm."

I blew out a breath and unclipped my seatbelt.

"Scars?" FFS!

"Yes, that's why he has all those tattoos on his arm. To cover up what his dad did to him. They're burns, I think. Scalds or something. You can see the skin is fucked if you look closely."

I almost put my hands over my ears as that explained why the skin on that arm was a lot rougher than the other. I'd noticed it in the barn that night.

I sat in silence, my mind a maze of thoughts and then Ella's face swam in there.

That niggling feeling that Connor had confided in her about his past rose to the surface again.

Maybe there *was* something between them? Maybe Nate was part of the deal too. The two boys seemed to have major issues with each other. It was all so messed up in my head, why couldn't it have been more straightforward? Fair?

I exhaled sharply and shot Tom a bleak look. "Thanks for telling me. I appreciate it but maybe we should leave it there. Imagine the backlash if he found out we'd been talking about him."

Tom looked relieved at my words and pushed his door open.

"Totally. As I've said before, I need all my fingers in working order thanks." He grinned.

I returned his smile and then exited the vehicle, walking around the back to join him. "I'm going to speak to my dad about it. He should have told me really."

Tom fell in beside me as we made our way to the entrance of the pub. The car park was busy. "Yes, you should. But don't tell him I told you though, Ella said no one is to know."

"I won't mention you when I speak dad."

Tom started to pull the main door into the pub open but stopped when I threw him another question. "Where do you think his dad is now?"

He shrugged. "No idea. I think Rachel has some type of restraining order against him so that he's not legally allowed anywhere near them."

I pondered his reply, worrying my lip.

"Shit." I blew out a breath. "Anyway, quiz time. You'd better be good Wade, as with most things in life recently, I'm useless. Especially when it comes to getting the right answers."

Twelve

When inside, the quiz question sheet we were handed looked ridiculously hard and was blatantly aimed at fifty-year-old farmers.

We managed to find an empty table in the back room which overlooked a beer garden. There were clusters of smokers out there, you could see the light from their cigarettes as they inhaled.

Tom cleared a couple of empty pint glasses from our table and went to the bar to order. I'd opted for diet coke, not really in a drinking mood due to anxiety about the whole Connor situation.

We didn't get the opportunity to speak about it again, as ten minutes before the quiz started, Nathan and another guy gate-crashed our table. Whilst Nate searched for a couple of spare chairs, Tom introduced the other guy as Ryan, Nathan's brother.

So, *this* was the Ryan, Connor had fleetingly mentioned. The 'responsible' brother. They were similar in appearance and carried that same brooding vibe but Ryan appeared much older and more serious.

I had been elected to write the answers down as Nate said that Tom's writing was illegible and half way through the quiz, I managed to ignore that churning feeling in my stomach. The banter around the table was fun and I didn't feel at all uncomfortable being the only girl in our group.

Ryan had a dry sense of humour and at almost twenty-eight years old, knew stuff. He had more suggestions for possible answers than any of us.

I saw a totally different side to Nathan. He acted differently in front of his brother, more grown up, balanced. He still drank fast though.

I took a sip of coke as Tom and Nathan went back to the bar, leaving me alone with Ryan with the gnome we had won as a booby prize for coming last in the quiz. We took it in good spirits of course.

I watched Ryan with a hint of a smile. "So, what do you do Ryan? I'm guessing it's farm related."

He returned my smile, but I noticed he looked tired. There were dark shadows beneath his eyes.

"I sell JCB's and so I should have got the one right about when the seasons fall, but to be honest, I'm not really with it tonight. I literally *just* arrived back after a two-week conference and I'm knackered." That explained the shadows.

"Do you work away a lot?"

"Yeah, I travel all over the country. I don't mind it, gets me out of this shit hole. How about you? Nate says you're staying with your dad at Two Oaks Farm. How you finding country living?"

"It's OK. I find it a bit cut off but I'm getting used to it. I might end up here more permanently next year if I get into Uni. There's a course I'm interested in at Scarborough. Save on the cost of halls and all that."

His head titled as he digested my words and he seemed genuinely interested.

"What course are you thinking about?"

I leaned my elbows on the table which brought our faces slightly closer. The pub was now quite busy and loud.

"It's just an Early Years course. I think I quite fancy teaching."

"Teaching kids? You are brave." He smiled, knocking back the last of his beer.

I embellished, saying. "Little ones anyway. Not sure about teenagers."

He placed the empty bottle on the table, looking thoughtful.

"Absolutely. That'd be my *worst* nightmare."

He paused to check his phone, the text he'd received appearing to puzzle him as his brow creased. I turned away and finished my drink.

After keying in a quick reply, Ryan pocketed the phone and asked. "What makes you want to be a teacher?"

"I don't know really. I've been told I'm good with my nieces and nephews. But it's hard isn't it, making that decision now. Sometimes I don't feel like I have any direction in my life at all."

Ryan pursed his lips and leaned back in his seat.

"You're young, that's the way it's supposed to be. That's why you should go to college, but stay in the halls instead of home. It would give you more freedom to go wild and do crazy shit, you know, make mistakes. That's what girls your age *should* be doing, not getting all serious about life and its many burdens."

I chuckled, he was very assertive but I totally wasn't the wild child type, much too boring. "Not sure about the going wild element but I'm definitely a pro at making mistakes."

"Tell me about it," Ryan put in, suddenly looking gloomy.

I arched an eyebrow, latching on to his change in mood. Here was another boy with secrets.

"You sound like you're experienced in the area," I declared, I was intrigued with the sudden long face. "Let me guess, female related perhaps?"

Ryan's eyes darted back to mine from the empty bottle, suddenly on high alert and I wondered if I'd crossed a line. We had just met after all. What if he'd had a girlfriend or even a wife that had died or something? Stupid runaway mouth of mine.

"Sorry, my mouth sometimes just blurts stuff out there," I apologised, taking a nervous sip of my coke, watching him from over the rim of the glass.

He rolled his shoulders after if trying to work out a knot then sat forward in his chair as if he was seeing me for the first time. I now had his full attention. "You're shrewd for a kid."

I wasn't annoyed that he called me a kid as he was much older me and I felt relieved that he hadn't taken offence at my rude judgement.

"So, I'm right," I put in softly, surprised that he'd admitted it. I delivered the words carefully, so as not to appear a stickler for idle gossip.

"Well, if you ever want an ear, I'm a good listener."

Before he could reply, I twisted my head to see Nate and Tom were still at the bar and added. "At least that's what I keep trying to convince everyone of around here. People from this village seem a bit on the closed off side."

"And I can imagine you witness that on a daily basis with your Connor. If I'm OK to call him that."

My heart bumped against my rib cage at the mention of Connor and how he said he was mine. Did he mean this due to the fact we were family, or did he also suspect something was going on between us? Maybe he was just really good at deflecting attention off himself.

"I suppose so." I replied with a shy smile.

153

His knowing eyes watched my lips and I knew from that look that he had his suspicions, maybe Nate had talked about it. I purposefully diverted our chat back again.

"So, this female of yours…"

He smiled and his cheeks dimpled, it made him look boyish and younger than his years.

"Yes, but not really mine at the minute. It's complicated."

His use of those particular words, made me straighten in my seat. There it was, that word, 'complicated' and my head started spinning like I'd just come off the waltzer. I'd heard that word spoken in the exact same way recently. I thought back to the club, racking my brains.

Ryan's smile dropped, his face becoming a mask. "What's wrong?" he asked, also stiffening.

I shook the thought away.

I exhaled and shot him a friendly, reassuring smile. "Nothing, sorry, déjà vu."

I was just about to add to that, but Tom appeared with the drinks. What was it with timing in this place!

Ryan recovered himself quickly and gave me a veiled look, for my eyes only. I read this as him wanting to change the subject. Maybe he wasn't comfortable talking about girl drama in front of his brother. I swallowed what I had been about to say.

"Sorry, the bar is mashed," Tom put in, juggling the glasses.

I thanked him for my drink and he looked between Ryan and I. Ryan was in the process of literally necking the bottle of Bud he'd just been handed by Nathan.

"Jesus Ry, where's the fire?" Nate put in, watching his brother's throat with bulging eyes.

Ryan wiped his mouth with the back of his hand. "Cheers guys but I have to go. It was good to finally meet you Harlow."

Nate lowered himself into his seat, staring as Ryan shrugged into his jacket. He must have been as broad as Connor.

"If you see Ella, be nice, OK?" Nathan said quietly.

His comment about Ella automatically switched the atmosphere.

Considering the pub was full, an odd silence fell around the table. Nathan looked down into his beer with a sullen expression, Ryan forcefully zipped up his jacket and Tom pulled out his iPhone and thumbed through it.

I drew the fresh drink towards me, my mouth suddenly felt quite dry.

Lowering his head, Ryan said in a stern voice. "Don't be driving the car Nate."

Nathan's gaze remained on the pale liquid in his glass.

"Whatever dad." He said in a quiet, small voice, his voice still slightly slurred.

Ryan was still, a serious expression on his face.

"I mean it Nate. Get a cab or walk, give yourself time to sober up before mom see's you."

Nathan nodded his head in agreement. "Yeah, I'll probably walk. Laters."

I eyed Ryan's leather jacket encased back as he walked away, wondering what the hell that was about. Tom's comment drew my concentration back to the table.

"I'm on coke Nate, I have to go past you on the way to Harlow's any way."

I glanced at the fizzy liquid in his hand. I hadn't realised Tom hadn't been drinking either.

It all got a bit weird after that and neither Tom or Nate spoke again. We finished our last drinks. I was still worried about the situation with Connor and I was at that point where I just wanted to leave anyway. It had been pleasant enough but definitely time to call it a night. My musings about Ryan's situation were still mixed and I started to feel the tell-tale signs of a headache.

I checked the time on my phone, noticing two texts from my mum, it was just after ten.

We left the pub with a 'well on the way' Nathan, whom we dropped off at the driveway to his huge house as promised.

As Tom pulled the car away, I suggested that he also drop me on at the bottom of the driveway, as it was almost ten thirty. Neither of us said anything about the weird tension with Ryan.

"Here we go. Are you sure you don't want me to drop you at the house, it's quite a walk from here?"

"No, it's fine." Tom's words broke me out of my trance and I turned to him, having been wondering if Connor would be home still.

"What you are thinking about, you look deep in thought."

I sighed, deciding to share my thoughts, we were alone and had already spoken about it anyway. The truth was out there.

"I was just wondering if Connor's still up and whether to ask him about his dad. I'm still trying to get my head around it all."

Tom released the wheel and pulled on the hand-break, the weathered gates into the farm rattled slightly with the wind.

"I'm just wondering when he last saw his dad."

"I think he saw him around two years ago, before they bought this place. Ella said Connor and Rachel lived in safety housing. They were in one of those places which is purposefully off the grid and Carter found them."

So, Connor's dad was called Carter.

I frowned, thinking about his comment about the house; like safe houses or witness protection places, or was that another TV thing? I shuffled back in my seat, contemplating his words.

There was a moment of heavy silence before Tom explained. "Carter put Connor in hospital and was arrested for a short time, so I heard." His voice was reflective, as if thinking about an uncomfortable past. "I suppose two years isn't that long a time to heal, emotional wise I mean."

"How the hell did Carter find them if they were supposed to be in hiding? Does he have contacts in high places or something?"

"No, it was quite sneaky really. Simple Ella said." Tom placed his hands back on the steering wheel. It was quite dark outside the car and the road was empty, it all felt a little on the eerie side.

"Carter phoned their house pretending to be someone else and got the address off the house keeper. Something like that, I think? Ella said."

I bobbed my head, digesting what he had shared. Sounded fairly simple to me, but there was a strange sensation twisting in my belly, like I'd forgotten something. Like when you leave a light on at home or have misplaced your phone.

To add to that, the niggle that Connor shared stuff with Ella resurfaced. The girl obviously filled a void I couldn't.

"Holy crap. Anyway, someone is home as the lights are on. I better go. Thanks for tonight Tom and for being a friend," I said, nodding towards the house.

"Just a friend?" he put in softly with a kind smile.

I mirrored his look and understanding flowed between us. "Yes, and a very good one."

Tom nodded his head, his face an open book before he replied in a low voice. "He's a lucky guy, just hope he doesn't fuck it up."

It was the first time I'd heard Tom swear. I decided against replying and squeezed his leg, silently thanking him for his understanding and support. He had obviously realised that I had feelings for Connor.

Tom pecked me on the cheek and I climbed out of the car and started off up the driveway, the gravel crunching under my feet. I could see the lights were on in the main house through the hedge.

I so hoped that Rachel and my dad were still out and I had the chance to speak with Connor alone. I had decided it was time for us to talk and if he felt comfortable, I would ask him to share some of the burden, I would listen with all my heart.

As I rounded the corner, I could hear voices, raised *angry* voices and I rushed towards the sound. The noise was coming from two men who were squaring up, circling each other in the yard, light from the house highlighting their rigid bodies. One was Connor and the other a stranger, tall and dark and scary looking. I didn't recognise him as one of the farm hands. I briefly noted the parked blue van which I didn't recognise by the barn.

What the actual fuck? I forced oxygen into my lungs and willed myself to calm the hell down.

It took me all of five seconds to process who he was, the two faces were almost identical, but the man I identified as Connor's father was bigger and much meaner looking. He grunted and fell backwards as his son suddenly rushed him, shouldering him in the stomach and panic clawed up my spine.

I yelled for them to stop and forced my feet to move, running towards them, my breath almost trapped in my throat, choking me. They were both on the ground rolling around, each trying to get on top of the other, blind punches catching skin and bone. There was blood on Connor's nose and I felt a surge of helplessness.

I screamed at them again, circling their entwined bodies, but my voice was ignored and the grunts and growls continued.

Terror clutched me. They were like *animals*; it was hard to believe they were even related. How could two people with the same blood *do* this to each other?

Connor angled his body and jetted to his feet before throwing a punch which hit his father directly on the jaw, knocking the older man to his knees.

"Stay down or I'll knock you the fuck out," Connor growled and spat aggressively next to the fallen man who had already started to push to his feet. His grim face full of murderous rage and determination.

It was at that point that Connor noticed me, his face darkening before he shot out, "Go, phone Mike now!" He shot at me over his shoulder, his face becoming swallowed by the shadows. I could see he was badly beaten and swollen.

I wanted to run to him and protect him somehow but his second growl shoved me into action and I dragged out my phone and searched for dad's number, all fingers and thumbs. I found it and pressed the screen with shaking hands, turning my back on the two guys going at it, hell for leather. Please answer, my God, please!

Tears were pouring down my face.

"Harlow?" Dad's voice bit into my ear and I stumbled over my words in my haste to explain.

"You need to come home! They're going to kill each other?"

"Who, what the hell are you saying?" Dad shot out.

"His dad is here! He's attacking Connor!"

"What the... Carter? Fuck. Go into the house and lock yourself in. I'm on my way." I heard Rachel's high-pitched squeal in the background before dad shushed her. From the sound of it, he was in the car.

"What do I do? Connor's face is—"

"Do what I tell you and get into the house. Connor can look after himself. Go now!"

Dad's harsh tone jerked me out of my stunned state. This couldn't be fucking happening. The call cut off and I spun back towards the two men, dropping my phone, my hair wrapping around my throat like a hand. My breath caught again as I attempted to scream. Connor's body was being battered.

He was on the floor and he didn't seem to be moving; fear jetted into me like lightening and I ran towards him.

Carter was on his feet and I could only watch with horror as he drew back his leg and kicked his son full on in the stomach, his target grunting in pain.

Connor's body curled further into itself in a foetal position but I could see he was conscious, but only barely.

I yelled for the man to stop but Carter drew back his leg for another blow and I lost it.

"*No! Get away from him! Stop, you'll kill him!*"

I ran and threw my body over Connor to try and shield him from the man with the demonic face.

Carter moved around me and booted Connor in the back.

It was like I wasn't there, like the larger man was in a murderous world of his own. He kicked his son again and Connor started coughing whilst trying to shove me away from him.

I pushed to my jelly-like legs and frantically scanned the area, seeing the piece of wood left over from when Connor had been patching the roof of the barn. Rushing over, I slid my fingers around it and heaved, my muscles straining with the weight. Adrenalin pulsed through me like lava. It was up to me, I had to do something and I dragged the wood over to where Carter stood staring down at his fallen victim. His back was facing me.

With a strength I didn't know was possible, I raised the piece of wood; my target, any part of Carter's body. Even if it only temporarily distracting him from finishing his son off, it was better than nothing.

I drew the beam of wood higher and then with all my strength swung it to smash it over Carter's head. He turned last minute, his eyes widening in shock as the blow came, smashing against his shoulder and the lower part of his face. It knocked him backwards and his breath whooshed from his body. I too fell back, landing on my side with a painful jolt and I scrambled away as Carter swayed back and forth, trying to recover.

As I sat there on my backside, with my hands either side of my body, bracing me up, Carter climbed slowly to his feet before turning to glare at me. He was noticing me now. His eyes filled with a murderous rage and my heart thumped so wildly, I thought it was going to burst out of my chest.

Carter staggered towards me like the drunks you saw in the city at night.

"You really shouldn't have done that." He dribbled out, spit running down his chin.

I shook my head, I needed to be strong. "I've phoned the police! They'll be here any minute! *Leave us alone*!" I yelled in a semi hysterical voice, sure that my turn was coming. I felt terror like I'd never experienced.

Cater would kill me easily and there was *nothing* I could do about it. I rolled to the side and then onto all fours, knowing that I'd have a better chance on my feet and praying that I could get there fast enough. I should have done as dad had ordered and ran to the house, but I hadn't been able to leave Connor.

Carter advanced on me as I came to my feet, backing away, my palms raised to ward him off.

I closed my eyes as my back hit the side of the barn and the realisation that there was no-where left to go, pooled painfully into my gut. This was it. My knees sagged. The range of emotions churning through me at that point was indescribable.

Carter grabbed me by the throat and started to squeeze. I felt my eyes bulge at the pressure.

Air was trapped in my lungs and he continued to tighten his grip around my neck. I lifted my hands and circled his wrists to try and drag his hand away and scratched his skin but it made no difference. I couldn't get my breath. The life was being choked out of me and my head started swimming.

I opened my mouth to plead with him but no sound came out and then suddenly, I felt Carter release me with a grunt. I fell to my knees, struggling for coherent thought as I dragged air into my deprived lungs.

A skirmish was going on beside me and I rocked to my knees, blinking back tears to see that Connor had knocked Carter down again. He had saved me. He was now pushing all his weight onto his father's back and the man's spine buckled. Carter's face was pushed into the dirt and he thrashed beneath his son's body attempting to rise.

"Get into the house Harlow. Now!" Connor bit out, his shirt was ripped and I could see angry looking welts on his bared torso, making me wince. I was breathing heavily, greedily refilling my body with oxygen.

The light from the house lit up Connors face. One eye was swollen, it was purple and angry looking, blood was crusted around his nose and his lip was split. I nodded frantically and pushed myself to my feet, running for the house as the sound of a car powered up the driveway. This time I was happy for the interruption. I spun in the direction of the lights, hope thumping through me.

Dad pulled the Land Rover into the yard, spraying pebbles everywhere and he wasn't alone. Rachel, Nigel and Clive were with him. The men jumped from the vehicle and descended, dragging Connor away by the arms as he struggled to free himself. Desperate to carry on attacking the older man.

His father, remained on the ground but was still moving, attempting to get to his knees.

After Connor was calmer, Nigel released him and he doubled over, struggling with his breathing. Clive and Nigel swung to Carter.

"You're trespassing mate." Nigel said aggressively as he grabbed him by the hair and drew Carter's head back. "Your lad proper fucked you up I'd say."

Carter's reply bubbled from his throat and was inaudible.

It was over, the nightmare was actually over and I sank to my knees again, tears streaming down my face as relief forced a bubble of hysterical laugher from my lips.

Rachel ran from the vehicle towards her son, her face sheet white in the dark as she threw her arms around him. I felt a twinge of sadness that I couldn't do the same and could only watch as the moisture streamed down her own face.

I heard him whisper my name and my heart leapt in my chest. I stood, staggering towards them.

"Rachel turned to look at me, her eyes running over my swaying limbs. "She's here, she's fine." She reassured him through sobs.

"Are you OK Harlow, did he hurt you," Dad began appearing at my side, running his hands over my body, searching for any possible sign of injury.

I cleared my gravelly throat. "No, I'm fine, honestly," my voice was husky from the damage Carter had probably caused to my vocal cords, but I didn't care, all could think about was Connor.

Dad's look of relief was palpable and he dragged me into his arms. I was determined not to lose it at that point but it was difficult. Shock forced my body to shake violently.

After holding me for a while until I was calmer, Dad told me to go into the house whilst the guys sorted Carter. The police were on their way.

I watched as my father and the two farm hands started to drag the hideous excuse for a man into the barn. Now I knew what real hatred felt like. Such a cruel horrible person and I wanted to run to him and kick him like he had his son. I turned away refocusing my attention on Connor.

Rachel was now checking his body, still sobbing heavily and Connor's eyes met mine over her shoulder. He looked beaten, and not just physically, like that fire inside him had burned out and my heart squeezed. How I wanted to put my arms around him and hold him close, support him in some way but I couldn't.

"I'm so sorry, is there anything I can do." I croaked. My eyes were puffy and I felt emotionally exhausted.

"Please go and put the kettle on love, I think we all need something sweet." Dad said calmly.

The man I had fallen for was on the ground and I had been relegated to tea maker, I had never felt so useless in my entire life.

I walked slowly into the house, feeling thoroughly confused and dazed by what I'd just experienced.

Eventually, the police arrived and took Carter away. I was watching from the window of dad's study. Rachel and Connor were safely in the house and dad had helped Connor upstairs to bed until the Doctor arrived. Both Rachel and my dad had suggested an ambulance, but Connor wouldn't have it. I lurked around in the background, doing anything I was asked and tried to be as helpful as possible.

Once the chaos had calmed, I sat in my room, listening to whispered voices before clearly hearing Rachel leave Connor's room and I decided it was my moment. He'd be sleeping no doubt, but I *had* to see him. The Doctor had left around an hour ago and had reported that luckily nothing seemed broken, but that Connor would need to go for a scan to check for possible cracked ribs.

It was almost one in the morning but I didn't care. I tiptoed lightly down the corridor, tugging at the lapels of my robe to secure it further against my body. I had removed my dirty clothes but hadn't showered or washed. The landing was freezing.

Connor's door was slightly ajar and I peered inside. He was propped up in bed, the covers pulled up to his waist and he appeared to be sleeping. Relief jetted into me as he didn't look like the bloody pulp I'd envisioned. Rachel had obviously cleaned up his face, one eye was swollen and badly bruised and there was the split lip but that was about it. As far as external injuries were concerned anyway. If his ribs *were* cracked, the pain would surely be horrendous. My heart sped up.

I pushed the door closed gently and quietly entered the room, thinking I would stay for a few minutes and then speak to him in the morning, I didn't want to wake him.

His breathing was shallow and I watched his T shirted chest slowly rise and fall as I approached the bed, stumbling slightly as I tripped over a gym bag on the floor. Seeing him like this was almost enough to break me.

"You'd make a lousy thief," Connor's voice startled me, making my heart race.

"Shit," I cried, clutching at my chest, "I thought you were sleeping."

He attempted to smirk and opened his eyes; one eye fully, the more battered eye slightly.

"I was before you came in like an elephant," he pointed out nonchalantly. It appeared his injuries had not curtailed his sense of humour.

"Great. Now I'm an elephant. Healthy enough to throw the insults around I see," I bounced back, smiling gently as I threw him an arched eyebrow.

The smirk changed to a grin, "Of course, insulting you is way too entertaining."

I rolled my eyes. "Well at least I'm a source of fun for you."

Connor paused before replying, the humorous twist to his lips fading before he cast me a serious look. "You're much more than that," he drawled slowly, his eyes searching my face. My pulse soared with hope.

"What—?"

He broke contact fleetingly as he swiftly changed the subject. "Did you enjoy the pub?" He put in casually.

"Connor—." I started, not wanting to head into an uncomfortable conversation or change the bloody subject to something so unimportant. My time on the farm had been gradually teaching me what was and what wasn't significant in life.

"Did you?" he questioned again, a little more firmly. Was he mad at me for going? I batted the thought aside. Now was probably not the time for intense discussions and so I didn't push it.

I brushed off his question with a quick-fire reply. He may not be ready to speak about whatever this thing was between us, but there was no way he was warding off a conversation about what I'd witnessed tonight.

"Why didn't you call someone?"

Connor snorted and shuffled further up in the bed, and I moved forwards to help but he held up his hand to ward me off. Stubborn as always, he may look battered and bruised but he hadn't lost his resilience.

"It was *my* problem," he stated. "And there wasn't time, he was just *there*. I was *trying* to get him to leave before my mom got back."

I lowered myself to perch on the side of his bed. I didn't ask for permission, it felt like the natural thing to do.

He shuffled further against the headboard but the movement must have been too much as he flinched and rubbed his ribs.

"Does it hurt?"

"Like a motherfucker," he rasped.

I cringed but not at the profanity, I could almost feel his pain. Connor misunderstood me as usual and apologised for swearing.

I shook my head, my lips twisting. "I think I'll allow the bad language under the circumstances. Can I do anything to help?"

He sighed, probably a sign that he was tired and I felt a smidge of guilt for keeping him awake. Maybe I should have left it until morning but I was so desperate to see him.

He leaned over and took a drink from the glass of water on his bedside table. "No, just talk to me. I find the sound of your voice calming. Well, *most* days," he said closing his eyes and leaning his head back against the pillows.

I grinned. "You're still a dick I see."

His own mouth curled into a smile and his eyes cut to mine. "You love it."

There were a few moments of silence between us as Connor rested his eyes again. I was toying with the thought of leaving, but my mouth switched onto autopilot.

"So that was your father?" I said, partly to myself.

He cleared his throat. "That was dear old dad," Connor replied his distaste evident.

"I'm sorry. You never talk about him."

"You can see why?"

I blew out a breath. "Yes. I'm sorry. *Really* sorry."

He remained silent for a while before replying partly to himself. "So am I."

"Why did he come here?"

Connor dashed a hand across his jaw. "He was looking for my mother," he paused momentarily and I saw a flash of annoyance cross his face at what was obviously an unsavoury thought. "Thank fuck she was out with Mike. Fuck knows how he found us again. He probably followed her from Gran's."

As I digested his words, a strange thought occurred to me, my hand flying to my mouth as realisation kicked in.

Connor's eyes followed the movement. "What's up?"

Panic chewed into me as I recalled the strange telephone call with 'the bank'. Tom had said in the car that Carter had made a fake call to their house in the past to find out their address. The memory of pulling the letter towards me and giving the address out over the phone jumped to the forefront of my mind.

I suddenly felt sick.

Connor sat forward with another grunt, obviously concerned by my now stricken face.

"Harlow? What is it?"

There was no way around it, I *had* to tell him. He would hate me. I could feel it.
I had led his father to the farm!

Regret bounced off me in waves and I couldn't control my reaction.

I had to come clean, the knowledge was like a huge burden sitting on my shoulders. I took a deep breath. "I'm sorry, I'm so sorry Connor. It was me! It must have been me. I gave him the address of the farm," I reeled, my hand now clutching at my tender throat in desperation.

I shot to my feet. "I didn't know it was him of course, but I remember his voice from the call."

Connor's expression shifted and his eyes bore into mine, the confusion on his face twisting his features. "What are you talking about?"

"I took a call on the phone from a guy saying he was from the bank. It must have been him—he asked for me to confirm the address and—I, I gave it to him," the words literally spewed from my mouth in one big whoosh.

Blatantly frustrated, Connor dragged a hand through his hair, shaking his head. "Are you sure?"

Moisture appeared at the corner of my eyes, I felt like such a failure. I had let them down, both Connor *and* his mother. Now they would hate me.

I assessed the damage to his face as he went silent, obviously trying to process the full extent of what I had confessed.

Suddenly he straightened and then drooped back against the pillows, the discomfort he felt by sitting up was written across his face.

"Motherfucker," Connor released with a sigh and my heart dipped. He was right, I was. I let the numbness wash over me. I knew he meant Carter but I decided I should take that particular label. It still probably wasn't strong enough thing to call me anyway.

We sat there is silence and I toyed with the idea of leaving to tell Rachel but his words stopped me.

Connor was watching me again.

"It's not your fault Harlow, you weren't to know."

I shook my head, totally in disagreement. I had been so stupid. "No, you're right. Call me any name you want and I'll accept that. I let you down."

Connor's eyes shot to mine. "Not you, never you. He's the motherfucker Harlow. The bastards done that before. You should have been warned instead of all the cloak and dagger shit. Then you would have been more prepared."

He paused before pushing his body closer and I felt a whoosh of relief. The thought of losing him and things going back to the way they used to be felt like a death sentence.

"No more hiding. I'll tell you anything you want to know and please, don't blame yourself. It was inevitable. He would have found us one way or another," he said firmly and some of the guilt lifted. "I mean it Harlow. You are not to blame yourself and besides, you saved me. *You actually fucking saved me*. You were so brave."

His smile was warm. I was surprised he was even conscious at the point where I'd hit Carter with the beam, but his next comment made me realise his words went much deeper than that and hope resurfaced.

"You make me want to be a better person."

I swallowed, almost overcome with emotion. "Really?"

"Yes, you are all I think about. I close my eyes and your face is all I see."

A tear slipped down my cheek as a further surge of emotion poured through me and I cried. Hard and loud and Connor pulled me into his arms and held me tight. Cradling my sobbing body, allowing me to offload.

When I had managed to calm myself, I drew back and Connor dropped his arms, his eyes searching my face which would surely be stained with all sorts, dirt, tears, as well as despair.

He wiped a tear away with his finger and leaned back. "I've never met anyone who can lift this darkness. Something I've carried my whole life, yet that's *exactly* what you do. You take it away."

I smiled, feeling my limbs start to relax.

"It may sound cringe, but it's true Harlow. I've had it, running away and trying to hide from it, so—I will if you will...?"

I wasn't quite sure what he was asking at that moment. My excitement and happiness about what he had just revealed had sent me into overload. All I knew was how to answer. "I will, yes. Absolutely."

He moved and covered one of my hands which rested on my lap with his own. His fingers were so long and capable looking. "But we need to move slowly. Mike, my mother. They need time to understand."

I nodded my head.

"These types of conversations are also better when I'm not pumped full of drugs." I hadn't realised the Doctor had given him a shot.

I thought back to my blunder and what a major fuck up it was. "I'm still sorry Connor."

"I know."

There was another one of those silences as we sat there together and I felt the anxiety I had experienced moments ago, start to dissolve.

Connor curled his fingers into my own and I placed my free hand just above his wrist on his tattooed arm. He didn't pull away but I could see he wasn't comfortable with the area I touched. I could now clearly see the welted pattern created by what look like scars on his inked arm. Tom had alluded to burns, I hadn't been able to comprehend what type of person could do that to a child, so I had pushed it out of my mind. It was too painful to consider.

Connor seemed to read my thoughts.

"When I was ten and scratched my old man's car, he poured water from the kettle on my arm, boiling water. Said it's only right to disfigure me the way I had his beat up piece of shit."

Pain jetted into me. "My God Connor, that's horrendous."

His eyes glazed over as if he were reliving the incident and I knew I had to pull him back. Now wasn't the time to be facing those demons.

"I think what you've done is beautiful."

I moved my fingers along the pattern on his arm. If Connor wanted to confide the whole story to me, there were better times. And at that moment, I was too weak to process something so monstrously evil.

I allowed the short silence before saying. "How did the fight start?"

I was careful with my choice of words. I needed to draw the answers from him without revealing the rumours I'd already been fed.

After a reassuring squeeze, Connor released my hand and moved back into the position he must have found the most comfortable, propped up against the pillows.

"The usual shit. He doesn't like to be challenged and hates the fact that he can't do whatever the hell he wants to me now. He'd come for Rachel. I wasn't going to let him get to her."

There was a thread of steel in his tone.

"Did she leave him because he was abusive?"

He exhaled sharply and rubbed the muscles in his neck. "Yes, but not like that, not with her. He saved the physical stuff for me. With mom he just ground her down emotionally, made her feel like a piece of shit. I'm sure you know the story."

"What do you mean?" I questioned, not wanting to worry him about people gossiping.

"I know people talk about it. You don't have to hide it from me."

I paused, deciding against denying it.

"Yes, you're right. I do know some stuff but I'd rather hear it from you."

If he was annoyed by my revelation, he didn't show it.

"There isn't much to say really. My dad's a worthless piece of shit and my mother left him."

I leaned forward on the bed and placed a hand on his duvet covered thigh, it was strong and warm beneath my fingers. His eyes flickered down to briefly witness the motion before he raised his face again. He was so beautiful, even with the battered face. He made me burn with just one look.

"It must have been horrendous. I can't even imagine it. My parents could really go at it when they used to fight but it wasn't ever abusive, at least I don't think so, just two people falling out about fairly mundane things."

"Carter knocked-up my mon with me when she was only sixteen and her family threatened to throw her out if they didn't marry. I doubt they had anything in common to start with, apart from a one-time fuck that backfired."

I could see the anger in his eyes give way to hurt. Connor was the product of that backfire, no wonder he didn't feel wanted.

"Your mother must have wanted the pregnancy though. There are ways of dealing with unwanted ones. She must have wanted you, even if your father didn't surely?"

"Who knows, she has a funny fucking way of showing it at times," He paused, almost reflecting on his sentence before brushing a hand through his tousled hair. "But then again, what do I have to compare it to?"

I was just about to speak but he cut me off, obviously done with the sharing, for now, anyway.

"Anyway, fuck that shit. I don't need you feeling sorry for me. That's the last thing I want from you. Pity."

I frowned, recoiling slightly, the tone was definitely back in his voice and I reminded myself that he wasn't a straightforward guy. He was hot one minute and then cold the next and if I was to be part of his life, I would have to learn how to deal with that. Connor had emotional wounds that had scarred him for life and maybe I was the one that could help him to learn to live with them.

His words echoed in my head. 'You make me want to be a better person.'

169

'Ditto.' I thought, then said. "Everyone needs some understanding now and then Connor."

I accepted defeat. The moment was lost.

"What I need right now is sleep."

Frustration bloomed in my chest as he shut me down and I could see he was about to turn on to his side.

"Is there anything you need before I go?" I questioned, trying not to sound too sympathetic, the soft stuff didn't seem to work on him. On the surface he was tough but underneath, he was just like any other guy with a past, terrified and alone.

Rising from the bed, I smiled down at him as he repositioned his body, his head turned to mine.

"Goodnight then." I whispered.

"Harlow?"

I twisted back towards the drugging sound of his voice. "Yes?"

"You asked me if there is anything I need before you go?" He said, his eyes on mine.

"Yes, anything?" I nodded. My eyebrows were raised with reassurance.

My heart soared at his words and as requested, I moved towards him, leaned in and pressed my lips against his gently to seal the end of our conversation with a goodnight kiss.

He was smiling with his eyes closed as I left his room, feeling much happier than when I had entered it.

Thirteen

Over the next week, Connor's recovery was surprisingly swift. Ella and Tom came by a handful of times and even Nate dropped by one day which surprised me. I had never taken him as the caring type. I was thankful that Connor had so much support from the village.

I had war wounds of my own, deep ugly bruises on my neck from Carter's hand. I covered them with a scarf, not wanting to worry my dad or Connor.

Dad explained that Carter had been sent back to prison and had been heavily fined for breaking the terms of his restraining order. I truly hoped we never saw the man again. The terror I had experienced during that night still played on my mind.

What also made it worse was the constant reminder that I had given the address to Carter. The police couldn't confirm anything as the man had used what they'd called a burner phone, but I of course knew the truth. My note about the call from the 'fake' bank was still on the fridge, a constant reminder of my fuck up. I couldn't bring myself to take it down.

I told dad before the police of course and I asked if he'd let me tell Rachel myself. I did and with a million apologies. She was good about it to be fair and dad just reiterated that you *never* give your address out on the phone unless you are certain who is calling. Rachel did say that he would probably have found them eventually but from the pinched look on her face, I knew she was still upset.

Due to this failing on my part, I made extra an effort with everyone.

Rachel and I buzzed around the house together, taking it in turns to take food up to the patient, who *never* seemed to get full. I was blown away by how much he actually ate. He also wasn't the easiest person to wait on and switched into one of his dark moods at the drop of a hat.

The Doctor visited and re-prescribed Connor's usual medication but he wasn't allowed to take it until he was off the heavier pain killers.

Everyone was doing their bit and my mother even sent a get-well card to Connor which I could tell Rachel appreciated. I'd started to speak to mum about him on our regular catch ups and she must have realised that I cared for him. The first Mrs Williams was more her old self and had started seeing Phil officially. She'd even reduced her drinking or at least that's what she said.

By the weekend, Connor was on his feet again and desperate to go back to work but my dad wouldn't let him. Light exercise had been suggested due to a scan revealing that Connor had two cracked ribs. It had been explained that he had to be patient and allow them time to heal on their own. Connor hadn't responded too well to the news of course and had done the exact opposite by starting to clear out a storage area in the main barn. Dad said he wanted to make it into a gym, which I agreed was a great idea, then Connor could stop making sneaky midnight trips to the hay barn to beat the crap out of a seed bag.

On Sunday morning Ella came around. She was hovering in the yard as I left the house, it was a bright sunny day and I needed to feel the sun on my skin. I'd just been texting my mum and pocketed my phone as I saw her.

"Hi. Connor's up and about now but I'm not sure where he is." I said breezily.

"I came to see you actually." She replied, instantly putting me on edge.

I played ignorant and batted down that feeling of uncertainty. I sure hoped she hadn't come to gossip about the fight.

Maybe I needed to take a chill pill, she may have wanted to offload about her 'complicated' life which I had suspected may involve Connor.

Or did it? 'Complicated', there was that word again. *It was Ella who had said it.* I couldn't remember at the pub but as I saw her, that word popped into my mind. It was the same way Ryan had described his current female problems. I batted the thought to the side, the guy must have been ten years older than Ella, wouldn't that be considered gross?

I inwardly rolled my eyes at myself and peeled my tongue away from the roof of my mouth.

"OK, cool, well I was going for a walk if you want to come?" I invited, motioning to the path which led to the fields. Rachel had mentioned baby lambs that I just had to see.

Ella nodded and fell into step beside me.

"So how is the patient today?" she questioned, pushing her hands into her pockets. I took this as a sign that she was nervous. Again, the girl had something to say and I now just wished she'd get the hell on with it.

My nose wrinkled. "Not too bad, although he did injure himself yesterday after going against advice to rest. They're making one of the outbuildings into a gym. I heard several 'F' words and stayed well away."

Ella shot me a sideways grin. "Yes, forever the hothead. At least it gives him something to focus on. Connor with too much thinking time is not a good thing."

'Really' I wanted to say, 'you obviously know him so well'. Did she fancy him or not?

"I just hope he doesn't over do it."

We weaved up the path between two hedgerows which cut off the view of the rolling fields. The trees rustled, the sun was high in the sky and the scent of freshly cut grass lingered in the air. I could hear one of dad's tractors in the distance.

A silence fell between us but I didn't feel particularly uncomfortable. From Ella's body language and expression, there was *definitely* something she needed to share. It didn't surprise me that she chosen me. There was a serious trustworthy girlfriend drought in the village. Natalie bitch face certainly wasn't one.

"I hear you and Connor are getting along?" she said and the looming dread rose to the surface. It was odd as I didn't identify jealous undertones in her words. Her voice was actually quite bright and friendly, but I decided I'd had enough circling around the subject. The fact that Connor confided in this girl still rattled my cage.

"Yes, things are good."

"Just good?" she probed.

I shot her a sideways glance. "Stop fishing Ella. As you said yourself, its 'complicated'," I threw her own words back at her and she cleared her throat and kicked a stone to the side of the path.

"That's guys for you I guess. Fucking unsolvable puzzles the lot of them."

As we turned the corner by a large oak tree, the hedge finished and field four came into view. Sheep were dotted before us. Some were being followed by their lambs who were still quite awkward on their feet. They were so cute.

I put my hands on the fence and stared out, delighted by the sight. Ella came to stand beside me. She didn't seem as interested in the animals and just looked ahead with a peculiar expression.

I pushed myself back off the fence and turned to face her.

"How about you? You have anything 'complicated' you want to talk about?" I pushed again.

She leaned forward against the fencing and twisted to face me, her copped hair had grown almost to her chin now and the brown tufts bounced in the breeze. She looked nice today in denim shorts and an oversized hoody that swamped her slender figure. She should dress more feminine. In a dress she'd look stunning.

I gave her another nudge.

"Fuck my life. It's probably not that difficult to explain but I've never really opened up to anyone about it. Well, apart from Connor. He told me his shit one nice and I told him mine."

Ella also swore far too much. Probably being around farm hands all the time and had a vocabulary made up entirely of bad words.

I cleared my throat. "You can talk to me you know. I won't say anything to anyone, I'm not like that."

Ella dashed a hand across her chin and I noted the chewed nails, another sign that she was troubled. Nail bitters always had secrets. Lisa forever had her hand in her mouth.

At last, the guts that she had held into place for so long started their spilling.

"Sorry for being so cagey but I have spoken to people in the past about it and they let me down. I find it hard to trust people now."

I bobbed my head in agreement and did the cross my heart sign with one finger. "I get that, but you can trust me. Come on, we've known each other a while now."

She grinned, feeling reassured.

"You have a boy problem I take it." I cursed the way that sounded, like I was a patronising mother. From her expression, she didn't take it that way.

The pregnancy story started circling my thoughts as I waited, basically holding my breath for her to spill the beans.

"Well, it isn't just one boy, there are two involved." Her attempt at small talk was forgotten and I pushed the sudden image of a three some from my immature mind.

Then another thought popped into my head. If she said Connor and Nate I'd throw up.

Due to all the weirdness, I now had my suspicions.

"Connor is one of them I take it?" The question pushed its way between the tightest of lips.

Ella's brow furrowed, her eyes impaling me. My own stare must have resembled glass at that point.

"Shit, no. Not Connor at all. *How could you think that*?" She physically recoiled.

Hope surged. Or was she lying?

My eyes studied her horrified face. She was no actress. She *must* have been telling the truth.

So, it wasn't Connor. We were surely running out of boys now. At least ones that I knew.

I was stumped and so wanted to point out. 'I thought that because of how weird you were with me that first day? Like you were warning me off him?' I almost fired back at her but of course I didn't. I was too busy revelling in the fact that her sex orgy didn't appear to involve the guy whose surname I had written after my own (to see how it looked) that very morning. It *definitely* worked.

"Well, *who* then?"

Then a thought occurred to me. "Nathan is one of them!" I blurted.

Ella's frown dropped away and a glint of surprise crossed her features.

"It's that obvious?" she said mirroring my comment about Connor during the night of the club.

I shook my head and rolled back on my heels slightly to give her my best pointed look.

"Not really. He just said something in the pub the other night which I thought was weird."

I paused to allow her to interject but she remained silent and pushed her nibbled fingers back into her pockets. "So, spill it. Surely, I'm half-right?"

A flush now stained her cheeks. Was she embarrassed because she revealed she's had a threesome?

"You don't have to be embarrassed. I know a few girls that have done it."

The frown was back.

"Done what?" she put in, now looking thoroughly confused.

I was starting to lose the will.

"Had a threesome," I blurted.

From the look on her face, I was totally barking up the wrong tree.

"Fuck, hell no! It's not like that at all!"

I can honestly say at that point, I was thoroughly bamboozled. Ella's reaction was off the chart. She dragged her hands from her pockets, slapped her hand against her mouth, which held the widest grin ever and burst into full on belly laughs. It was rather high pitched with the occasional pig grunt in there. It was *not* attractive.

I grinned, the infectious laughter lighting up my own face.

"What? It's like we're speaking in two different languages," I chided in between giggles.

We both stood there laughing like hyenas for a few minutes, the ice was well and truly broken again.

 Once we had both recovered, I staggered over to a tree stump which looked a fair enough sized for both our arses. Ella followed me, rubbing at her now red eyes. Running from laughter I must add*, not* from crying.

"Sorry, I just got the giggles. The thought of the two guys in question together in any way intimately is wrong in every sense of the word."

The penny wasn't just dropped, it was hurled at my head.

Ryan's face and his own confession about it being 'complicated' connected the dots.

"Because they're brothers." I put in at last. Ping! "Nathan and Ryan." At last.

Ella grinned as she turned to face me, knowing that it had clicked. I felt like a bit of a dummy having not totally realised it after quite a few hints looking back.

"Yes, Nathan and Ryan," she nodded, "and no threesomes were involved as that would be repulsive. For them anyway."

I chuckled to myself at her cheekiness and then stopped when her voice became serious again.

"And yes, complicated as Nate doesn't know about Ryan and I don't know what to expect if he does find out, but it won't be good."

Boom again! Now that explained those moments of strange atmosphere I'd witnessed.

"So, which one was the dad?" I puffed before I could reign in the thought.

Ella rolled her eyes at that one. "*There wasn't a baby*! Eck, that story is so last year."

"So, you were *never* pregnant?

"No way! You go away for a few months in this village and you're either pregnant or on drugs." Ella explained drily. I was surprised I hadn't offended her, if I had she recovered really quickly which made her more believable. If she had got pregnant and was lying about it, I'd have known it. I was usually good at reading people when they were full of it.

I patted her on the shoulder.

"Sorry. Just call me the 'jump to conclusions' girl."

"It's fine, really. It never bothered me to be honest, well the rumours didn't."

"So, Nathan and Ryan?" I prompted, feeling my phone vibrate in my pocket. I left it of course, this girl was at last opening up and I didn't want any distractions. The fact that she also had no feelings for Connor was the cherry on top. I wanted to do a little victory dance on the spot.

I thought briefly about the two boys and how different they were and Ryan Lane, how the hell would *that* work? I blew out a breath, I needed to be supportive, not appear like an overly judgemental type.

"So, it's a triangle type thing? Who came first, Nathan or Ryan, I'm confused. And no pun intended." I grinned. My God, I was suddenly dirty minded girl.

I jammed a hand through my hair, frustrated by my own lack of patience.

"Sorry, you go. Give it me from the top," I said encouragingly, doing the 'zipped mouth and throw away the key' gesture with my fingers.

So, the basics of it were. Ella and Nate had been involved in an on and off 'thing' a few years back. They snogged and did bits one night at a party after Nate had sent Ella a dick pic by mistake. This led to Ella winding him up on and off about it until one night they left the friend-zone and slept together. Ella said it was one of those stupid drunk moments that she immediately regretted the next day.

She spoke about it in such a blasé way that I imagined Ella had already had a few one-night stands under her belt.

She explained that Nathan became hooked and didn't want to go back to being just friends, to the point where he started to make a nuisance of himself.

Ella said after weeks of being hounded by Nathan, who had started to behave like a jealous boyfriend that their original friendship had not been repairable. A rift was created in the group of friends and going to parties and other events had become awkward, to the point that Ella had taken herself off the grid for a while and travelled to see her aunt. Ping! The supposed pregnancy months in the USA.

And then came the bit about Ryan. The 'complicated' section.

Ella had returned to Pickering and was waiting for a taxi at the train station at the same time Ryan had come up from London. They'd shared a cab and got talking. She explained to me how she'd always had this huge crush on Ryan and that *he* was the real reason she went to Nate's parties with the hope of running into him.

Over the months that followed her return from her aunts, Ella said that she and Ryan had started to see each other on and off, to the point where things had headed into more serious relationship type of waters.

"My parents would freak out if they knew I'd been seeing someone almost ten years my age and the fact that he's one of the Lane boys, would probably give my mother a stroke."

Ella puffed with frustration as we faced each other across the log. I had both my feet up now and was sat crossed legged, drinking in all the information. I had actually missed talking about these types of shenanigans. My girlfriends back home were full of stories like this, not *exactly* like this of course.

"Does Ryan know you slept with Nathan, cos that conversation won't be easy?" I said with a pondering edge. Talking about exes was probably not the easiest of discussions with budding boyfriends.

She worried her lip and I knew the answer before she opened her mouth.

"He doesn't know and I don't know how to tell him."

I allowed myself to process that one for a moment. "Does Nathan know about you and Ryan?"

Ella shook her head. "No, no one knows, only Connor. Nate guesses there's someone else I think."

The comment about Connor still needled me a bit. The fact that they were close.

"I take it you and Ryan are—" I paused, struggling now to get the words out. She put me out of my misery and supplied. "No, not yet. We've done other stuff but Ryan wanted to wait unit its out in the open and we don't have to sneak around anymore. He wants to speak to my dad. Like a proper old-fashioned guy."

She must have seen the look that flashed across my face and put in. "Not about marriage! You're right, you do jump to conclusions."

I smiled and raised my hand in an 'apologies, please continue motion'.

"It's just such a mess, isn't it? Why the heck did I have to get pissed and shag the younger brother of the guy I've wanted for so long?"

Ella stretched her legs out and flicked a blade of grass off her bare leg. My eyes roamed over her face, wondering what type of relationship advice I'd be worthy of giving.

"I suppose you have to tell Ryan about Nate, it's the right thing to do. Play it down though, it was a silly drunken mistake and you're young. These things happen. What you have to worry about is how Nate will react when he finds out about you and Ryan. The guy's wired most of the time and think of how that's going to affect them as brothers going forwards."

She groaned and rolled her eyes before pushing herself to her feet. She held out and hand and I let her pull me to mine.

Although I had obviously not completely taken away her troubles, she appeared more relaxed and less flushed. A problem shared and all that.

"Thanks for listening. There isn't anyone else I can talk to now. Connor has been so withdrawn lately. Ryan is the one I usually rely on, he's so intelligent but of course, I can't really share this particular problem just yet."

We started a slow walk back to the farm. Ella spoke about Ryan, Ryan and more Ryan, it was like the Ryan floodgates had been opened and I was surprised she had managed to keep her mouth shut for such a long time.

At the house, she pulled me in for a hug and thanked me again. I told her to text me if she needed anything. Her situation was complex. I'd had little to no experience of relationships myself and so what further advice could I give? Be true to yourself, follow your heart and be honest. As long as I had listened, that was the main thing. Hopefully it would all work itself out.

I walked Ella to the gate.

"Let me know if you fancy a meet up in the pub or we could do something else sometime, we could go to the cinema. My dad could drop us off?"

She brightened and I knew at that point that now the misunderstandings were gone. We could start to build a friendship.

Of course, there wasn't that much time for that, soon I would go home and back to what I now considered to be an extremely boring lifestyle compared to the village.

I shooed away the thought of having to leave and how much I'd miss everyone, especially one particular someone.

As I made my way into the house, I checked my phone and the text I'd received was from Connor asking where I was. I decided to head to his room without replying.

It turned out that he did have a TV screen in his room but that he only used to it to play video games. It was also usually muted or set at a low volume.

He had since explained about what his dad used to do to him and was quite open about it now. He also told me about his arm and the hearing in his ear.

When I questioned him about how he'd managed in the nightclub with the noise, he explained that it wasn't necessarily the level of sound but the device itself. Connor said as a teenager, the sight of a TV would be a major trigger for aggression and he'd play up, irrespective of whether it was turned on or not. As Rachel and my father were more into reading, they never purchased a TV for the house. Dad also preferred the radio than watching what he would call the crap on telly.

I always made sure I positioned myself on the side with Connor's good ear so he wouldn't have to ask me to repeat myself. He was definitely touchy about the whole hearing thing, who wouldn't be.

I knocked and opened the door and there he was in all his glory. Bare chested, half sprawled on his bed holding a video game controller, his concentration entirely focused on his game. His jean encased legs were stretched out in front of him and he was leaning against the headboard. His torso was still bruised but the marks had faded.

"Sign me in then," I instructed as I threw myself onto the bed to join him. He rolled his eyes and handed me his controller before leaning over to grab the other.

"You're back for another beating then. You've got guts I'll give you that," he said with a curl to his lip.

"Get ready for an ass-whopping," I cooed.

He darted me an arched eyebrow.

"We're on the same team Harlow."

"I know. I was speaking to the bad guys."

We both started the game with huge grins which was cool, it felt so normal to be in his company now.

I was thoroughly enjoying myself, attempting to play Call of Duty, although I was absolutely rubbish and eventually resorted to shouting at the screen. We were part of a team and I was the worst shot ever and just kept getting mowed down by helicopter fire. Connor explained that if you shot enough players, it opened up bonuses and you were given extra firepower as a reward.

Someone with a call sign 'NinjaWarrior129' really had it in for me and ended up named as my nemesis at the end of the second match.

Connor was clearly amused at how poorly I played the game, but I gave it my all.

As I waited to respawn (I was starting to learn the lingo), I leaned further back against the pillows and eyed Connor who appeared totally engaged with the gameplay.

"Stop it," he said, still heavily concentrating, there were deep groves in his forehead.

I beamed. "What?" I said innocently with the sweetest of smiles.

"You know what. You're trying to put me off."

I shuffled further towards him, imagining a few delightful ways I could put him off. He shot me a knowing look before turning back to the screen and healing my player.

Unexpectedly, there was a brief tap on the door and dad walked straight into the room, I jumped back like I'd burnt myself. He would have chosen that *exact* point when I'd been about to blow in Connor's ear. Like Maid Marion does to Robin Hood in that movie Prince of Thieves when he's practicing archery.

As he saw us together on the bed, he was stunned at first and then embarrassment must have kicked in. Red stained his weathered cheeks.

"What?" I asked innocently enough. Did he think we'd been up to something? The thought of my dad thinking about boy stuff was mortifying.

He was now blatantly uncomfortable and didn't know where to look. We were only sat on the bed together, it's not like I was straddling the guy! Dad needed to take a serious chill pill.

"I just came to see if you needed anything Connor?" Dad began his voice a mumble. Sheepish is the best way to describe his expression. I bet he was regretting bursting in now. I found it quite amusing but decided not to wind him up.

"Nah I'm good," Connor replied nonchalantly as he placed the controller on the bed in front of him and gave dad a sympathetic look.

"Ah OK. Anyway, I can see you've got your hands full so—"

At his words, both Connor and I glanced at each other, both highly amused but managing to contain ourselves. Poor choice of words dad.

"Not now, but I did have a minute ago," Connor announced with a twist to his lips.

His comment made my dad's eyes almost bulge from his head. His mouth did a fishlike thing. I surprised a giggle and shoved Connor's arm in a 'stop playing with him' motion.

"I'm joking Mike. We're good here but thanks anyway," Connor put in, thankfully coming to dad's rescue. I imagine he was now a freshly rehabilitated inpatient person who would certainly knock in the future.

Dad still looked uncomfortable and he darted another glance between us.

The air was tense and fizzed with a mischievous element.

"Right. Good, well. I'll see you both later." And off he went, exiting the room even faster than he'd entered it, purposefully leaving the door open. He even made sure it was wider than it was before.

Connor and I both burst out laughing. It was hilarious, the panic on my dad's face. He so didn't expect to see me in there.

I climbed off the bed as it was almost time to call my mother. Connor took a glass of water from his bedside table and swung his legs down, rising to his feet. I admired his strong, tanned throat as he drank and the way his Adam's apple moved. He was so manly considering he was only a few years older than me

His room was quite masculine and there were no posters or anything on the walls. It was decorated in grey and black and was much larger than the room I had. His double bed was also rather comfortable. From a sitting up point of view, I hadn't of course had the opportunity to lay down in it… yet. I smiled at the 'yet' I added.

"What are you smiling at? You almost gave your dad a heart attack?" Connor drawled before draining the rest of the water and placing the glass aside. He walked towards me around the bed with sure footed strides.

I could feel the heat from his body.

I flicked a strand of hair behind my ear and his own hand lifted to do the same to the other side. It was a gentle gesture and the skin on my neck prickled.

"You were the one winding him up," I pointed out, a little shyly, considering the handful comment had of course been related to my breasts.

Suddenly, Connor's eyes darkened and scanned my throat. He must have noticed the trace of bruising which was still present on my neck. I hadn't worn my scarf for the last day or so.

His fingers traced the area softly before moving to skim across my collar bone. Goosebumps flittered across my skin at the contact.

"That fucker," he whispered in a gruff voice. "No one will ever touch you again Harlow," he said with a determined promise in his eyes.

He cocked his head to the side thoughtfully.

"You have such tiny ears," he commented.

"I'm tiny everywhere," I croaked.

His gaze then lowered to my cleavage and his eyes darkened before they travelled back to my face. I didn't actually mean 'there' but he checked me out anyway.

"I'm a bum man really," he confessed with a teasing glint. This was probably a good thing due to the fact my boobs were not really anything to shout about.

"You don't have to go. You can stay here with me. We don't have to play Xbox; we can do something else."

There was a suggestive light in his eyes and my tongue flicked nervously over my lips. I knew I should leave, the atmosphere between us simmered. The door was also wide open and I didn't have the nerve to shut it. I could hear my dad whistling quite loudly down the corridor. No doubt warning us that he was still in 'hearing' distance.

"I need to call my mom really," I explained.

He nodded his head in understanding. "K, well, say hi from me."

"I will."

"Do you talk to her about me? I bet you do," Connor said arrogantly.

"You are so full of yourself," I berated with a laugh.

"Do you?" he said again, this time more seriously. The split on his lip still angry looking although it had partially healed.

"Yes, actually I do. It's not all *good* stuff though so your ego isn't to get any bigger," I whispered, popping a kiss on his cheek.

As I drew back, he shot me a suggestive smile. "I'm big everywhere," he whispered, echoing my pattern of words from before.

I dramatically rolled my eyes.

"Whatever. Get some rest," I ordered and moved to turn away but he caught my elbow and gently swung me back.

"It's just too much fun pissing you off."

There was a moment of thick silence before he said. "You fancy a drive to the beach with me tonight?" There was a slight tremor in his voice.

My heart leapt in my chest. "Yes, OK," I replied a little too soon and with much more eagerness than I should have. Didn't they say you should always play it cool at first?"

He returned my smile and his eyes almost glittered.

Thoughts of playing it cool vanished as I thought about his health. "Are you OK to drive though?" I asked.

He escorted me to the door by my elbow

"I'll be fine. You should go before I change my mind and keep you in here." He announced, turning me gently and placing a palm in the hollow of my back. I trotted forward through the doorway.

"Oh and Harlow…" I spun back to face him.

"Yes?"

One mouth-watering muscled arm was rested on the door frame above his head, his tattooed skin close to my face.

I lifted my eyes to meet his assessing stare, it was as if he was looking at me for the first time again.

"It isn't a date," Connor pointed out in a semi playful / serious tone.

I raised my eyebrows and beamed up at him. It was too a date and we *both* knew it really.

I purposefully lifted my chin up towards his, confidence thrumming within me.

"If you say so."

And with that I twisted and sashayed off down the corridor, ensuring I gave him a view of my backside and that perfect Monroe sway which I had mastered the art of after many years of practice. I knew my bum would look pretty fantastic in the black skin tight jeans.

I heard him inhale sharply before he chuckled quietly to himself and closed his door.

I had definitely won that round.

Fourteen

The drive to the coast was a vast improvement on my last two experiences in Connor's car. We spoke about a variety of topics and I thoroughly enjoyed being in his company. It felt comfortable and the banter flowed naturally between us. The old animosity had well and truly gone now and I was grateful that he had started to open up more.

I told him about my exams and he explained how he'd dropped out of school and didn't have any GCSEs. It didn't bother me as there were other routes to travel career wise and he was already well involved with the farm. I also knew he was naturally intelligent, mature and a hard worker. After what had happened to him as a child, he'd had to grow up fast.

Connor was encouraging about my idea of studying teaching and the fact that this could bring me to Yorkshire on a more permanent basis was now even more appealing.

I thought about my mum and how disappointed she'd be if I did say I wanted to study away. No doubt she'd get over it given time and at least she had Phil on the scene now.

Connor pulled the Ranger into a parking place, high above the sea and then unclipped his seat belt.

"Let's do this," he said, leaning across me and releasing my belt. He was so bossy and always in control but I liked it.

We both climbed from the car; the sun was starting to set but it still cast a pretty glow across the ocean and the breeze was fairly gentle considering how the sea was crashing against the rocks beneath us.

Connor took my hand and walked me over to a gap in the fence where there were steps leading downwards.

I glanced down at my footwear with a frown. Strappy sandals were not the right thing to be walking down fairly steep steps. I'd had an image of walking hand in hand on the beach, but it appeared we needed to hike down there first.

Guiding me to the slope, Connor turned and with a cock of his head glanced purposefully down at my feet before looking back at me with an unimpressed eyebrow.

"Yes, I know, not the best idea I get it," I grunted. Annoyed at myself.

"Take off your shoes," he commanded, his deep voice firm. It sent another flutter of heat across my skin which had nothing to do with the sun.

I did as he instructed and stood before him on the top step, sandals in hand, awaiting his next move.

"Jump on," Connor beckoned and turned to offer me his broad back. OMG, he's offering a piggy back and he's only recently recovered from busted ribs, the guy was mental.

"Connor, I don't think—."

He cut me off. "Don't think, don't speak, just climb on and I'll do the rest."

He was very determined and I caved, shoving my sandals into my rucksack before carefully climbing onto his back. I had to step on the fence to give myself a boost, he was so tall.

I curled my denim short clad legs around his waist, totally aware of every inch of my body. I tingled where we touched and held my breath.

Connor grabbed my legs with his arms to secure me. It was difficult to get my head around the fact that Connor was now between my legs and the thought sent my pulse racing.

I placed my arms around his neck and held on for dear life as he negotiated the rocky steps. As we ascended, I noted the concrete was severely corroded from the tide, I sure hoped they were safe.

It was fairly quiet, just the sounds of the sea and Connor's breathing. My breasts were pressed against the sold muscle of his back and they felt heavy somehow.

"Connor, are you sure you're OK to carry me?" I said into his good ear.

"I'm fine, you weigh, like, nothing."

I knew he'd have no problem carrying me under normal circumstances, he was so strong and I was quite small but the guy did have busted ribs and bruising almost everywhere.

He carried me easily. We had a few wobbly moments which caused a bit of relieved chuckling here and there.

We were almost at the bottom and I could smell the salt from the sea. As we rounded a corner and travelled down the last few steps it opened up onto a secluded sandy cove. It was perfect. There was one other person there walking his dog. The waves swept up and down the beach like a caress.

Connor placed me on the sand, it was cool against my toes and I scrunched my feet up to feel it against my skin. We looked out to sea for a minute before Connor caught me around the waist and tugged me towards him, his eyes watching my lips before he lowered his head and kissed me. A dog barked in the distance and when his lips meet mine, nothing else mattered.

The breath was almost yanked from my lungs as our mouths moved together, greedily, like they had been craving the contact for so long.

His kiss was demanding and as usual he took control, his hands moving along my back and then up into my hair. I wanted him to carry on kissing me more than I wanted air. It felt so perfect and I pushed myself up onto my tip toes to give him deeper access.

I imagine we stood there on the sand in the sea air, locked together for quite some time but it still wasn't enough. I was alive when he was touching me and I wanted more, so much more.

I moaned my disappointment against his mouth as he drew away.

Connor stared down into my upturned face, running his thumb down my cheek, a content expression on his face. I looked up into his eyes, thinking how long his eyelashes were for a boy.

"You're so sweet, pure. You don't really belong with me Harlow," he said, his voice husky from our kiss.

I smiled reassuringly. "I can be annoying when I want to be," I put back gently with a smile.

His grin was brief.

"You shouldn't want me. I'm not an easy person to be with. I'm moody. I get irritable quickly and struggle with my moods. Especially when I'm off my medication."

I pulled back slightly and pushed a chunk of hair back from my eyes. His voice was suddenly quite grave.

"I don't care, I'm done pretending and as for your moods, I think I've seen my fair share, I know what to expect now and it doesn't scare me." I replied, running my hands up his chest to rest them there.

Connor placed his own hands on the top of mine. Covering them with his strong fingers, it made me feel safe.

"Why were you so mean to me when we met?" I questioned shyly, not sure I wanted to hear the answer. If he had genuinely thought me a self -involved princess with nothing to say for herself, it would have made me sad.

He half shrugged, unsure himself it appeared.

"I think it must have been a self-preservation thing. I resented you before we even met."

My brow creased at that. "Really?"

He nodded, running his thumb gently across my fingers, almost like he was apologising. "I was probably jealous. Mike talked about you all the time, day and night. He cared so much for you. I'd never had that from my dad. I guess I craved it. When he showed me your picture, you were so fucking perfect, it wound me up even more. Then when I saw you at the party, I felt an immediate attraction and that also pissed me off. I felt out of control again. Not necessarily the way I'd felt as a kid, but I didn't like the way it made me feel. I can't stand weakness.

You lit up the room, I made sure I kept my distance and sat as far away from you as I could on purpose, so as not to let you in. I remember the way everyone hung on your every word and I knew I needed to mess with you. Like a boy who pulls the wings off daddy long legs and enjoys watching them suffer. As I said, so fucking perfect." He paused for thought, obviously troubled by his past behaviour and snap judgements. "I was a dick. Forgive me?" He said, taking my hand.

"I'd forgive you anything, even the Natalie's of this world." I replied with a smile. I popped her name in there to see how he reacted.

He grimaced. "So, she told you. Thought she would. That is most *definitely* over. Want to paddle?" he suddenly said and I barked out a laugh. He was so spontaneous and I relished in the opportunity to be juvenile with him.

"I thought you'd never ask."

We raced over to the water and I dropped my bag and watched Connor as he removed his trainers. I helped him roll up the bottom of his jeans and he complained that I was tickling him. He had large calf muscles and my hand brushed against the hair on his legs.

I tried to help him to his feet and he almost pulled me over, he was so much larger than me. We laughed and crashed into each other and he occasionally pecked me on the lips. It felt so loving that my heart squeezed.

We walked hand in hand over to the edge of the water as it lapped the sand, it was icy against my feet but I ploughed further into it, until the sea caressed my own almost non-existent calf muscles.

We laughed, splashing around and spoke about our past experiences at the beach and the places we had travelled. Connor explained that he intended running his own farm one day and that my dad had offered to help him get started. It didn't bother me. I wanted my father to help him. We briefly spoke about Natalie again and he did so with no feeling at all, I understood that she'd just been a release for him and that no feelings were ever involved. He spoke about Ella like a little sister and how they'd confided in each other and my jealousy about this also started to fade.

We shared a few more passionate kisses whilst the water splashed against our legs. It was perfect in every way.

The tide was coming in and approaching where we'd left our stuff and so we left the water and headed back up the beach towards our exit route.

Connor explained that when he moved to the farm two years ago, he'd found this particular cove and that he visited often when he needed some alone time. *This* was the place he escaped to the night he'd the fight with his mother. Not to Natalie as I had first assumed.

He said he'd found it hard when his mother and my dad first got together but after a few months, eventually got used to the idea. He also explained that it had been obvious that my dad was the right guy for Rachel. He was so calm and didn't have an aggressive bone in his body. Connor said Mike didn't even raise his voice in an argument.

The Mike he was describing was not the father I remember growing up. My mum and dad used to go at it like two crazy people at times. Although merely in a vocal way.

It was all about being with the right person. I was now with the right person in Connor, for sure. I was the soft to his hard, the gentle to his tough. Surely, we evened each other out?

In the car on the way home, I fell asleep feeling the happiest and most content I have in months.

Connor woke me gently by rubbing my shoulder and I squinted from the light coming into the car from the house. It appeared someone was still up. We'd left a note to say we'd gone for a drive and so it wasn't like we hadn't told anyone.

It was dark outside as we walked side by side towards the house and I experienced a moment of guilt as I wondered what our parents would say if they'd seen us on the beach together. Behaving like a boyfriend and girlfriend. I batted off the thought, there was no point worrying about it, as I had to go home in a few days. The thought sank like led in my stomach. I had one more year of school to get through. How would I cope without him?

As we got to the door, Connor kissed my mouth and said he'd see me in the morning. I was curious about where he was going at such an hour but I didn't want to come over like a bunny boiler who needed to track his every move. Connor would hate being smothered. Maybe it was seed thwacking time?

As I made my way in through the front door, I heard Connor's car start up, so wherever he was going it wasn't close. The light was still on in the hall but it was dead quiet.

I started to remove my sandals, my toes still had sand on them and it reminded me of our perfect evening together.

I attempted to swallow a cocktail of guilt and misery over the thought of leaving again but decided to shelve the feelings about going back home for now. I needed to establish why I felt guilty being with Connor when it also felt so right.

As I rolled it around my head, I realised it wasn't because our parents were married. I certainly didn't see Connor as a sibling. It was the sneaking around part. You constantly felt like you were looking over your shoulder. I imagined that is what Ella and Ryan would feel like.

As for Connor and I. What were we? No label had been made. He hadn't asked me to be his girlfriend or anything.

I approached the stairs, lost in thought as Rachel appeared from dad's study.

"Did you have a nice time?" she asked in a low voice.

She had a tone that I couldn't quite put my finger on.

"Yes, thank you. Great," I answered and threw her a shy smile, suddenly feeling uneasy.

Her next words were even harder to read.

"I hope you know what you're doing Harlow," she began. "Some men are not easy to love."

I turned to face her. My expression purposefully guarded but said.

"I know, but I have to try." Laying my heart open.

She smiled and nodded her understanding, but I could see she was worried.

I had known Connor a matter of months, but I knew when the fight broke out that I was in love with him. Full-on, hard-hitting love and I was *terrified* of being hurt but I had to go with it.

I could feel Rachel's eyes drilling into me as I said goodnight and headed up the stairs. She was right, but I was lost and there was no turning back. Life has no undo button.

I needed Connor Barratt like I needed the air in my lungs.

The last week of my summer holiday flew by at an alarming speed and the thought of going home and leaving Connor was now making me feel sick on a daily basis.

We kept our hands off each other when we were in company, but I witnessed Rachel and my dad exchange knowing glances. They knew something was going on. I imagine most of our friends also had an idea, they too exchanged enough looks behind our backs, ones they thought we didn't see.

Eventually, we held hands going into the pub which was witnessed by Tom and Ella who were there eating supper with their parents one night.

Tom was very quiet for a couple of days afterwards but then must have got used to the idea, especially when a new pretty Veterinary Nurse started working at his practice. She was called Milly and seemed really sweet. She also liked him. I could tell. We met in the village for drinks one night and she full on belly laughed about his hoof rot story.

On the night before I was due to leave, Rachel and my father had purposefully eaten out, probably to give Connor and I some alone time.

We were downstairs in the floral room, with the fire lit. The flames bounced shadows across the leather bound books. It was so romantic. Connor was wearing jogging pants and a tee and I was in my PJs. I was laid with my back against his chest and we were talking about the next time we would see each other. My Mother and Phil were going to the coast during the half term in October and it was the plan for Connor to travel down and stay whilst my mum was away. I wasn't sure if we'd ask my mum or whether I'd smuggle him in. It was one of those wait and see ideas.

As I snuggled into him, enjoying the fact that we had the house to ourselves, I ran my fingers up his thigh. A mixture of nervous emotion and excitement thrumming within me. My heart was fluttering like a bird against my ribcage and Connor twisted his head to peer down at me.

I moved my hand further along his leg but he stopped my fingers as they fell short of my intended target. Uncertainty raised to the surface and I craned my head to meet his gaze, unsure of what to do next.

He stroked the back of my hand.

"No, not here and not now. The timing has to be perfect."

It felt pretty perfect to me, well apart from the fact that our parents could actually appear at any moment.

He manoeuvred himself on the sofa so we were facing each other.

"I can't actually believe I'm saying this. You know I want to. So, fucking much it's insane but I want your first time to be right. Not here and certainly not on the sofa or the floor."

"We could go upstairs." My voice was thick, it didn't sound like me.

"No Harlow. Not when you're leaving tomorrow. It's not right."

A sliver of relief seeped into me. I wanted to sleep with him, but I wasn't fully ready to have sex for the first time and then be separated from him. Being intimate in that most special way and then not being able to be together for a month would be unbearable surely.

He pulled me onto his lap and kissed me. It was deep, loving and totally sexy and I moved against him, feeling he was hard.

He pulled back and knowingly grinned at me.

"That's for another time." He chuckled, his eyes heavy with desire and my pulse skyrocketed. The fact that he wanted to wait, made me love him even more.

For at least another hour before our parents arrived back, we fell asleep together on the sofa and were awakened when a car's headlights shone in through the window.

Connor pulled me to my feet.

"What you thinking?" he questioned softly.

I peeped up at him with a dirty grin.

"They were another forty minutes. We could have fit it in." I pointed out with mischievous wink.

An amused look spread over his features and he slowly shook his head.

"Not the way I do it. That would only cover foreplay." He boasted playfully.

I blushed a full-on girlie blush.

"I'll hold you to that." I replied with a naughty grin, accidently on purpose catching him 'there' with my hand as I moved to push myself to my feet. His voice caught in his throat at the contact.

At that moment, I felt thoroughly feminine and enjoyed the power that came with it. I felt confident and less like a school girl.

Leaning up, I pecked him on the cheek and slid from the room quickly, having now most definitely given him something to think about.

"Maybe lock your door." Connor warned cheekily before I jetted up the stairs to my room.

As I lay in bed that night, I held my breath as I heard Connor pass by, wondering if he'd try the handle.

He didn't of course and I wasn't sure how I felt about that.

The morning I had been dreading came soon enough. I said goodbye to dad and Rachel and thanked them for giving me the best summer ever. Tears were involved and even dad was upset, not bawling his eyes out, but I spotted some moisture.

Connor drove me to the station and he was deathly quiet in the car. I felt like I was slowly dying. October half term seemed ages away.

The car journey felt so short and there was so little time left. My heart was aching and I knew he felt it too from his body language.

At the platform, he took my face in his hands and kissed me, promising to call me every day and I felt tears sting my eyes (again). His last image of me would be red eyed with snot running down my nose, knowing my luck.

We both stared at each other as the announcement was made to signal my train was about to leave. Connor had briefly boarded to put my case in the rack. How things had changed from when I'd first arrived.

We stood there on the platform.

"Time to go," he said, his voice sounded pained and I know he too was struggling.

"I could just stay?" I put in weakly, feeling severely depressed and knowing I had to get with the program. This was real life, people got together and had to go away to study, it's what happened. I knew I couldn't just chuck away my schooling over a boy. Even one I was in love with.

He was firm with his reply. "No, you need to finish you're A-Levels or you'll have wasted the first year. I'll Face Time you tonight and I'll see you in October and fuck it, I'll probably be down sooner than you think. May have a few cows with me though. And I mean the furry ones on all fours."

I smiled weakly but at that point I didn't care. I just needed to be with him. "But this is where you are, so it's where I want to be."

"And you will be. We'll make it work Harlow." It was as if he could hear my heart breaking. Inside I was screaming.

A thousand thoughts were racing around in my head and I felt like my world was being ripped away. I started to feel sick and panicky and I took a deep breath and hugged him, taking in that heady scent.

"Here." Connor gently pulled my arms from around his neck and uncurled my fingers before placing a small envelope in my hand. I looked up at him, puzzled and then went to open it.

"No, it's for the train."

I tried again and he stopped me a second time, so I gave in and pushed it into my pocket.

"I'll call you later. You'd better pick up." I said feebly, now feeling anything but confident. Where had the girl from last night gone?

"Harlow, you're only a few hours away. And yes, I'll pick up. I want to introduce you to *other* things we can do together on the phone."

He winked suggestively and I grinned, probably still blushing at his words.

"See you."

"Yeah. See you." He mirrored.

As I turned to get on the train, I twisted back to face him and caught his expression. He wasn't as calm as he was attempting to appear, I saw the strain on his face.

"I love you," I mouthed and he smiled, his eyes igniting.

I stepped back and the doors closed with a sense of finality, the train slowly moving away from the platform. My heart ripped in two as the first boy I had ever loved was swept away.

I must have stood by the door staring at the flashing countryside for well over five minutes before I headed to find my row.

Lowering myself into seat 13B, I realised that I was, by coincidence sat in the seat where the book engrossed 'ham woman' had been on the journey over.

I managed a smile, thinking back to the girl I had been. Fresh faced, probably a bit too full of herself, worried about the little things and so stressed at the thought of seeing her father again.

My time on the farm had changed me and I swallowed down the pain at the thought of being distanced from Connor.

I was tough, I could do this. I *had* to think about myself too.

When I was back at college next week people would sit up and take notice of the *real* me. I was a Williams and I was determined to make my mark. I'd work my fucking brains out and get the highest grades possible to allow me to be successful in my own right. The better grades I got, the more opportunities I'd have. I'd make my mother, father and Connor proud and the Samantha Jones's of this world could go fuck themselves. As could the silly school boys who panted after her. Adapting myself to fit in was no longer an option. They would see the real Harlow Williams.

I was also on my way home to my mother, much wiser about life in general and in a real relationship, well, sort of. Although I had told Connor I loved him.

To be painfully honest, I wasn't *really* sure *what* our relationship was. So much had been unspoken but I'd needed him to know, know how I felt. I didn't regret it, putting it out there. I could see how those three special words had affected him.

The train rattled along the track but this time I didn't feel any motion sickness.

I had grown this summer, gone were the thoughts about looks and material stuff. I was now more confident and felt comfortable in my own skin. As I said, the new me. She was tougher too. The silly stuff didn't matter anymore.

As the train entered the tunnel, I remembered the envelope Connor had given me and slid it from my pocket.

I carefully ripped it open. It was a note. The words flickered as light dipped in and out of the carriage. The train shot from the tunnel and my spirits lifted with it.

Will you be my girlfriend?

My heart soared with immense pleasure and I dragged the words to my chest, hiding them from nosy eyes, *this* was *mine*, those words just for me.

I must have had the biggest grin on my face and just when I thought my lips couldn't get any wider, I turned the paper over and had a second surprise.

I love you.

I inhaled sharply. I was so happy, I wanted to scream into the carriage.

A few people glanced at me with knowing eyes and I shot them a shy smile.

I pulled out my phone and texted my new boyfriend my reply.

YES! XXXXX

My life was now officially… perfect.

THE END

Meet Connor and Harlow again in Ella and Ryan's story, COMING SOON…

Excerpt

There was a faint trace of blood at the corner of Nathan's mouth where Ryan had hit him. From the slight amount of damage, the older and much bigger man must have pulled his punch. Unfortunately, Nate's next words made an already explosive situation so much worse.

"Just remember brother." He almost spat, his beaten face un-weakened, apart from a section of jaw which was rapidly changing purple.

"When you get between her legs, remember I was there first."

There was no containing it, I was helpless as all hell broke loose. The second punch hit its intended target at full force and the sound of bone contacting bone reverberated between their two bodies.

Printed in Great Britain
by Amazon

87718903R00119